W9-AGP-782

MARKED FOR DEATH?

The first death looked accidental. The second was as obvious as a murder could be. And now her fiancé had narrowly escaped two potentially fatal "accidents." A horrified thought crept into Patricia Allison's mind—would her Jim be the third victim?

Superintendent Hannasyde thought otherwise. For no one had a better motive for murder than Mr. James Kane. . . .

THEY FOUND HIM DEAD

An ingenious mystery in the best English tradition

GEORGETTE HEYER

THEY FOUND HIM DEAD

BANTAM BOOKS · TORONTO · NEW YORK · LONDON

*This low-priced Bantam Book
has been completely reset in a type face
designed for easy reading, and was printed
from new plates. It contains the complete
text of the original hard-cover edition.*
NOT ONE WORD HAS BEEN OMITTED.

THEY FOUND HIM DEAD

*A Bantam Book / published by arrangement with
Doubleday & Company, Inc.*

PRINTING HISTORY
*Doubleday edition published October 1938
Serialized in England in* WOMAN'S HOME JOURNAL

Bantam edition / January 1970

2nd printing ... January 1970	5th printing .. September 1971
3rd printing ... February 1970	6th printing .... June 1972
4th printing .... May 1970	7th printing ..... March 1973
8th printing .... June 1977	

*Bantam Books are published by Bantam Books, Inc. Its trade-
mark, consisting of the words "Bantam Books" and the por-
trayal of a bantam, is registered in the United States Patent
Office and in other countries. Marca Registrada. Bantam
Books, Inc., 666 Fifth Avenue, New York, New York 10019.*

PRINTED IN THE UNITED STATES OF AMERICA

CHAPTER ONE

MISS ALLISION thought that Silas Kane's sixtieth-birthday party was going off rather better than anyone had imagined it would. Such family gatherings—for the Mansells, through long business partnership with Silas, might almost be ranked as relatives—were, in Miss Allison's sage opinion, functions to be attended in a spirit of considerable trepidation. Nor had this one promised well at its inception. To begin with, Silas was at polite variance with old Joseph Mansell. Their disagreement was purely on a matter of business, but although Joseph Mansell, a husband and a father, had existence outside the offices of Kane and Mansell, Silas and his business were one and indivisible. He was not, at the best of times, a man who contributed largely to the gaiety of an evening party. He was invariably civil, in an Old-World style that seemed to suit his neat little imperial and the large stock-ties he wore, and he would listen as patiently to a discussion on Surrealism as to the description of the bird life on the Farne Islands which was being imparted to him at the moment by Agatha Mansell. Both subjects bored him, but he inclined his head with an assumption of interest, smiled kindly and coldly, and said Indeed! or Is that so? at the proper moments.

Miss Allison, glancing from his thin, pale face, with its austere mouth, and its calm, aloof eyes, to Mrs Mansell's countenance, wondered whether a realization of her host's complete indifference to her conversation would shake Agatha Mansell's magnificent assurance. Probably it would not. Mrs Mansell had been to college in the days when such a distinction earned for a woman the title of Bluestocking and the right to think herself superior to her less fortunate sisters. She had preserved through thirty years this pleasant feeling of superiority and an alarmingly cultured voice which could make itself heard without the least vulgar effort above any number of less commanding accents.

"We were disappointed at seeing no gannets," announced Mrs Mansell. "Of course, when we were on Ionah last year we saw hundreds of gannets."

"Ah, is that so indeed?" said Silas Kane.

"I saw a film about a lot of gannets once," suddenly remarked young Mr Harte. He added disparagingly: "It wasn't too bad."

Neither Silas nor Mrs Mansell paid any heed to this contribution to the conversation, and young Mr Harte, who was rising fifteen, returned unabashed to the rending of a drumstick.

Young Mr Harte was not really a member of the family, but his mother, by reason of her first marriage with Silas' nephew James, ranked in the Kanes' estimation as a Kane. James had been killed in the Great War, and although the Kanes bore no ill will towards Sir Adrian Harte, they could never understand why Norma, who was left in comfortable circumstances, had taken it into her head to marry him.

Neither Norma nor Sir Adrian was present at this gathering. Norma, who had developed in her thirties a passion for penetrating into the more inaccessible parts of the world, was believed to be amongst pygmies and gorillas in the Belgian Congo, and Sir Adrian, though invited to the party, had excused himself with a vague and graceful plea of a previous engagement. He had sent in his stead, however, his son Timothy, in charge of Jim Kane, his stepson, who was even now trying to catch Miss Allison's eye over the bank of flowers in the middle of the table.

Timothy had come to stay. Jim had brought him down in his cream-coloured sports car with a charming note from Sir Adrian. Sir Adrian had providentially remembered that Silas, upon the occasion of Timothy's last visit, had said that he must come again whenever he liked and for as long as he liked, and Sir Adrian, confronted by the task of amusing his son during the eight weeks of his summer holidays, decided that the day of Timothy's liking to visit Cliff House again had dawned. Miss Allison, sedately avoiding Jim Kane's eye, wondered what young Mr Harte would find to do in a household containing herself in attendance upon an old lady of over eighty years, and Silas Kane. He enlightened her. "Are there any decent films on in Portlaw this month, Miss Allison?" he inquired. "I don't mean muck about love and that sort of thing, but really good films, with G men and gangsters and things."

Miss Allison confessed ignorance but said that she would obtain a list of the entertainments offered.

"Oh, thanks awf'ly; but I can easily buzz into Portlaw on my bike," said Mr Harte. "I sent it by train, and I dare say it'll be at the station now, though actually when you send things by train they don't arrive until years after you do." He refreshed himself with a draught of ginger beer and added with a darkling look across the table: "As a matter of fact, it was complete drivel sending it by train at all; but some people seem to think nothing matters but their own rotten paint work."

Jim Kane, at whom this embittered remark was levelled, grinned amiably and recommended his stepbrother to put a sock in it.

Miss Allison glanced down the long table to where her employer was seated. Old Mrs Kane, who was over eighty, had been carried downstairs to grace her son's birthday party, not against her wishes (for she would have thought it impossible that any function should be held at Cliff House without her), but firmly denying any expectation of enjoyment. "I shall have Joseph Mansell on my right and Clement on my left," she decreed.

Miss Allison, who filled the comprehensive role of companion-secretary to Emily Kane, ventured to suggest that more congenial dinner partners might be found than the two selected by her employer.

"It is Joe Mansell's right to take the seat of honour," responded Mrs Kane bleakly. "And Clement is senior to Jim."

So there was Emily Kane, sitting very upright in her chair at the end of the table, with Joe Mansell, a heavy man with gross features and a hearty laugh, seated on one side of her, and on the other, her great-nephew Clement, the very antithesis of Joe Mansell but equally displeasing to her.

Clement, a thin, desiccated man in the late thirties, with sparse hair rapidly receding from his brow, did not seem to be making much effort to entertain his great-aunt. He sat crumbling his bread and glancing every now and then in the direction of his wife, who was sitting between Joe Mansell and his son-in-law, Clive Pemble, on the opposite side of the table. Miss Allison, separated from Rosemary Kane by Clive Pemble's impressive form, could not see that sulky beauty, but she knew that Rosemary had come to the party in what the family called "one of her moods." She had many moods. On her good days she could brighten the dullest party by the very infection of her own tearing spirits, but her good days were growing farther and farther apart, so that during the past six months, reflected Miss Allison, glancing back in retrospect, it had been more usual to see Rosemary as she was to-night, with her eyes clouded and her full mouth drooping, boredom and discontent in every line of her lovely body.

Clement, who was a partner in the firm of Kane and Mansell, was a man of considerable substance, and, since he was heir to his cousin's private possessions, a man of large expectations also. Miss Allison supposed that Rosemary must have married him for these reasons, for there did not seem to be any other. She was obviously impatient of him, and as careless of showing her impatience as she was of showing her predilection for the society of one Mr Trevor Dermott. Mrs Kane, who thought Clement a poor creature, had claimed the prerogative of extreme old age to tell him two days before that if he did not look after his wife better she would run off with "that Dermott." Miss Allison, mentally contrasting Trevor Dermott's handsome face and noble form with Clement's uninspiring mien and manner, could not but feel that so passionate a creature as Rosemary might be pardoned for throwing her cap over the windmill.

Matters between the Clement Kanes were certainly becoming uncomfortably strained. In the drawing room, before dinner, Rosemary had sat a little withdrawn from the rest of the company, preoccupied and ungracious, while Clement, trying to appear unconcerned, all the time watched her. Like two characters out of a problem play, thought Miss Allison, who preferred drama to be confined to the stage. And really it made things rather awkward and unreal when two members of a very ordinary family behaved in this neurotic manner. Even Clive Pemble, who was not sensitive to atmosphere, seemed to be aware of tension. He had made several hearty efforts to engage Rosemary in conversation, but though her lips smiled mechanically, her replies were monosyllabic and discouraging. Miss Allison had a fleeting suspicion that the beautiful Mrs Clement Kane was seeing herself in a tragic role and banished it nobly. "Cat!" said Miss Allison to herself.

On the opposite side of the table Betty Pemble was chattering to Jim Kane, from time to time appealing to Clive to corroborate her statements. There was no trace of her mother's majesty in Betty. She had enjoyed a certain measure of success as a girl through a natural ingenuousness which was pretty in a debutante but slightly tedious in a woman of thirty-five. She had a vivacious way of talking, pleasing manners, and a good heart, but her habit of telling interminable and incoherent stories about her own experiences made her a wearisome person to be with for more than an hour or two together. Fortunately Clive Pemble profoundly mistrusted clever women, and if he sometimes was bored by his wife's conversation, this boredom was more than compensated for by her blind faith in his omniscience. She was often heard to say that Clive was a Rock, and Clive, who knew that he was no Rock but a man like other men, and hated the knowledge, found this faith in him a comfort and a stay. So when Betty told Jim Kane that if there was the least hint of thunder in the air she simply couldn't sleep a wink and demanded inevitably: "*Can* I, Clive?" he smiled placidly and replied with perfect good humour: "No, rather not!" Other men, thought Miss Allison, would have brained the silly wench.

Between Betty Pemble and her mother the last member of the party was seated, taking a polite interest in an anecdote about Betty's children. Knowing his attention to be fully engaged, Miss Allison allowed herself to steal a look at Mr James Kane's admirable profile.

The Kane family tree was a spreading one, and while Silas was the last representative of the senior line, Jim was the last of the junior. Nor could any two people have been more dissimilar.

The original founder of the family's fortune had left four sons. From the eldest son's marriage to Emily Fricker had sprung Silas. Clement was the grandson of the second. The third, emigrating to Australia, had drifted out of the Kane circle, his only surviving descendant being a granddaughter, of whose existence the English Kanes were no more than vaguely aware. The fourth son had left one daughter, who died a spinster, and one son, who was killed in Gallipoli. To this son and his wife Norma had been born Jim, the last of the Kanes.

The last of the Kanes bore very little resemblance to the rest of the family and was not a member of the firm of Kane and Mansell. He was a large fair young man with a frank smile and a pair of direct grey eyes which had a habit of gazing in Miss Allison's direction. He worked at the Treasury, and although this was a very respectable occupation his cousins Silas and Clement could never feel that he was a really serious or responsible person. He professed no interest in the manufacture of netting, and he spent a great proportion of his spare time engaged in sports which held no lure for his cousins at all. At Cambridge he had got his Blue for Rugger, a circumstance which seemed right and commendable (though strangely un-Kane-like) to Silas and Clement. But when he continued to play Rugger on Saturday afternoons, after he had come down from Cambridge, the cousins shook their heads and were afraid that he would never settle down. They thought it a great pity, for they were fond of Jim. Clement said he had a very sound brain if only he could be brought to take life seriously; and Silas, watching in astonishment Jim's handling of a speedboat, feared that the poor boy had taken after his mother. He disapproved of the speedboat as profoundly as he disapproved of the flighty-looking sports car, but, all the same, he let Jim keep it in his boathouse at the bottom of the cliff and, little as he understood the lure of such sports, derived a queer pleasure from recounting his young cousin's exploits to such people as Joe Mansell, whose nephews and cousins achieved no speed records and broke no limbs at Twickenham.

Since young Mr Harte, upon her right, was fully occupied with the consumption of ice pudding, and Clive Pemble, on her left, had become involved in the intricacies of his wife's anecdote, Miss Allison had leisure to observe the last of the Kanes. Having decided some months previously that it was no part of a companion-secretary's duties to fall in love with any member of her employer's family, she had assured herself that she was wholly impervious to Mr James Kane's charm of manner and made up her mind to demonstrate clearly to him her utter unconcern. Unfortunately he seemed to be insensitive to snubs, and, in spite of having received from her a very cold greeting upon his arrival at Cliff House, he had had the audacity to try to catch her eye three times during the course of dinner. She was happy to think that upon each occasion she had managed to avoid his gaze.

At this moment the object of her reflective scrutiny turned his head. Miss Allison demonstrated her indifference by blushing hotly and thereafter devoted her attention to his stepbrother.

It seemed a very long time before old Mrs Kane rose from the table. Jim Kane held open the door for the ladies to pass out of the room, and Miss Allison's kind heart overcame her judgment. He was looking rather worried and certainly puzzled. She was afraid all at once that her studied disregard of him had hurt his feelings, and, instead of going out of the room without paying any heed to him, she raised her eyes to his face and gave him a faint smile. His brow cleared; he smiled back at her so warmly that she almost repented of her humane impulse.

In the drawing room it was her first duty to see Mrs Kane comfortably ensconced in her favourite chair, a footstool under her feet and her ebony cane within her reach. In the performance of these offices she was slightly hindered by Betty Pemble, who said: "Oh, do let me!" and brought up too high a footstool and tried to insert a cushion behind her hostess. As Mrs Kane came of a stiff-backed generation and despised women who could not sit up without such soft support, this piece of thoughtfulness was not well received. Nor did Mrs Pemble's next utterance tend to make her more popular. "I think Mr Kane is *simply* marvellous!" she said.

Emily's faded blue eyes stared glassily at her. "In what way?" she asked.

Mrs Pemble, forgetting that she was addressing a lady over eighty years old, said: "I mean, when you think of this being his sixtieth birthday, it just doesn't seem *possible,* somehow."

Emily looked at her with contempt and confined her response to one blighting dissyllable. "Indeed!" she said and, turning to Miss Allison, requested her to close one of the windows. "There is a nasty fog creeping up," she announced. "I can feel it in my bones."

"No more than a sea mist, I believe," said Mrs Mansell.

"You may believe what you choose, Agatha," said Emily, "but I call it a nasty fog."

"Yes, I think it's a kind of a fog," said Betty.

Emily looked at her with renewed dislike. Betty plumped herself down upon the rejected footstool and said: "I simply *must* tell you what Peter said to me when I told him I was going to Uncle Silas' birthday-party! You know the children always call him Uncle. They absolutely worship him. But of course he's simply marvellous with children, isn't he? I mean, he has a kind of way with them. I suppose it's a sort of magnetism. I always notice how they go to him. I mean, even a shy mite like my Jennifer. It's as though she just can't help herself."

This portrait of her son drawn in the guise of some kind of boa constrictor did not appear to afford Emily any marked degree of gratification. She said dampingly: "And what did Peter say?"

"Oh God!" muttered Rosemary and, jerking herself up out of a deep chair, walked across the room towards Miss Allison and suggested to her that they should go into the conservatory.

Miss Allison realized with a slight sinking of the heart that she was to be made the recipient of confidences. Mrs Clement Kane had some few months before suddenly taken what appeared to be a strong liking to her and had signified it by recounting to her with remarkable frankness her various emotional crises.

"What a Godforsaken party!" Rosemary ejaculated as soon as she was out of Emily's ear-shot. "I can't think how you manage to put up with living here day in day out."

Miss Allison considered this. "It isn't as bad as you might imagine," she said. "In fact, it's really rather a pleasant life, taken all round."

Rosemary looked at her in wondering dismay. "But the utter boredom!" she said. "I should go mad."

"Yes, but I'm rather placid, you know," replied Miss Allison apologetically.

"I envy you. Cigarette?"

Miss Allison accepted one.

"It must be great to be able to take what comes, as you do," pursued Rosemary. "I wish I were like it. But it's no good blinking facts: I'm not."

"Well, I don't say that I should choose to be anyone's companion," said Miss Allison. "Only I'm a fool at shorthand and have no talents."

"I expect you have, really," said Rosemary in an absent voice and with her gaze fixed broodingly upon a spray of heliotrope. "I told you I was getting to the end of my tether, didn't I? Well, I believe I've reached the end."

There did not seem to be anything to say in answer to this. Miss Allison tried to look sympathetic.

"The ironic part of it is that having me doesn't make Clement happy," said Rosemary. "Really he'd be better off without me. I don't think I'm the sort of person who ought ever to marry. I'm probably a courtesan *manquée*. You see, I know myself so frightfully well—I think that's my Russian blood coming out."

"I didn't know you had any," remarked Miss Allison, mildly interested.

"Good God, yes! My grandfather was a Russian. I say, do you mind if I call you Patricia?"

"Not at all," said Miss Allison politely.

"And please call me Rosemary. You don't know how I hate that ghastly 'Mrs Kane.' There's only one thing worse, and that's 'Mrs Clement.' " She threw away her half-smoked cigarette and added with a slight smile: "I suppose I sound a perfect brute to you? I am, of course. I know that. You mustn't think I don't see my own faults. I know I'm selfish, capricious, extravagant and fatally discontented. And the worst of it is that I'm afraid that's part of my nature, and even if

I go away with Trevor, which seems to me now the only way I can ever be happy, it won't last."

"Well, in that case you'd far better stick to your husband," said Miss Allison sensibly.

Rosemary sighed. "You don't understand. I wasn't born to this humdrum life in a one-eyed town, surrounded by in-laws, with never enough money, and the parlourmaid always giving notice, and all that sort of ghastly sordidness. At least I shouldn't have that if I went away with Trevor. We should probably live abroad, and anyway he would never make the fatal mistake of expecting me to cope with butcher's bills. It isn't that I *won't* do it, it's simply that I *can't*. I'm not made like that. I'm the sort of person who has to have money. If Clement were rich—really rich, I mean—I dare say I shouldn't feel in the least like this. You can say what you like, but money does ease things."

"Of course, but I was under the impression that you were pretty comfortably off," said Miss Allison bluntly.

Rosemary shrugged her shoulders. "It depends what you call comfortable. I dare say lots of women would be perfectly happy with Clement's income. The trouble is that I've got terribly extravagant tastes—I admit it freely, and I wish to God I hadn't, but the fact remains that I have. That's my Russian blood again. It's an absolute curse."

"Yes, it does seem to be a bit of a pest," agreed Miss Allison. "All the same, you've got any amount of English blood as well. Why not concentrate on that?"

Rosemary looked at her with a kind of melancholy interest and said simply: "Of course, you're awfully *cold,* aren't you?"

Miss Allison, realizing that to deny this imputation would be a waste of breath, replied: "Yes, I'm afraid I am."

"I think that must be why I like you so much," Rosemary mused. "We're so utterly, utterly dissimilar. You're intensely practical, and I'm hopelessly impractical. You don't feel things in the frightful way that I do, and you're not impulsive. I shouldn't think you're terribly passionate either, are you?"

"No, no, not at all!" said Miss Allison.

"You're lucky," said Rosemary darkly. "Actually, of course, I suppose the root of the whole trouble is that Clement could never satisfy me emotionally. I don't know if you can understand at all what I mean? It's difficult to put it into words."

Miss Allison, hoping to avert a more precise explanation, hastened to assure her that she understood perfectly.

"I don't suppose you do really," said Rosemary rather thoughtfully. "It's all so frightfully complex, and you despise complex people, don't you? I mean, I've got that awful faculty of always being able to see the other person's point of view. I wish I hadn't, because it makes everything a thousand times more difficult."

"Does it? I should have thought it made things a lot easier."

"No, because, don't you see, one gets torn to bits inside. One just suffers doubly and it doesn't do any good. I mean, even though I'm in hell myself I can't help seeing how rotten it is for Clement, and that makes it worse. I'm simply living on my nerves."

Miss Allison, who from the start of this conversation had felt herself growing steadily more earthbound, said: "I expect you need a change of air. You've got things out of focus. You must have—have cared for your husband when you married him, so——"

"That's just it," Rosemary interrupted. "I don't think I did, really." She paused to light another cigarette and said meditatively: "I'm not a nice sort of person, you know, but at least I am honest with myself. I thought I could get on with Clement, and I knew it was no use marrying a poor man. I mean, with the best will in the world it just wouldn't work. I knew he was going to come into money when his cousin died, but I didn't in the least realize that Cousin Silas would go on living for years and years. Which of course he will. Look at Great-aunt Emily! I don't know that I actually put it all into words, but subconsciously I must have thought that Clement was going to inherit almost any day. They all say Cousin Silas has a weak heart, you know—not that I believe it."

"Would money make so much difference to you?" asked Miss Allison curiously.

"I don't know," replied Rosemary. "I think it would. Not having enough of it makes me impossible to live with. I'm not a good manager. I hate everything to do with domesticity. It isn't in my line. I can't help getting into debt, because I see something I know I can't live without another moment—like this bracelet, for instance—and I buy it without thinking, and then I could kill myself for having done it, because I do see how hateful it is of me."

"I suppose," suggested Miss Allison somewhat dryly, "that it doesn't occur to you that you might send the bracelet back?"

"No, because I have to have pretty things. That's the Russian in me. C'est plus fort que moi. To do him justice Clement knows that. He doesn't grudge it me a bit, only it worries him not being able to make both ends meet. Now he says we shall have to move into a smaller house and do with only two maids. It's no use pretending to myself that I don't mind. I know I shouldn't be able to bear it. I feel stifled enough already."

"When are you moving out of Red Lodge?" inquired Miss Allison, with the forlorn hope of leading the conversation into less introspective channels.

"On quarter day, I suppose. I believe the people who've bought it would like to move in sooner, but I don't really know. We don't discuss it."

This magnificent unconcern made Miss Allison blink. She said practically: "But oughtn't you to be looking for another house? It'll be rather awkward if you don't, surely?"

Rosemary shrugged. "What's the use?" she said.

Miss Allison, feeling herself to be unable to cope

with the problem, said apologetically that she thought she ought to go back to the drawing room.

"I often think," remarked Rosemary, preparing to follow her, "that you placid people must find life very easy. I wish I did."

Not thinking this observation worthy of being replied to, Miss Allison merely smiled and stood aside for her to pass into the drawing room.

Their reappearance coincided with the arrival of the gentlemen from the dining room. As the door opened old Mrs Kane abandoned even the smallest show of interest in the diet of Betty Pemble's children and looked towards it. Her deeply lined countenance, with its close mouth and pale, rather starting eyes, had in repose a forbidding quality, but as her glance fell on Jim Kane her whole face seemed to soften, and her mouth to relax into one of its rare smiles. She said nothing, but when he came across the room towards her she looked pleased and made a little gesture towards a chair beside hers.

He paused by a table to stub out his cigarette before coming to her, and then drew up the indicated chair and sat down.

"Well, what have you got to say for yourself?" inquired Emily.

He smiled. "That sounds as though I've done something I shouldn't. Have I?"

She gave a grim chuckle. "I'll be bound you have. When are you coming to stay?"

"Next week. May I?"

She nodded. "They don't give you long enough holidays at that Treasury," she said. "Where's your mother gone gallivanting off to now?"

"Belgian Congo," replied Jim. "It's no use asking me precisely where in the Congo, because no one can make out the address on her last letter. It looks like Mwarro Gwarro, but we can't help feeling that that's improbable."

"Pack of nonsense!" said Emily, but without rancour. "At her age too. Leaving the boy—what's his name—with us, are you?"

"That was the general idea," Jim admitted. "Not mine, but Adrian's. Do you mind? Adrian says Cousin Silas was kind enough to invite him."

"I dare say. He won't bother me," said Emily. "I like young people about the place. Miss Allison can look after him." A gleam stole into her eye; she added sardonically: "You'd better talk it over with her." She looked towards her companion and nodded imperiously. Miss Allison came to her at once. "My great-nephew wants to talk to you about his stepbrother," she announced.

Jim Kane had risen at Miss Allison's approach but shook his head at her glance of mild surprise. "No, I don't," he protested. "I mean, not about Timothy."

"Well, you don't want to talk to an old woman when you might be talking to a pretty young one, I hope," said Emily. "Miss Allison, show my great-nephew the orange tree in the conservatory."

She dismissed them with a nod. Jim Kane said: "I wish you would. I haven't been able to exchange two words with you so far."

"Go along," said Emily, clinching the matter.

So Miss Allison entered the conservatory for the purpose of the tête-à-tête for the second time that evening. Mr James Kane, who had a disconcerting habit of going straight to the point, said bluntly: "Have I offended you?"

"Offended me?" replied Miss Allison in a voice of studied lightness. "Dear me, no! Why should I be offended with you?"

"I don't know," said Jim. "I got the impression during dinner that you weren't liking me much."

"Nonsense!" said Miss Allison bracingly.

"Is it nonsense?" asked Jim.

"Of course. I mean—have you seen the white magnolia?"

"Yes, thanks. Why have you been snubbing me?"

"I don't think I have," said Miss Allison feebly.

"You know you have."

Really, thought Miss Allison, this tête-à-tête is worse than the last. She said rather haltingly: "Well, you must remember that I'm in a—I'm in a somewhat difficult position. I'm Mrs Kane's companion, you know."

He looked puzzled for a moment; then his eyes crinkled at the corners. "I get it. I mustn't ask my great-aunt's companion to marry me. A bit Victorian, isn't it?"

"Not at all. Anyway, don't be silly!"

"I'm not being silly. Will you marry me?"

"No, certainly not!" said Miss Allison with quite unnecessary emphasis.

Mr James Kane did not appear to be noticeably cast down by this brusque rejection of his suit. He said: "Because you'd rather not, or because you're Aunt Emily's companion?"

"Both," said Miss Allison in a hurry.

There was a moment's silence. Then Jim said in a level voice: "I see. All right, I'm sorry. Let's look at the magnolia."

Feeling like a murderess, Miss Allison led the way to the magnolia.

"Improbable-looking flowers, aren't they?" remarked Jim.

"Yes; so waxen," agreed Miss Allison. "The orange tree is over here."

"I've lost all interest in orange trees," said Jim. "Do you think you'll be able to cope with my young stepbrother till I come down?"

"Are you coming down?" asked Miss Allison involuntarily.

"Next week. Not if you'd rather I didn't."

"Of course I wouldn't. Please don't be absurd!"

"Come now, that sounds a lot more hopeful!" said Jim. "At least you can't dislike me!"

Miss Allison made no response.

"I shall persevere," said Jim.

"If ever I marry," declared Miss Allison, "it will be a millionaire."

"It?" said Jim.

"Well, you know what I mean."

"Rather! I see lots of 'em trotting about the city. Failing a millionaire, wouldn't a young man in comfortable circumstances do?"

"No," said Miss Allison firmly. "I must have pots of money. I *need* it."

Jim grinned appreciatively. "You've been talking to Rosemary."

She laughed. "Yes, but I ought not to have said that."

"A companion's life seems to be stiff with embargoes," he remarked. "The sooner you give it up the better. Would Aunt Emily's consent be any use to you?"

She shook her head.

"Then it *is* pure dislike?"

"No, it isn't!" said Miss Allison, unable to stop herself. "I mean—I mean—I'm going back into the drawing room!"

Mr James Kane stepped between her and the way of escape. "All in good time. What *do* you mean?"

Miss Allison said bitterly: "You're one of those loathsome people who when given an inch grab an ell!"

"Me to the life," agreed Jim. "But let's get this straight. If you weren't my great-aunt's companion would you turn me down?"

Miss Allison, instead of assuring him that she would, replied a trifle incoherently: "It isn't so much Mrs Kane. There's your mother too. She might well object to your getting entangled with a penniless companion-secretary."

"Good Lord, is that all?" said Jim, relieved. "You needn't worry about my mother. She won't care two hoots. Do you like coloured stones, or do you prefer diamonds?"

"I hate all jewelry!" said Miss Allison.

"Ah," said Mr Kane, "I can see you'll make a Frugal Wife."

Before Miss Allison could think of a suitable retort their privacy was invaded by young Mr Harte, who strolled into the conservatory with the air of one who is sure of his welcome and said cheerfully: "Hullo! What are you doing?"

"Oh, just looking at the magnolia!" answered Miss Allison. "What do you think of it?"

"Swell!" said Mr Harte, somewhat unexpectedly.

"If you start that American film talk here you'll get thrown out on your ear," Jim warned him.

"Sez you!" replied Mr Harte indulgently. "I say, Miss Allison, do you know what I think?"

"No, what?"

"Well, it's suddenly occurred to me that I shouldn't be at all surprised if somebody got murdered here to-night."

Miss Allison was slightly taken aback, but Jim, accustomed to the morbid processes of his relative's mind, said promptly: "Nor should I. What's more, I know who'll be the corpse."

"Ha ha!" said Timothy. "Very funny!"

"But why should anyone be murdered?" inquired Miss Allison.

"Oh, I don't know!" replied Timothy vaguely. " 'Cept that it's absolutely the right sort of layout for a murder."

"Idiot!" said Jim.

"Of course, I know there won't be one really, but all the same, it 'ud be jolly good fun if there was," said Mr Harte wistfully.

CHAPTER TWO

WHEN she went back into the drawing room Miss Allison was more able to understand why the notion of murder had occurred to young Mr Harte. A certain atmosphere of drama seemed to have spread over the room. To this the Clement Kanes were largely contributing, Clement by gazing hungrily at his wife whenever opportunity offered, Rosemary by looking stormier than ever and casting into the pool of conversation remarks calculated to convince the company that her marriage was on the verge of shipwreck. These were met by a high-nosed stare from Agatha Mansell and several downright snubs from old Mrs Kane; but Betty Premble, who found Rosemary "interesting", soon moved across to a chair by her side and began to talk to her. The interchange was curious and unsatisfactory, for Rosemary, who despised as suburban any woman who not only lived upon amicable terms with her husband but presented him with two healthy children into the bargain, looked upon Betty with contempt, while Betty massacred Rosemary's narrated spiritual reactions by capping them with similar ones of her own.

"I feel stifled in Portlaw," announced Rosemary in unencouraging response to an encomium bestowed by Mrs Pemble on the invigorating properties of the air. "It's as though I couldn't breathe."

"I know exactly what you mean," agreed Betty. "I felt the same when we were living in a flat in town. It was simply tiny—*literally* you couldn't move in it—and I used to say to Clive that I felt absolutely *cooped* up."

"I don't think actual space matters so much as room

for one's Essential Ego to expand," said Rosemary a trifle loftily.

"Yes, I do utterly agree with you there," replied Betty. "Atmosphere means a most frightful lot to me too. I mean, I'm awfully sensitive to beauty—and, funnily enough, both my children are, too, even Peter, who's only three and a half. I mean, if a picture is out of the straight, I *simply* can't rest until I've put it right. It seems to kind of hurt me."

"I'm afraid," said Rosemary, with a faint, superior smile, "that I shouldn't even notice a crooked picture."

"Yes, I'm frightfully absent minded too. I seem to go into a sort of dream, and I forget simply everything. I often think that's where my Jennifer gets it from—it's quite extraordinary the way that child daydreams! I mean, everybody says so, it isn't only just me. The children absolutely love coming down to stay with Granny and Grandpa by the sea. They simply *live* on the sands. Of course it's just coming home to me, and Clive feels exactly the same, really far more so than with his own people. It's quite a joke in the family!"

Rosemary looked faintly disgusted by this sample of the humour prevalent in the Mansell household and said in a voice of suppressed passion: "How odd that you should be glad to come here while I would give my soul to get away! The sameness! . . . Doesn't it get on your nerves? But perhaps you don't suffer from your nerves as I do."

It was not to be expected that Betty Pemble would allow so insulting a suggestion to pass unchallenged, and she replied warmly that, as a matter of fact, she was One Mass of Nerves. "I simply never talk about myself, because I think people who tell you about their ailments are absolutely awful; but actually I'm not frightfully strong. I get the most terrible nervous headaches for one thing. I mean, I could scream with the pain often and often. I think it's from being terribly highly strung. Both my children are exactly like me too. Frightfully sensitive and easily upset. They kind of feel things inside, the same way that I do, and bottle it up."

Her mother, who happened to overhear this remark, said robustly: "Nonsense! You spoil them, my dear child; that's all the trouble."

Mrs Pemble turned quite pink at this and at once joined issue with her parent, declaring that Agatha just didn't understand, and that everyone said she managed her children better than anyone else. As Mrs Mansell appeared to be unconvinced by this universal testimonial, Betty at once appealed to Clive to support her, interrupting him in the middle of a discussion with Jim Kane on the probable outcome of the Surrey vs Gloucester Match. By the time Mrs Mansell's stricture had been repeated to him, and various incidents illustrative of Betty's skill in handling her progeny recalled to his mind, Joe Mansell, Mrs Kane and Clement had all become involved in the discussion, Joe advancing as his contribution to it that he liked to see kids enjoying themselves; Clement, with a meaning glance at his wife, deploring his own lack of children; and Mrs Kane stating that in her young days children never had any nerves at all.

This was an observation calculated to rouse the ire of the most good-tempered mother, and when it was promptly seconded by Mrs Mansell, Betty Pemble, reinforcing her own arguments by the pronouncements of a host of sages somewhat vaguely referred to by her under the general title of People, set about the formidable task of convincing two stalwarts of the Victorian age that they did not understand children's little minds.

While this battle raged, Rosemary relapsed into brooding silence, Jim Kane seized the opportunity to engage Miss Allison in conversation, and Joe Mansell moved across the room to where Silas was sitting and suggested that they might have a word together.

Silas Kane said: "Why, certainly, Joe!" in his slow, courteous way and got up out of his chair. "We shall be quite private in my study."

Joe Mansell followed his host to this apartment, a severe room looking out onto the shrubbery at the side of the house, and remarked that having Betty and the children staying at the Cedars brought quite a lot of life into the place.

"Ah!" said Silas. "And are they with you for long?"

"Oh, about a month, I expect. Betty likes the children to have a thorough change, you know. Not but what they tell me it's very healthy at Golders Green—very. Still, it's not like the sea. Between ourselves, it's a fortunate thing that we're able to have them, for things aren't too good on the Stock Exchange at the moment. The wife and I suspect Clive's finding things a bit tight—just a bit tight."

"Ah, I dare say!" said Silas, sorrowfully surveying a post-war world. "The times are very unsettled."

"Yes," agreed Joe. "No stability, wherever you look. But that's not what I want to talk to you about." He tipped the long ash of his cigar into the empty grate and cleared his throat. "I don't know whether you've thought any more about Roberts' proposition?"

An inflexible expression came into Silas' chilly grey eyes. He fixed them on his partner's face and replied: "No. I am of the opinion that this is not the moment to be launching out into speculative ventures."

"I think myself there are excellent prospects. Expansion, Silas! One's got to move with the times, and there's no doubt—in my opinion not the slightest doubt—that if we decide to push our nets in Australia it will not be many years before we shall be amply repaid for the initial capital outlay."

"Yes?" said Silas, putting his finger tips together. "You may be right, Joe, but I cannot say that Roberts' scheme attracts me."

"Clement is in favour of it," offered Joe Mansell.

"Possibly," said Silas rather ironically. "But I'm thinking that it is not Clement who would have to bear the brunt of that capital outlay you mentioned. I'm sorry to go against you, Joe, but I don't see my way."

Joe Mansell looked at him resentfully, thinking that it was easy for an old bachelor with no one dependent on him to sit tight on his moneybags and say that it was not the time to be launching out into speculative ventures. He was mean; that was what was wrong with Silas. Always had been, and his father and grandfather before him. Not but what old Matthew Kane had never been afraid to spend money if he saw a good return, judging from the fortune he'd left. He'd made money hand over fist, had Matthew, the founder of the business. It made Joe Mansell feel more resentful than ever when he looked about him, as now, at the evidence of Kane wealth and thought of the Kane holding in the business, comparing it with his own share. And now, when there was a chance to expand, he'd have to watch some other firm seize the opportunity, just because Silas was too conservative to consider new ideas and too well off to think it worth while tapping a fresh market. He'd listen to all the arguments with that damned polite smile of his; he'd agree that there might be something in the scheme; he'd say it was very interesting, no doubt; but when you got down to brass tacks with him, and it came to talking of the capital he'd have to advance to start the show, you'd find yourself up against a brick wall.

But Silas, watching Joe with veiled eyes, was thinking that it had always been the same tale with him. He'd no judgment: he rushed into things. It was just like him to allow himself to be talked over by a plausible fellow with an American accent. He was lavish with other men's money, was Joe. Clement, too, of whom he'd thought better, lacked judgment. All he cared for was to make more money to spend on that flimsy wife of his. Well, those weren't the methods by which the firm had been built up. He said as much, but with his usual civility.

"One must move with the times," Joe repeated. "I believe you'd get a good return on your money."

"Perhaps, perhaps," Silas agreed. "But I'm not as young as I was. I doubt whether I should live to enjoy any return."

Now he's getting on to his weak heart, thought Joe. It's my belief he'll live for ever.

"Well, I won't disguise from you, Silas, that I'm

strongly in favour of the plan—strongly in favour of it! As a matter of fact, things aren't too easy for me about now, what with reduced dividends and having to help Clive tide over a bad patch. Not to mention Paul's troubles."

"Indeed! I'm sorry to hear that," Silas said, wondering what concern of his were Joe's bad investments, or Joe's son-in-law's financial embarrassments, or the alimony his son's wife had to be paid.

"I wish you could see your way to it."

"Yes, I wish I could, since you're so much in favour of it," said Silas.

That was the sort of remark that made one want to brain Silas. Joe Mansell controlled his temper with an effort and heaved himself up out of his chair. "Well, I hope you'll think it over carefully before you finally turn it down," he said. "Roberts gets back from London tonight and will be wanting your decision. Paul's in favour of it, too, you know; and though I say it of my own son, I'm bound to admit he's got a shrewd head on his shoulders. He was sorry, by the way, not to be able to be here tonight."

"Indeed yes, we were sorry too," said Silas mendaciously. He disliked Paul Mansell, whose shrewdness verged on sharpness, and who had been divorced from his wife. A flashy fellow, with his oiled hair, and his waisted coats, and his habit of running after Patricia Allison. No doubt he saw himself managing the Australian side of the business. A nice thing that would be!

They went back to the drawing room. Old Mrs Kane was looking tired; her face had set into deeply carved lines, and she was making no effort to attend to any of the conversations in progress about her. Agatha Mansell, finding her monosyllabic, had transferred her attention to Rosemary and was lecturing her in a kind, authoritative way on the many improving pursuits she might with profit engage upon. When her husband preceded Silas into the room she looked across at him with a question in her eyes and, upon his slightly shaking his head, got up, announcing that it was growing late.

With the Mansells went Clive and Betty Pemble, to be followed in a few minutes by the Clement Kanes, Clement having lingered to ask Silas what his decision was on the Australian project. Upon hearing that his cousin disliked it, he said in a dispirited tone: "You may be right. All the same, we might have seen big profits. It's a pity Mansell isn't in a position to advance the necessary capital himself."

"I fancy you would none of you be so anxious to risk your own money," replied Silas dryly.

Clement flushed. "I don't think there would be much risk. However, you've a perfect right to refuse, if you feel like that about it. Come, Rosemary; are you ready?"

Silas escorted them to the front door. Emily roused herself and addressed Jim abruptly: "There's a nasty fog outside. You'd better stay the night."

He shook his head. "Thanks, Aunt, but I must get back. It isn't thick enough to worry me. Besides, I shall leave it behind me."

"Don't tell me!" said Emily snappishly. She added: "High time that child was in bed."

Young Mr Harte was affronted but stood in too much awe of Emily to expostulate. He was indeed experiencing considerable difficulty in keeping his eyes open.

"Good Lord, yes!" said Jim, becoming aware of his relative's presence. "You'd better go up, Timothy."

Mr Harte said with dignity, and in muted tones, that it was unnecessary for Jim to stick his oar in. He cherished in his bosom a considerable affection for his stepbrother and passionately admired his athletic prowess. He quoted him upon all occasions and acquired reflected glory from retailing his exploits upon the Rugger field or the race track, but would have thought it unseemly to give Jim any cause to suspect this veneration. So when Jim, bidding him farewell, said: "I'm coming down next week," he betrayed no flattering pleasure at these welcome tidings but merely replied that he would try and bear up till then.

Silas came back into the room as Jim was saying

good-bye to his great-aunt. He wore the satisfied expression of a man who has sped the last of his guests, and remarked that he fancied the party had gone off very well.

"H'm!" said Emily. She looked at him under her brows. "Joe tried to get you to advance money for his harebrained scheme. I hope you sent him off with a flea in his ear. Such nonsense!"

"I'm afraid Joe and I don't see eye to eye over it," Silas answered. "You off, my boy?"

"He'd better stay the night. There's a fog."

"Why, certainly!" Silas agreed. "But it's only a bit of a mist, Mother. Nothing to alarm anyone. I shall take my usual walk."

"You still stick to that, sir?" Jim said, smiling.

"If I didn't I should not enjoy a wink of sleep all night," replied Silas. "Wet or fine, I must have my stroll before going to bed."

"Fiddle!" said Emily in an exasperated voice. "If you didn't think you had insomnia you'd sleep the clock round! *I* don't have insomnia: why should you?"

"Indeed, I wish I knew," said Silas.

"One of these days you'll catch your death of cold. Don't say I didn't warn you! Miss Allison, be kind enough to ring the bell! I'm tired."

Jim Kane lingered until the business of assisting Emily into the carrying chair was accomplished and contrived, while the butler and footman were bearing her up the shallow staircase, to exchange a few final words with Miss Allison. Then he sallied forth to brave the dangers of the sea fret, and Miss Allison, holding Emily's ebony cane, the rug which she used to cover her knees, and her handbag, went sedately upstairs in the wake of the carrying chair.

Emily Kane, with her companion and her maid, occupied a suite of rooms in the west wing of the house. Miss Allison followed her there, arriving in time to see Ogle, her maid, helping her to an armchair in her bedroom. She laid down her various burdens and would have left Emily in Ogle's jealous charge had not Emily said: "Don't go! What did that hussy say to you in the conservatory?"

"Nothing much," replied Patricia. "I've heard it all before, anyway."

"She'll run off with that Dermott yet," prophesied Emily. "Good riddance to bad rubbish is what I say! Not that I want a scandal in the family. We'll leave that to the Mansells. Them and their precious son! You take my advice and send him to the rightabout."

"I will," promised Patricia.

Emily began to sip the glass of Horlick's Malted Milk which Ogle had put into her hand. "If my son would take something hot going to bed it would do him more good than trapesing about on the cliffs at this hour of night," she remarked. "Fresh air indeed! There's a great deal of nonsense talked about fresh air these days. I've no patience with it. Why he doesn't catch his death of cold I don't know."

"I expect he's hardened to all weathers by this time," said Patricia consolingly.

"That remains to be seen. He's as pigheaded as his father was. Never knew a Kane who wasn't. Jim's as bad as the rest of them, I warn you—— Here, take this away!"

Ogle relieved her of her empty glass and went out with it. Emily said: "I've had a very dull evening. Don't you start being discreet with me, young woman! That hussy's working up for mischief, or I don't know the signs. What's the matter with her?"

"Well, as far as I can gather, she wants more money. On account of her Russian blood."

Mrs Kane stared for a moment and then gave a cackle of laughter. "She does, eh? It would do her more good to have a few children, and you may tell her I said so."

Patricia laughed. "I expect you will tell her so yourself, Mrs Kane."

Ogle came back into the room and began to make ostentatious play with a dressing gown. Patricia bade her employer good night and went away to her own bedroom.

Mr James Kane's proposal kept her mind occupied for quite some time but did not trouble her dreams. She slept as soundly as ever and did not wake until the housemaid entered the room at a quarter to eight with her early-morning tea.

"If you please, miss, Pritchard would like a word with you," said this damsel, evidently thinking the request an odd one.

Miss Allison blinked and said sleepily: "Pritchard wants a word with me? What on earth for?"

"I don't know, miss. He didn't say, but he looks ever so queer," replied Doris eagerly.

Miss Allison sat up. "Is he ill?"

"Oh no, I don't think so, miss! He never said he was ill, but I'm sure there's something wrong. It struck both Mallard and I he looked queer."

It seemed to Miss Allison that there must be something very wrong indeed to make Pritchard, who was almost the perfect butler, request an interview with her before ever she was out of bed. She got up and slid her feet into her slippers. "All right, I'll see him at once. Ask him to come upstairs, will you?"

"He is upstairs, miss," said Doris. "He's waiting on the landing."

Miss Allison put on her dressing gown and sallied forth on to the passage. Pritchard was standing at the head of the staircase. Miss Allison would not have described his appearance as queer, but he certainly looked rather worried. At sight of her he apologized for disturbing her at an unreasonable hour and said in a lowered voice: "I wouldn't have troubled you, miss, if I had not thought the matter serious—not to say disturbing. The master, miss, is not in his room, and his bed has not been slept in."

Miss Allison stared at him rather blankly. Various explanations chased one another through her head, only to be dismissed as inadequate. She said mechanically: "Are you sure?"

"You may see for yourself, miss," replied Pritchard, leading the way to Silas Kane's room.

The sight of the bedclothes turned neatly back, the uncrushed pillow, the pyjamas laid out, was oddly frightening. There could be no doubt that Silas had not slept in his bed. Miss Allison pulled herself together and said briskly: "Have you sent out to search the grounds? Mr Kane went for his usual walk last night, I know. He may have had a heart attack."

"Yes, miss, I thought of that at once. There's no sign of him been seen yet, but I've sent Edwards and Pullman along the cliff walk. I believe the master generally went that way. I thought it best to tell you at once, on account of the mistress."

"Quite right. There's no need to say anything to alarm Mrs Kane until we know more. Did you see Mr Kane go out last night?"

"Not precisely, miss. I saw him when Mr James left, and I understood from him that he meant to take his usual walk. I happened to mention the fact of there being a considerable sea fret, but the master made nothing of it. You know his way, miss. He told me I need not wait up, and I consequently went up to bed and thus did not actually see him leave the house."

Miss Allison nodded and went back onto the landing. Her appearance there coincided with the opening of Timothy Harte's bedroom door. Timothy stuck a tousled head out and desired to be told what all the row was about.

Miss Allison allowed this grossly unfair description of her quiet colloquy with the butler to pass unchallenged and merely said that nothing was up. Timothy looked severely from her to Pritchard and said with a marked nasal intonation: "Say, sister, get wise to this! You can't put nothin' across on me!"

"Say, brother," retorted Miss Allison, not to be outdone, "let me advise you to scram!"

Timothy grinned and, apparently construing this request as an invitation, came out onto the landing. "I thought you looked as though you might be sporting," he remarked. "Honestly, what is up?"

Pritchard gave a warning cough, but Miss Allison

judged it wisest to admit Mr Harte into their confidence. "We don't quite know, but we're afraid Mr Kane may have been taken ill on his walk last night or have met with some accident. He doesn't seem to have come home."

Timothy's eyes grew round, but the most partial of observers could scarcely have supposed his expression to denote anything but profound relish of these disturbing tidings. "I *say!*" he gasped. "I jolly well *told* you so! I bet I had a kind of instinct about it!"

"Don't be so absurd!" said Miss Allison rather irritably. "How could you have had an instinct, as you call it, that Mr Kane would have a heart attack? Besides, you never told me anything of the kind."

"Yes, I did!" said Timothy. "At least, not about a heart attack. But I distinctly remember saying that I shouldn't be a bit surprised if someone was murdered here in the night. Actually, I never thought about it being Uncle Silas, but I probably had a sort of premonition all the same."

The butler looked outraged and startled, but Miss Allison, unimpressed, said: "If that's your idea of a joke, it's a bad one. There's no question of murder, but we are rather worried about your uncle, and that kind of suggestion isn't in the best of good taste."

"Sorry," said Timothy. "As a matter of fact, he isn't my uncle, though. Actually he isn't any relation at all."

"Well, you go and get dressed," replied Miss Allison. "Then you can help look for him."

It seemed good to Timothy to follow this advice. He said: "Sure thing!" and disappeared into his room again.

"I'll do the same," said Miss Allison. "You've warned Ogle not to say anything to Mrs Kane, I hope? Not that I think she would."

"The female staff knows nothing as yet, miss. I thought it best to speak to you first."

"Don't tell them anything, then, till we know just what's happened. I'll be down in a few minutes."

She dressed in haste but was beaten in the race by Mr Harte, who was downstairs ten minutes ahead of

her, having decided that excessive ablutions in a moment of stress would be frivolous.

He did not await her arrival but went out at once to
take part in the search for his host. Just as Miss Allison reached the hall he came into the house with a
very white face and said jerkily: "I've met them. I say,
it's pretty ghastly, Miss Allison. He's dead."

She did not say anything for a moment. Silas Kane's
death was a possibility she had already realized; the
news of it merely confirmed her fear.

"They're bringing him up to the house," said Timothy. "Honestly, I didn't think anything like this would
happen, Miss Allison."

"No. Of course not." She turned as Pritchard came
into the hall from the servants' wing and said as
quietly as she could: "Master Timothy has told me,
Pritchard. How did it happen? Have you any idea?"

The butler looked very much shaken. "They found
him at the foot of the cliff, miss. Just where the path
runs along the edge. He must have missed his way in
the fog. You'll excuse me, miss, but I'm a bit upset. I
do not know when I have been so upset. To think of
us lying in our beds with the poor master smashed up
like that on those wicked rocks! Not that one could
have done anything. If only he hadn't gone out! That's
what I keep on saying to myself, over and over. It'll
just about kill the mistress, this will."

Miss Allison returned a mechanical answer. She did
not think that Mrs Kane was of the weak stuff to be
killed by shock, or even by grief, but the task of break-
ing the news of Silas' death to her was not one to
which she looked forward. After a moment's reflection
she decided to postpone it until Emily had had her
breakfast and with this end in view went off in search
of Ogle.

It was a point of honour with Ogle always to dis-
agree with Miss Allison, of whom she was profoundly
jealous, but her adoration of Emily made her on this
occasion acquiesce in Patricia's decision. In acqui-
escing, however, she took the opportunity to tell Patricia

that she knew Emily far better than anyone else did and could assure the anxious that Emily would bear up under this shock as well as she had borne up under all the other shocks incident in a long life.

She was right. When Miss Allison, standing beside Emily's bed, said: "I have some very bad news for you, Mrs Kane," Emily looked her over piercingly and rapped out: "Well, don't beat about the bush! What is it?"

Patricia told her. Emily made no outcry, shed no tear. Only her face seemed to set more rigidly, and her eyes to become fixed upon some object beyond Patricia's vision. Her thin hands, their fingers bent with gout, lay motionless upon the quilt; she did not speak for some moments, but at last she brought her gaze to bear upon Miss Allison's face and said harshly: "What are you waiting for? Is there anything else?"

"No, Mrs Kane. Would you like me to go away?"

Emily smiled wryly. "I suppose you want to stroke my hand and tell me to have a good cry?"

"No, I don't," replied Patricia frankly. "It is my business to do exactly what you wish. Only you must tell me what that is, because I've never faced this situation before, and I don't know what to do."

"Good girl!" approved Emily. "I dare say you think I'm a heartless old woman, eh? When you reach my age you'll know that death doesn't mean so much as you think it does now. Go downstairs and make yourself useful." She paused, and for the first time Patricia saw a twinge of some emotion contract her features. "Clement," she said. "Yes. Clement."

Miss Allison nodded. "Of course. I'll ring him up immediately."

Emily looked at her with rather a curious expression in her face. "He'll come here," she said. "He and that wife of his."

"You need not see either of them, Mrs Kane."

Emily was shaken with sudden anger: "You little fool, I shall have Clement here for the rest of my life!"

"I hadn't thought of that," admitted Patricia. "Still, if you can't bear the idea of living in the same house with him, you could always have a house of your own, couldn't you?"

Emily's eyes narrowed. "You think I'm going to be turned out of the house that has been mine for over sixty years, do you? Well, I'm not! When I leave it, it will be in my coffin, that I promise you!"

Miss Allison, from what she knew of Clement Kane, thought it extremely unlikely that he would make the least attempt to dislodge his great-aunt, but she wisely refrained from saying this and instead went away to inform him of the tragedy.

She found Timothy downstairs, awaiting her. Silas' death had shocked him into a silence which had lasted throughout breakfast, but he seemed now to be restored to his normal self, though he apparently thought it proper to speak in lowered tones. While Patricia talked to Clement Kane on the telephone he stood watching her with a portentous frown on his brow, and as she put down the receiver he said in a voice fraught with suspicion: "I say, Miss Allison, will there be an inquest?"

"I suppose so," replied Patricia.

"Ah!" said Timothy with deep meaning. "Well, do you know what I think?"

"Yes," said Patricia.

"What, then?" demanded Timothy, put out.

"You have a sort of instinct that Mr Kane was murdered," said Patricia calmly.

Timothy was disconcerted and said rather lamely: "Well, I have. What's more, I bet I'm right. Don't you think I'm probably right? Honestly, Miss Allison, don't you?"

"No," said Patricia. "And if I were you, I wouldn't talk about it any more. It sounds silly."

This damping rejoinder offended Timothy so much that he walked away, informing a Jacobean chair that some people (unspecified) didn't seem to be able to see what was under their noses and would look pretty silly themselves when the truth was discovered.

CHAPTER THREE

CLEMENT KANE, very gently laying the receiver down, sat for a minute or two without moving. To Miss Allison he had uttered conventional exclamations of surprise and distress, but when their brief conversation was ended, neither surprise nor distress was discernible in his face. It was singularly expressionless. He sat looking at the telephone and presently drew a long, slow breath. He got up and felt in his pocket for his cigarette case, selected and lit a cigarette, and walked across the room to put the dead match tidily in an ash tray. He stood smoking for several minutes, then he stubbed out the cigarette, gave his cuffs a twitch, and walked upstairs to his wife's room.

Rosemary always breakfasted in bed. She said that she knew she was quite unbearable in the morning, and as she saw no possibility of improving, it was really more sensible to segregate herself in her own room. Clement found her with the remains of her breakfast thrust on one side and a large box of carnations lying across her knees. He did not permit himself to look at these for more than a second; he knew who must have sent them, but it would be beneath his dignity, besides provoking a nerve storm in Rosemary, to request her not to encourage Mr Trevor Dermott's advances.

Rosemary cradled the carnations in her arms; two pale-pink blooms brushed her cheek; she said: "Lovely, lovely things! Isn't it funny how some people can't understand that flowers are quite literally a necessity to anyone like me?"

"If they're such a necessity to you, I can only say

that I'm surprised you don't pay a little attention to the garden," said Clement in a peevish voice.

She shrugged her shoulders. "I've told you often and often that it's just no use expecting me to do things like that. I'm not that sort. I wasn't brought up to it."

He saw the sullen look descend on her face and said quickly: "I know: I wasn't blaming you. I didn't come up to talk about anything like that. Miss Allison has just been on the telephone. Really, it is so unexpected and—and shocking that I am almost unable to realize it. Silas is dead."

She let the flowers fall, ejaculating: *"What?"*

"Yes—yes! A dreadful accident. Death must have been instantaneous, I understand. He took his usual walk last night in the fog—there was a considerable fog, wasn't there? You remember we were obliged to drive very slowly on account of it? Well, as I was saying, in the fog he must have lost the path just where it winds close to the cliff edge and gone over. It doesn't bear thinking of, does it?"

She fixed him with a wide, glowing stare. "Dead? Cousin Silas actually *dead?* Clement, I can't believe it!"

"No, it doesn't seem possible, does it? I am very much distressed to think that such a thing should have happened."

"Yes, of course," she agreed. "But I do believe in being absolutely honest with oneself, and you must see, Clement, that it'll make the most tremendous difference to us. It's almost as though there's a Providence that steps in when one's almost desperate. Like that thing Mummy took up last year. Right Thought, or something, where you simply fix your mind on what you want and utterly believe it'll come to you, and it does, as long as you don't do anything about it."

Clement felt doubtful whether the exponents of whatever this odd creed might be would relish Rosemary's description of it. Nor did he feel that fixing one's mind upon the death of a relative could really be called Right Thought. He ventured to say so, but quite mildly, and added that, though he quite understood what Rosemary meant, he thought she should be careful of what she said. One would not like to seem callous.

She brushed this aside impatiently. "My dear Clement, I know I have a lot of faults, but at least I'm honest. I can't pretend to be sorry Cousin Silas is dead, because I'm not. Perhaps I am callous. Sometimes I think there is something inside me which is quite, quite cold. Not that I've any reason to mourn for Cousin Silas. I didn't like him, and he never understood me. I suppose you'll be the head of the firm now, won't you?"

"Well—I believe—that is to say, I know—that I shall have the biggest holding in the business. I really haven't considered it yet."

"And Cliff House?" she pursued. "That's yours, too, isn't it?"

"Yes," he said reluctantly. "I suppose it is."

She sank back against her pillows, clasping her hands across her eyes, her head a little thrown back. "No more poky, hateful houses!" she said. "No more of this foul housekeeping! Do you know, Clement, I do honestly believe the sordidness of it all was killing the Essential Me?"

His gaze dwelled on the lovely line of her lifted jaw. He said: "That's all I ever wanted wealth for: to give you the things that will make you happy, Rosemary."

She murmured: "Darling, you're terribly, terribly sweet to me!"

He bent over her, crushing the carnations, and kissed her throat, and her chin, and her parted lips. "You're so beautiful!" he said huskily. "You ought to have all the things you want. Thank God I shall be able to give them to you at last!"

"Darling!" sighed Rosemary, gently disengaging herself from his grasp.

He went away to the office, uplifted as he had not been for many weeks, thinking of his inheritance in terms of pearls for Rosemary, furs for Rosemary, huge expensive cars for Rosemary.

The news of Silas' death was before him. In the outer office faces composed in decent grief met him; the head clerk, speaking in hushed tones, begged on behalf of the staff to offer condolences. He went immediately to Joseph Mansell's room and found him there with his son Paul and the tall lean man with the goatee beard who was Oscar Roberts.

All three were deep in discussion, but the talk was broken off as he entered the room. Joe Mansell rose ponderously from his chair and came forward, saying: "I'm glad you felt able to come to the office, Clement. This is a terrible business! Poor old Silas! And only yesterday we were all at Cliff House to celebrate his sixtieth birthday! I know how you must feel it. I was only saying to Roberts just now that Silas was almost like a father to you. Poor fellow, poor fellow! It was that heart of his, I suppose?"

"I don't know," Clement replied. "I only heard over the telephone, and I didn't ask for details. Really, I was so shocked I could scarcely take in the bare fact of Silas' death."

"No wonder, no wonder! When I heard of it I could not believe my ears. Bowled over! It doesn't do to think of the years I've known Silas. Right from the cradle. He will be a great loss to the firm."

Paul Mansell, who had been contemplating his well-manicured hands with smiling complacency, looked up and murmured his agreement with this sentiment. The fourth member of the party, observing father and son with a distinct twinkle of amusement in his deep-sunken eyes, said in a slightly nasal drawl: "Well, I guess talking won't mend matters. I'd like to offer my sincere condolences, Mr Kane. Maybe the old man and I didn't see eye to eye, but I sure did respect him. It seems out of place for me to be here to talk business today, but time presses, and I have to consider the interests of the firm I represent."

Joe heaved a gusty sigh. "Yes, yes, I'm sure we all

appreciate your viewpoint. Silas would be the last person to want us to neglect the business, eh, Clement? Dear me, it will seem strange not to have him at the head of affairs!"

"Strange and melancholy," said Paul, gazing at the top of the window frame.

"Yes indeed. Well, we shall look to you now, Clement, to fill his place. Ably, I am sure, you'll do it. We've often said, between ourselves, how like you were to Silas. You have his hard head, without his—how shall I put it?—conservatism! Poor Silas! He was getting old, you know. I've thought several times his years were telling on him. Losing grip—just losing grip a little."

Clement's harassed look deepened. He said in his quick, worried way: "I haven't had time to look to the future yet. I shall have to consider my position, of course; but at present I haven't thought about it."

"No wonder," said Joe sympathetically. "I'm sure we all understand how you must be feeling. But, as I said to Paul, you'll be the first to appreciate Roberts' position. In actual fact, I believe I'm right in saying that we are all three of us agreed on the subject?" He paused, but Clement stood frowning down at the floor and said nothing. Joe glanced momentarily towards his son and resumed with a rather false air of heartiness: "Well, well, we've talked it over so often that we needn't go into it again now. As you know, Roberts came down from town last night to get Silas' final answer. Naturally things will have to remain in abeyance until after probate, but I fancy we shall have no difficulty in coming to an agreement on the future policy of the firm and can give our friend here his answer now. What do you say, Clement?"

There was a short silence. Clement was thinking of what the upkeep and the probable refurnishing of Cliff House would cost him; of death duties and the super-tax he would have to pay; of the pearls Rosemary must have. Silas had been right: this Australian project was a chancy business. It meant locking up a lot of

capital without any certainty of an adequate return.
Easy enough for the Mansells to talk so lightly about
it. They wouldn't be risking anything. He looked up
and said: "Really, I don't think I am in a position to
say anything definite at the moment. I shall have to
look into things carefully. The whole situation has al-
tered. I don't feel I ought to commit myself rashly before I see just how I stand. I'm sure Mr Roberts will
understand that it is quite impossible for me to give
him an answer today."

Oscar Roberts replied before Joe Mansell could
speak: "Why, surely, Mr Kane! I reckon it wouldn't be
reasonable to expect you to decide anything at a moment's notice like this."

"Exactly! This has come upon me so unexpectedly
that really I hardly know what is happening. I only
came to the office to inform you of Silas' death, Joe, in
case you shouldn't have heard about it. I'm going up
to Cliff House immediately to see my great-aunt and to
make the—er—the necessary arrangements." He
glanced at his wrist watch. "Yes, I see I'm late already.
I have to pick my wife up on the way. I shall have to
ask you to excuse me."

He hurried away. Oscar Roberts sat still, with his
long legs crossed, a faint, imperturbable smile on his
lips. Paul Mansell said with an unpleasant ring in his
voice: "So that's how it's going to be, is it?"

Joe had been standing rather foolishly gazing at the
door through which Clement had gone, but he turned
as his son spoke and said robustly: "Nonsense, my
boy, nonsense! It's very natural he should feel all at
sea just at first. Mr Roberts quite understands that."

"Sure," said Roberts amiably. "I don't want to
hurry him unreasonably. You know my position, Mr
Mansell. I want the best I can get for my firm, and you
make the best. If I can fix things with you I'll be glad
to do so; if I can't—well, I'll have to negotiate with the
next best."

"Quite, quite!" Joe said. "We fully appreciate your
position, and I think I may say—yes, I am sure I may

say—that we shall be able to give you a definite answer at no very distant date."

On this note of optimism they parted. No sooner had Oscar Roberts left the room than Paul said furiously: "The damned skunk! I suppose you see what's going to happen now he's got his hands on the money-bags?"

"We mustn't leap to conclusions," Joe said. "He hasn't had time to find his feet yet, that's all it is."

"Oh, that's all it is, is it?" Paul said. "Just hasn't found his feet! Well, if you ask me, he is finding them a dam' sight too quickly! When I think that we've got rid of that old fool Silas only to find Master Clement——"

"Paul, my boy! Paul!" Joe interrupted, losing a little of his high colour. "You're talking very wildly—very wildly indeed!"

"Yes, and I feel wild!" his son threw back at him. "Like a fool I thought that if once Silas was out of the way we could see our way clear. Now we've got a——"

Joe brought his open hand down upon the desk between them. "Hold your tongue!" He saw Paul staring at him and said in a milder voice: "It's very tiresome; but I don't despair of Clement by any means. He'll come round. Why, he's been in favour of the scheme all along! But this—this tragic business of Silas' death—— My dear boy, you can't be too careful what you say. Anyone hearing you might well wonder——"

"Whether I had anything to do with Silas' death?" Paul said, looking him in the eye.

Joe made a gesture with one hand. "Of course, it would be a preposterous idea; but we don't want to give people the least cause to suspect that we did want him dead. And when you talk of having believed that once he was out of the way—well, it's injudicious, my boy, extremely injudicious!"

Paul lit a cigarette and flicked the match into the grate. "Naturally I only meant that we've heard so much about Silas' weak heart that I couldn't help envisaging the possibility of his death."

"Naturally, naturally!" Joe agreed. "But though the very notion is absurd, one has to be careful. There's bound to be an inquiry, and one doesn't want the least hint of suspicion—not that any sane person could possibly imagine for a moment . . ."

"Well," said Paul blandly, "if the police suspect foul play, I fancy they'll be more interested in Clement's movements last night than in mine." He paused and inhaled a deep breath of smoke. "What makes you think there was foul play, Dad?"

Joe started. "I? Good God, I don't think it! Nothing of the sort! Nobody could think such a thing! Nobody who knew Silas!"

He was wrong. Mr Timothy Harte, having spent an awe-inspiring hour watching the proceedings of the police, inspecting the scene of the accident, and cross-examining Pritchard and Ogle, told Miss Allison that he was now quite sure that Silas had been bumped off. Miss Allison took instant exception to this vulgar and unfeeling expression and said that he was talking nonsense.

He looked her over with a sapient eye. "You can say it's nonsense if you like, but, all the same, I bet you think it was murder."

"I do *not!*" said Patricia emphatically. "I think it's all absolutely horrible, and that you're making it worse by trying to turn it into a cheap thriller." She walked away from him, up the stairs to Mrs Kane's rooms, conscious of a faint wish that Mr James Kane was present to quell his stepbrother.

She was a young woman not easily shaken out of her calm, but the events of this fateful day were, she suspected, a trifle on her nerves. Policemen and ambulances, official questions, servants whispering together, and a general atmosphere of surmise and suspicion were not conducive to a calm frame of mind. Nor was relief to be found in Mrs Kane's presence.

Emily was in her own sitting room, motionless in a straight-backed armchair, staring before her with blank, cold eyes, her shrunken mouth compressed, as though guarding secrets. Miss Allison knew herself to be overwrought when an odd fancy seized her that there was something ruthless about her employer.

Emily brought her gaze slowly to bear upon Miss Allison's face. "Well?" she said. "So they've taken him away?"

"Yes," replied Patricia.

"Nice scandal!" Emily said. "Inquests! Post-mortems! My husband would turn in his grave!"

"It's very unpleasant," agreed Patricia. "But it's only a matter of form."

Emily looked at her queerly. "It is, is it?"

Coming immediately after Timothy's sinister pronouncements, this grim utterance made Patricia feel uncomfortable. She met Emily's look and said after a moment: "What do you mean, Mrs Kane? What are you thinking?"

"I?" said Emily sharply. "I don't think anything. All I know is that my son is dead. What I think won't bring him to life again. Yes, what is it?"

Ogle, in the doorway, brought the news of Mr and Mrs Clement Kane's arrival. Emily gave a short laugh and said: "Show them up." To Patricia she added brusquely: "You needn't go. In fact, you're to stay."

In a few minutes Ogle ushered the Clement Kanes into the room. Rosemary was wearing a blue linen frock, but Clement had found time to procure a black arm band. Emily observed this immediately and said: "I'd like to know what you've got to mourn about!"

This was not a very promising start to the interview. Clement replied that to wear an arm band was usual, a mark of respect. He tried to make a speech of condolence but was interrupted before he had uttered half-a-dozen words. "Never mind that!" Emily said. "I don't want your sympathy. I don't want anyone's sympathy, if it comes to that."

"I think I should feel like that too," remarked Rosemary critically.

"You?" said Emily. "You'd spend a twelvemonth

telling everyone what your emotions were. *I* know you!"

Rosemary took this in very good part, merely saying with a certain amount of interest, "I wonder if I should? Do you think I analyse myself too much? With my type that's always a danger, of course."

Miss Allison felt that Rosemary came off the best from this encounter. Emily could only glare at her, folding her lips more tightly than ever.

Clement, always ill at ease in his great-aunt's presence, began to speak of future plans. Miss Allison guessed, when he said that he knew Emily would not wish to be alone in the house, that Rosemary had made up her mind to move into Cliff House immediately. She dreaded an explosion from Emily, but Emily heard Clement out in unencouraging silence. Watching her, Miss Allison felt that behind the mask of age Emily's brain was working hard. There was something rather terrible about this stout, alert old lady who sat so still and looked so bleakly out of eyes that were arctic blue and expressionless.

"Of course," Clement was saying, "we only wish to do what will be most agreeable to you: that goes without saying. But naturally I know how much supervision an estate entails, and it seemed to me—that is to say, I wondered—whether you might not prefer us not to wait for probate—which, you know, may take some time—but to come and stay with you as soon as possible."

Under his great-aunt's unwinking stare his voice dwindled and finally ceased. Rosemary took up the thread, saying: "It seems rather silly not to move in now, don't you think? Particularly as the people who have bought our house want possession as soon as possible."

"I suppose," said Emily, "that one of your maids has given notice."

"Both," replied Rosemary with complete candour. "Cook gave notice yesterday, because she says she can't get on with the kitchener, and this morning that *devil* of a house-parlour-maid said she was going, too, because cook's leaving made her feel unsettled. I mean, I simply can't face it."

"You can move in here when you like," said Emily.

Miss Allison, seated by the window, looked up from her needlework in momentary surprise, then bent her head again over the embroidery.

"Darling, how *angel* of you!" said Rosemary. "You've simply saved my life!"

"Very kind—very kind indeed!" Clement said, looking at the floor. "I need hardly say that we look upon this house as yours, Aunt Emily."

"Oh, utterly!" agreed Rosemary. "I loathe having to look after a house, and I haven't the least intention of interfering with anything here—except, of course, quite small details, like having my own rooms redecorated, which I absolutely *must* have done. I'm one of those people who are ridiculously sensitive to colour, and I *know* that if I had to have a blue sitting room, for instance, it would get on my nerves to such an extent that I should probably go mad. But as for ordering meals, or telling the servants what to do, I should be quite, quite hopeless. I shall beg and implore Patricia to carry on just as usual."

Miss Allison smiled but said nothing. Emily, having listened to this speech with an expression of contempt on her face, turned her eyes towards Clement and addressed him abruptly: "I've invited Jim to stay next week. If you don't like it you'll have to lump it."

"My dear aunt!" protested Clement. "You have every right to invite whom you please, and as for my not liking to have Jim here, good heavens, I shall be extremely pleased to see him!"

"I'll tell him," said Emily sardonically. She moved her hands in her lap. "There's another thing. What you do with the business is no concern of mine; but if you mean to take up with that plausible American I'll have you know that your cousin was set against it. I dare say you and those Mansells think yourselves very clever, but there's not one of you has the head my son had!"

Clement reddened and replied with some annoyance: "Really, Aunt, it is quite unnecessary for you to tell me that. I spoke to Silas about it last night, and I may say that upon reflection I fully agree with his view of the matter. Not that Roberts is an American. He has lived for some years in the States, but he is of English birth."

"That's neither here nor there," said Emily. "He dined here last week, and I didn't take to him. What's more, he talks like an American. That's enough for me."

Clement permitted himself to smile rather superciliously and to give the faintest shrug of the shoulders before changing the subject. He told his great-aunt that she must prepare her mind for the unpleasantness of an inquest, to which she replied that she was not born yesterday.

By the time the Clement Kanes took their departure Clement at least had won Miss Allison's sympathy. It seemed to her that he was behaving towards Emily with patience and considerable restraint. Indeed, so unresentful of snubs did he show himself to be that Patricia ventured to ask Emily, when he had gone, what she found to dislike in him.

"He's a fool," Emily said harshly. "A weak fool! and that wife of his!" Her fingers worked on the silk of her gown. "A nice pair to succeed my son! A nice pair for me to live with for the rest of my days!" A faint colour crept into her cheeks. Between their puckered lids her eyes stared straight ahead. "I wanted Jim," she said, more to herself than to Patricia. "It ought to be his, all of it! Clement! He's only half a man!"

Patricia said nothing. The note of hatred in Emily's voice was inexplicable and rather shocking.

"And his father," said Emily, with concentrated venom, "was just such another! I've always hated 'em —the whole pack of them! Jim's the only one worth tuppence." She pulled the shawl more tightly about her shoulders and said: "I won't see anyone else. If any of those Mansells call, you can send them about their business."

Both Agatha Mansell and her daughter called during the course of the day, but although Agatha insisted upon seeing Patricia, she accepted without comment the message that Mrs Kane felt unable to receive visitors. Betty Pemble, however, assured Miss Allison that she quite understood and gave into her charge an untidy posy of mixed flowers, the touching offering of her children, who (according to her account) had thought of it quite by themselves upon being told the sad news of Uncle Silas' death.

"I just told them that dear Uncle Silas has gone away on a long journey," she said. "They're such mites, you know, and I've never let them hear about Death or have ugly toys or stories about ogres and things. I mean, I do frightfully believe in keeping their little minds free from everything but happy, beautiful things, don't you?"

"A waste of time," pronounced Agatha. "Children are singularly heartless creatures."

Not from conviction, but with the object of preventing Mrs Pemble from entering upon an involved argument in support of her offspring's sensibilities, Miss Allison made haste to take the flowers and to agree that all ugly things should be kept from the young. Betty, who had hitherto believed Miss Allison to be hard and "what-I-call-unsympathetic" was pleased and told her earnestly that when one of his Pemble aunts had sent Peter a golliwogg for Christmas she had instantly taken it away from him and given him instead a sweet little woolly lamb.

"Yes," said Agatha magisterially, "and had *I* been his mother I should have given him a good spanking for screaming from sheer temper as he did. I well remember the occasion. Not that I see what a golliwogg has to do with Silas Kane's death."

She turned to Patricia and desired her to recount the precise circumstances of the accident. She did not ap-

pear to believe that Patricia was unable to gratify her
curiosity, for she continued to question her long after
Patricia had confessed almost entire ignorance. Her
manner was so majestic and her voice so overpower-
ingly cultured that Patricia found herself apologizing
for knowing so little. It did not occur to her until that
masterful presence was withdrawn that Agatha Mansell, who despised gossip and considered accidental
deaths sensational and therefore vulgar, had been
oddly anxious to possess herself of all the facts of the
case.

Two more callers visited Cliff House to leave cards
and sympathetic messages. One was Paul Mansell, who
contrived to waylay Miss Allison in the garden and to
pay her unseasonable addresses; the other was Oscar
Roberts, who said naïvely that, having enjoyed the old
lady's hospitality, he wanted to do the civil thing.

Mr Harte, having looked Paul Mansell over with the
mercilessly critical eyes of the youthful male, informed
Miss Allison dispassionately that he seemed to be a
pretty good tick. Oscar Roberts, however, whom he
encountered in the drive, instantly won his approba-
tion. Unlike Emily, Mr Harte had no prejudice against
Americans. America for him was an Eldorado popu-
lated in its wilder regions by venal sheriffs and heroic
cowboys; and in its towns by bootleggers, gangsters,
kidnappers and G men. That another side to American
life might exist he was happily unaware, so that when
Oscar Roberts addressed him in the accents of his favourite film star he believed that he stood in the presence of one who might at any moment produce a gun
from somewhere about his person and accorded him a
reverent admiration that was strong enough to enable
him to pardon Mr Roberts for having committed the
awful solecism of hailing him as "son."

They fell easily into conversation, Oscar Roberts
being apparently amused by so much obvious admiration and having the tact neither to disclaim American
citizenship nor to correct Timothy's ideas of American
life. A polite reference to Silas Kane's death opened

the floodgates of Timothy's confidence. He reiterated his belief that Silas had been bumped off, and although Mr Roberts looked rather startled for a moment, he did not make any snubbing remarks but, on the contrary, listened to Timothy's various theories with perfect gravity and even allowed himself to be led off to inspect the scene of the accident. Appealed to, he agreed that no doubt some evil-minded person might have pushed Silas off the cliff.

"Well, don't you think that's probably what did happen, sir?" said Timothy, bent on acquiring an ally.

Oscar Roberts stroked his pointed beard and suggested mildly that the possible murderer must have taken a big chance on Silas' choosing to walk along the cliff that night.

"No, because everyone knew that Uncle Silas took a walk along here every night!" said Timothy, triumphantly disposing of this objection.

"Is that so?" said Roberts. "Kind of a habit with him, maybe?"

"Yes, because of not being able to sleep."

"Well," replied Roberts, shaking his head, "I'll say that certainly looks as though you might be right, son."

Timothy looked up at him with glistening eyes and in a burst of gratitude invited him to come back to the house for tea.

Ocsar Roberts declined the invitation, but on the way to the drive across the gardens they encountered Miss Allison, who had come out in search of Timothy, and Timothy immediately begged her to add her persuasion to his. Oscar Roberts, however, intervened before she could speak and countered with an invitation to Timothy to accompany him back to Portlaw for tea at his hotel.

Patricia could not but feel grateful to anyone who offered to relieve her of Mr Harte's company on this very trying day, as Timothy seemed anxious to go with his new friend she gave permission, only qualifying it by insisting on his first washing his hands and brushing his hair.

He went off to do this, leaving her to stroll towards the drive with Roberts. She said: "It's really most awfully kind of you. Are you sure he won't be a nuisance?"

He replied with his slow smile: "Why, no, Miss Allison. I've got a kind of fondness for kids of his age. I'm at a loose end just now, and I'll be mighty glad of his company." His smile grew. "Guess he hopes I'm one of those gunmen he sees in the movies."

She laughed but said with some misgiving: "He's a dreadfully bloodthirsty child. I do hope he hasn't favoured you with his 'theories' about Mr Kanes' death? I've done all I can to squash him, but without much success."

"I shouldn't worry," he answered. "Kids just naturally get those ideas."

She felt impelled to say: "Of course, there's nothing in it. It was an accident. I don't want you to get a false impression from Timothy."

He looked down at her with a twinkle in his eyes. "Any impression I get won't come from Timothy, Miss Allison," he said deliberately.

CHAPTER FOUR

GREATLY to Timothy's disgust, the inquest on Silas Kane's death contained no thrills. A verdict of death by misadventure was returned, a post-mortem examination having established the fact that Silas must have had a heart attack. His own doctor gave some highly technical evidence and annoyed Timothy by agreeing that, although an attack was unexpected, he would not go so far as to say that he was surprised that Silas should have had one. The excitement of his birthday party, coupled with overfatigue, might well have produced it.

Joseph Mansell and his son both corroborated the statement that Silas had been in the habit of working too hard, Joseph adding that in his opinion Silas' powers had been declining for the past few months.

Clement was a still more disappointing witness. Questioned, he would not say that his cousin had been in failing health. He had not been a young man; things had certainly tired him. He had not discussed Silas' health with him; he had not noticed any particular signs of weariness or excitement in him on the night of his death.

No persuasions had availed to keep Timothy away from the inquest, but he professed himself disgusted with the result. When it was over Oscar Roberts took him and Miss Allison, who had been present in obedience to Emily's command, to refresh themselves with lemonade and ices before returning to Cliff House. He seemed to be considerably amused by Timothy. He allowed the boy to air his views, recommending him to get it off his chest once and for all, advice which Timothy followed, bitterly announcing his dissatisfaction with the methods of the Portlaw police.

"They jolly well ought to have found out what everybody was doing when Uncle Silas was killed," he said.

"They did," replied Patricia. "You know perfectly well they made all the proper inquiries."

Timothy snorted. "I don't call it making proper inquiries just to ask people where they were and not to try and prove they weren't there at all. Why, they didn't even *ask* Jim, and he was at the party."

"You unnatural viper!" said Patricia calmly. "Besides, what had Jim—I mean, your stepbrother—to gain by murdering his cousin?"

"I know, but——"

"The fact of the matter is, son, that you can't have a murder without motive," said Roberts.

"There were motives!" replied Timothy instantly.

"Look at Clement! He's getting simply pots of money out of it."

Patricia removed the lemonade straw from her mouth to expostulate. "You definitely must *not* go about saying your Cousin Clement had a motive for murdering Mr Kane!"

"He isn't my cousin. I'm a Harte," said Timothy loftily. "I'll bet Mr Roberts thinks he had a pretty good motive."

"Sure I think it," agreed Roberts. "But I've a notion that if I were Mr Clement Kane I wouldn't run the risk of bumping off an old man who had a valvular disease of the heart. Guess I'd wait a piece for Nature to do its work."

Timothy shook his head. "Not if you wanted his money absolutely at once."

"He didn't," said Patricia. "The Clement Kanes are quite well off."

Timothy was silenced for the moment, but the consumption of a large strawberry ice inspired him afresh. "Well, what about the Mansells?" he demanded.

Patricia glanced round the teashop apprehensively. "For heaven's sake shut up!" she begged.

"Yes, but they had a motive. I know *all* about the Australian show. I'll bet Mr Roberts——"

"No, no, sonny, you won't drag me into that!" interposed Roberts. "Next you'll be telling me I've got a motive. See here, now! This kind of talk isn't going big with Miss Allison at all. What do you say we drop it?"

Patricia looked at him. "I believe you're as bad as he is," she said.

"No, no," he assured her. "But when a man falls off a cliff edge, Miss Allison, folks just naturally get to wondering about it. You can't blame Timothy. It's kind of inevitable."

"But surely you don't think——"

"I don't know enough about the family to think anything," he said with a shade of reserve in his voice.

When Emily heard about the proceedings at the inquest she smiled grimly and said she had expected nothing else. Something in her tone impelled Clement, who had driven Patricia and Timothy back to Cliff House, to inquire a little sharply what she meant.

"If you don't know what I mean it won't hurt you," replied Emily.

Clement reddened. "Well, I certainly don't, Aunt. I should have thought it was obvious that Cousin Silas' death was due to the fog, coupled with one of his heart attacks."

She fixed him with one of her blank stares. "Pray, who said it was not?"

Timothy, scenting an ally, said: "I do."

Emily looked at him. "You do, do you? And why?"

"Well, partly because he was so frightfully rich, and partly because I had an instinct there was going to be a murder."

The word sounded ugly. Clement's eyes snapped behind his pince-nez; he said in an angry voice: "How dare you say such a thing? It seems to me you let your stupid imagination run away with you! I thought you were old enough to know better."

"Leave the boy alone," said Emily. "He's entitled to his opinion as much as you are to yours. So my son was murdered, was he, Timothy?"

"Well, I don't absolutely *know* he was," replied Timothy with a touch of caution, "but I do think it looks jolly suspicious. What's more, I'm pretty sure Mr Roberts thinks so too."

"Roberts!" Clement exclaimed. "What has Roberts to do with it? You've no right to discuss this affair with a stranger! Really, I think it high time Jim came down and took you in hand!"

But Mr James Kane, when he arrived, three days after Clement and Rosemary had taken up their residence at Cliff House, showed little disposition to take his stepbrother in hand. His energies were concentrated upon Miss Allison, who had had by that time such a surfeit of the Clement Kanes, Paul Mansell and Mr Trevor Dermott that she greeted him with unfeigned pleasure. This circumstance led Mr James

Kane to leap to unwarrantable conclusions. He had the audacity to catch Miss Allison up in his arms and to kiss her, not once but several times. Miss Allison apparently decided that it would be useless to struggle with anyone so large and muscular. She submitted to Mr James Kane's rough handling, merely remarking as soon as she was able that she very much disliked people who grabbed ells when offered inches.

Mr Kane only laughed, so Miss Allison, setting her hands against his chest and pushing hard, explained severely that her gladness at seeing him arose purely from boredom.

"My poor dear," said Mr Kane lovingly.

"For goodness' sake let me go!" begged Miss Allison. "What on earth would anyone think if they saw us?"

"They'd think we were going to be married, and they'd be right," replied Mr Kane.

"They'd be far more likely to think you were philandering with your great-aunt's companion," retorted Miss Allison.

"Vulgar little cat!" said Mr Kane, tucking her hand in his arm. "Now that we've settled that, tell me what's been going on here."

"Nothing much. You saw pretty well what it was like at the funeral, didn't you?"

"General impression of piety, that's all. Who's got on your nerves? Rosemary?"

"No, your repulsive little brother. You'll have to sit on him. He will go about looking for clues and saying Mr Kane was murdered."

Jim looked interested. "Really? What put that into his head?"

"The films he sees, of course. I do what I can to squash him, but Mrs Kane encourages him, and so does Mr Roberts—at least, I don't know that he actually encourages him, but I've got an uncomfortable feeling that he suspects Timothy's right."

"Half a shake!" Jim interposed. "Who is Roberts? Do I know him?"

"No, I shouldn't think so. He's the agent for the Australian firm which wants to do business with Kane and Mansell. Rather nice, and awfully decent to Timothy. They struck up an acquaintance after Mr Kane's death. Timothy invites him here, and Clement dodges him when he comes."

"Why?"

"I don't know. Timothy, I hardly need say, has a theory that Mr Roberts is on to something and Clement's afraid to meet him. Actually, I expect it's because Clement doesn't want to be badgered about the Australian business."

"Timothy seems to be doing what he can to liven things up," commented Jim. He had guided Miss Allison across the lawn towards a seat under a big elm tree and now invited her to sit down. Taking his place beside her, he said with an appraising look cast at her profile: "Come on, my love, tell me what's the matter."

She was silent for a moment. He possessed himself of her hand. "Let me remind you that the keynote to a successful marriage is Mutual Confidence."

She smiled at that. "I dare say. I think I've probably exaggerated things in my mind. It—it just seems to me that people are behaving rather abnormally. There's a certain atmosphere in the house—well, you'll see for yourself."

She refused to be more explicit, but there was much that she might have told her betrothed.

There was the attitude adopted by Emily. Emily hated Clement, yet when he had proposed moving to Cliff House immediately, she had not demurred. She had acquiesced, and since his arrival she had ceased to snap at him. Patricia had no fault to find with this, but when she saw Emily looking at Clement she knew that the implacable old lady resented his presence and would always resent it. But after her first outburst she had not spoken again of her dislike, nor had she uttered one word in criticism of Clement's wife. Only she watched them both, her face wooden in its impassivity.

Clement seemed to Miss Allison to be ill at ease, but she thought the new responsibilities resting on his shoulders might account for this. He was often irritable; he fidgeted, frowned, grew querulous over trifles, and looked more harassed than ever. He complained of his partners' stupidity once or twice; it was as though he invited Emily to comment on the firm's policy, perhaps to support him with her ruthless certainty. Miss Allison saw him as a weak man, mistrusting his own judgment, needing the approval of a stronger character before he could be brought to make a decision.

It was plain that he could expect no help from Rosemary. Rosemary was passing through an emotional crisis. She told Patricia that she had reached a turning point in her life, and that it was tearing her in two. Patricia was uncharitable enough to suspect that she was revelling in the drama she had created, and received this piece of information with a marked lack of sympathy. What sympathy she felt was for Clement and for Trevor Dermott, both helpless in the snare of Rosemary's beauty, but her pity for them was charged with contempt. She thought them fools to be slaves to Rosemary.

Yet in Trevor Dermott, whom she profoundly disliked, there was a quality which Rosemary might find disturbing if ever he awoke to a realization of the part he was hereafter destined to play in her life. Miss Allison called him privately the Flamboyant Male but suspected that his flaunted masculinity was an integral part of him and no pose assumed to match his vigorous good looks and lusty body. Stupid he might be, but his hot brown eyes, lacking intelligence, held a spark of purpose. He was of the type that must snatch what it desires: it was too evident that he desired Rosemary, so delicately playing him on the end of her line.

"You can't go on living with a fellow like Kane, a fellow who's only half alive!" he said.

Rosemary looked at him thoughtfully. He supposed her to be comparing his splendid physique with Clement's thin, stooping frame. He did not preen himself, but he laughed, sure of his superiority. Actually no comparison was in her mind. He attracted her strongly; she was loath to let him go; but Clement, possessing his cousin's fortune, was beyond comparison. She said seriously: "Clement *needs* me, Trevor."

It was true; she did not disguise from herself the fact that she needed Clement's money, but she began to feel rather holy. This was reflected in her face, uplifted to Dermott's. He said: "My God, and don't I need you? Are you going to sacrifice us both to a man who doesn't satisfy you, can't so much as start to understand you?"

She sighed. She saw herself immolated upon the altar of wifely duty, the victim of a tragic love affair. That she saw herself gowned by Reville, wearing a long mournful rope of pearls, only made the vision more picturesque: it did not lessen its pathos. "It was just a beautiful dream, Trevor," she said, not very originally but with deep feeling.

"I don't dream," replied Dermott, grasping her arms above the elbows. "Will Clement let you divorce him?"

"No, never."

"He'll have to divorce you, then."

"But, Trevor, you don't understand!" Rosemary said, genuinely distressed. "You *must* realize how important it is for me to have money! It's no use blinking facts, and there's no doubt—I mean, I know myself so well!—that not having any money was what ruined Clement's and my life together. I've simply got to face it."

His grip on her arms tightened until it hurt her He gave an uncertain laugh, his eyes searching hers for the reassurance he needed. "Pretty mercenary, aren't you?"

"You can call it that, if you like."

"I don't know what else to call it!"

"Of course I realize—I always have—that I'm a hateful person," Rosemary said. "I'm not trying to excuse myself; I was just made like that."

"You talk a lot of damned rubbish!" he said roughly. "Have you thought of what's going to happen if you decide to stay with that dried-up stick of a husband of yours?"

She made a slight effort to free herself, but his grip did not slacken. She was afraid her arms would be bruised by it, but the sense it gave her of his strength pleased her. "We can still see each other," she offered.

"Oh no, we can't!" he retorted. "I'm not a lap dog to be whistled up when you please. If you choose Clement and his blasted fortune, it's good-bye, my dear!"

He let her go as he spoke, so certain of his appeal for her, of what her ultimate decision must be, that he dared to utter this threat. His eyes glowed as they rested on her, but he would not touch her again, though his flesh ached for her. "Think it over!" he said. "I won't go on like this."

He saw her face troubled; a trick of the light seemed to show the fineness of the bones under the delicate skin. His voice thickened; he said: "Oh, my sweet— my lovely sweet! I'd be good to you. I'd give you everything. You know you love me!"

A gentle melancholy possessed her. Her eyes filled with tears. She said: "Yes, I do. It *hurts* me! But I must think of Clement. Please don't be unreasonable, Trevor. You don't know how dreadfully, dreadfully difficult it all is!"

A sense of frustration crept over him, but he still could not believe that he might lose her. He repeated: "You'll have to make up your mind once and for all. I mean it."

"Not now, Trevor!" she begged. "I can't. It's no use expecting me to. I just can't."

"No, not now, but this week. I'm going to London tomorrow. I shall be back on Saturday, and I shall want your answer then."

He had had no previous intention of returning to town, but he thought his absence might clinch the matter. The mere contemplation of four days to be spent without sight of her made his heart faint within him;

he could not believe that she might be able to bear them with equanimity.

Her mouth drooped a little, but she accepted the ultimatum without demurring. She would miss him very much, but she thought perhaps the temporary separation would be a good thing for him. If it could be avoided she did not want to lose him altogether; probably four days spent apart from her would chasten him enough to make him agree to her terms.

Most of this was told to that most discouraging of confidants, Patricia Allison. ("I can't imagine what it is about me that induces neurotic idiots like Rosemary to tell me their life stories!" Patricia said despairingly to Mr James Kane.)

"What I can't bear," said Rosemary intensely, "is the thought that I've got to hurt Trevor. *That's* what I've got to face."

Miss Allison was feeling tired. She had left Emily in Ogle's jealous charge and was on the point of going to bed when Rosemary had waylaid her and dragged her off to her own room for a private conference. "Well if that's all you've got to face, you're lucky," she said.

"Ah, but don't you see how much, much worse it is to hurt Trevor than to be hurt myself?" said Rosemary.

Miss Allison shook her head, stifling a yawn. "No."

Rosemary gave her one of her long critical looks. "I expect you're one of those lucky people who don't feel things very deeply," she said.

Miss Allison agreed. It was the easiest thing to do.

"I so terribly want your advice," Rosemary said earnestly. "I'm afraid Trevor may do something desperate."

"Well, I can't stop him," replied Patricia. "I dare say he'll get over it."

"You don't know what it is to be the victim of a *grande passion,*" said Rosemary.

Miss Allison felt extinguished. Rosemary thrust her slim fingers up through her hair. "Sometimes I feel as though I should go mad!" she announced, apparently holding her head on by main force. "What am I to *do?*"

"Snap out of it!" recommended Miss Allison, gratefully borrowing the expression from Mr Harte's vocabulary. "Sorry to be so unsympathetic, but from what I've seen of Trevor Dermott I think you'd better be careful. He doesn't look to me the sort of man you can play about with safely."

Rosemary raised her head from her hands. "I suppose you think it's all terribly silly," she said. "I dare say it seems so to you. But you don't know what it is to be desperately in love, do you?"

This was too much for Miss Allison. She said in an affronted voice: "Considering I've just got engaged to be married——"

"Oh yes, but that's so different!" Rosemary interrupted with a smile of immeasurable superiority. "I mean, you've fallen in love in a sensible way, haven't you? I envy you awfully. I would give *anything* to be able to take things in that quiet way. I know I spend myself too much. It wears me out. Of course, personally, I can't imagine being swept off one's feet by Jim. I know you don't mind my saying that, do you? It isn't that I don't like him. I think he's very nice, in a dull sort of way. What I mean is, he isn't a bit out of the ordinary, is he?"

"We ought to hit it off splendidly, then," said Miss Allison, nettled.

Rosemary's interest in another person's affairs was always evanescent. Her mind had already reverted to the drama of her own life, and she only smiled absently at this remark and said: "I don't think Clement could live without me, do you?"

"I've no idea," replied Miss Allison. "Do you mind if I go to bed? I'm rather sleepy."

"Oh, are you?" said Rosemary, faintly surprised. "I don't feel as though I should ever be able to sleep in this room. I think it's the paper. I lie awake counting those damned baskets of flowers."

"Why not try turning the light out?" suggested Miss Allison.

"My dear," said Rosemary earnestly, "if I do that they close in on me. They do, really. It's my nerves. I've told Clement it's got to be repapered at once. I can't stand it. Do you think I should like a shaded apricot paint?"

"Yes, I'm sure you would," said Miss Allison, edging towards the door.

"I think you've probably got marvellous taste," remarked Rosemary. "The awful part about me is that I think I shall like a thing, and then when it's done I find I loathe it." She sighed. "I suppose you want to go to bed. I don't a bit. I feel as though every nerve in my body was stretched taut. Do you ever get like that?"

"Often," said Miss Allison.

"I don't suppose you do really," said Rosemary. "If you did, you'd never be able to live in the same house with that ghastly maid of Aunt Emily's."

Miss Allison laughed. "Oh, there's no harm in Ogle. She's jealous of anyone trying to come between her and Mrs Kane, that's all."

"She hates me," said Rosemary. "She spies on me. She hates Clement too. I've got a sort of sixth sense that tells me she does."

"I think you're mistaken," said Patricia, not because she did think so but with the unhopeful object of nipping this obsession in the bud. "She just doesn't care tuppence for anyone but Mrs Kane."

But Ogle's dislike of the Clement Kanes was so bitter that it superseded her mistrust of Miss Allison. She said: "Them to be in the master's place, driving my dear into her grave with their nasty ways!"

"Nonsense!" said Miss Allison.

Ogle shot a smouldering look at her under her thick low brows. "You may call it nonsense if you please, miss. I'm only an ignorant old woman that never had any fine education, but I know what I know, and no one'll ever persuade me different." She went on folding Emily's clothes away, handling them tenderly, as though they were a part of Emily. "Forty-five years I've been with her. I know her better than Mr Silas did, better than the old master did." She paused and added grimly: "He was a bad husband to her. Light come, light go. But she never said anything. She was never one to talk about her troubles."

"You should not tell me this," Patricia said gently.

"You could learn it easy enough from others besides me. She's too old to have more troubles."

"I know it's unfortunate that she should dislike Mr Clement, but perhaps she'll get used to him. He's very kind to her, after all."

"She won't get used to him!" Ogle said fiercely. "She'll eat her heart out, with no one but me to turn to! Everyone leaves her but me. There's no one cares what becomes of her. She took a fancy to you, but you don't mean to stay."

Patricia said guiltily: "I'm going to be married."

"Yes, miss, she told me. You're going to marry Mr James. Why don't you stay with her, the both of you?"

"We couldn't do that. This is Mr Clement's house. Of course, I shall stay till she finds someone else to take my place."

Ogle rolled up a pair of stockings, her hands trembling a little. "Some worthless madam to plague her life out! You're the only one she ever had that wasn't a worriting fool! But you don't care! No one cares but me!"

Miss Allison felt that the news of her approaching nuptials could scarcely be said (in Oscar Roberts' phraseology) to have gone over big either with Ogle or with Rosemary.

Emily, however, had seemed pleased; and Clement, though it was evident that he thought his cousin might have done better for himself, congratulated both parties and said that Miss Allison would be a great loss to everyone at Cliff House. Young Mr Harte was no believer in marriage and was inclined to look upon his stepbrother's engagement as yet another instance of a promising career blighted, but he admitted that Miss Allison was quite a decent sort.

"Anyway, she's not half as bad as that Malcolm dame you were nuts on two years ago," he said.

This handsome tribute failed to please. Jim said in a dulcet voice: "My little pet, what a gift from heaven you are! It may interest you to know that I don't even remember what the Malcolm dame looked like."

"She was a bit like the other one you were gone on," said Timothy helpfully. "I forget her name, but she had red fingernails, and——"

"If you don't shut up I'll wring your neck!" said Mr James Kane.

This ferocious threat made Mr Harte aware suddenly that he had hit upon a subject for blackmail. His eye brightened; he said: "I bet Miss Allison doesn't know about the others."

"There weren't any others," said Jim. "Don't try to be funny!"

Mr Harte drove his hands into the pockets of his trousers and said with a grin: "Say, buddy, let's talk business!"

Jim sighed his resignation. "You're barking up the wrong tree. My life's an open book."

"Sure it is," agreed Mr. Harte. "The way I figure it——"

"Talk English!"

"Right!" said Mr Harte briskly. "Will you take me with you when you have the speedboat out?"

"I might."

"Nix on that!" said Mr Harte, reverting to a foreign tongue. "I've got the drop on you, and don't you forget it!"

Miss Allison arrived on the scene a few minutes later to find Mr Harte, in a highly dishevelled condition, ensconced on the branch of a tree well above Jim's reach. She shook her head regretfully. "You should have wrung his neck while you had him," she said.

"I know I should," replied Jim. "Blackmail's his latest racket."

"Do you swear to take me out *every* time with you in the boat?" demanded Mr Harte.

"No. Do your worst!" said Jim.

"You are a rotten cad!" said Mr Harte, disgusted. "I've a jolly good mind to blow the gaff."

"Ha!" exclaimed Miss Allison. "I knew it! You've got a guilty secret. Timothy, is there another woman in his life?"

"Hundreds of them!" said Timothy with relish.

Miss Allison appeared to be overcome and begged Mr James Kane, in throbbing accents, not to touch her.

"Curse you, you have been my ruin!" groaned Mr Kane, shaking his fist at the tree.

"I say, Jim, you will take me, won't you?" said Mr Harte, abandoning blackmail.

"Yes, and drop you overboard with a weight tied round your ankles. Come down!"

"Is it pax if I do?" inquired Mr Harte suspiciously.

"All right," agreed Jim.

Mr Harte descended, gave his trousers a perfunctory brush with his hands, and said darkly: "I know one person who'll probably have a fit when he hears about Miss Allison and you getting married."

"Talking about serpents' teeth . . ." began Miss Allison hastily.

"No, you don't!" interrupted Jim. "Go on, Timothy; who is it?"

"Mr Mansell," replied Timothy. "Not old Mr Mansell; the other one. I shouldn't be a bit surprised if he tried to poison you, or something. He's batty about Miss Allison."

"What, that bounder?" said Jim. "Fellow with waved hair and a wasp waist? Pat, I thought better of you!"

"Nor was your trust misplaced," answered Patricia cheerfully. "I think he's a horror."

"He is too," nodded Timothy. "I jolly well hope he comes oiling round you again before he knows about your being engaged to Jim. Then Jim can dot him one on the boko." This programme appealed to him so strongly that his eyes gleamed with simple pleasure, and he added: "It 'ud be a pretty good lark if he did come and start making love to Miss Allison! I should think you could knock him out *easily,* couldn't you? I say, let's lay a trap for him! I bet Clement would be as pleased as punch if you beat him up."

"Why?" demanded Miss Allison.

"Because he can't stand him, of course. He had a stinking row with him on the phone yesterday. I know, 'cos I was in the room, and when Clement rang off he woffled a whole lot to me about people bothering his life out, and never seeing any point of view but their own, and being sick to death of the whole Mansell family."

Jim told him he ought not to repeat such confidences, but they did not come as news to him. Clement had already unburdened himself to his cousin, complaining of the enormous death duties Silas' estate would have to bear, of the weight of responsibility Silas had left him. He had even touched upon the Australian project, but though Jim could sympathize he felt himself to be quite unqualified to advise.

Clement made it plain that he was being badgered by his partners. It seemed to Jim that one half of his mind liked the Australian plan, while the other half shrank from it. He vacillated as Silas would never have done, mistrusted all the Mansells' arguments in favour of the scheme, and ended by absenting himself from the office on the score of having so much to do in picking up the threads of Silas' private affairs that he had no time for more than flying visits to the office. The ingenuity he displayed in evading Oscar Roberts lent a certain amount of colour to Timothy's theory, but Roberts cornered him at last by the simple expedient of stating calmly that when he came to Cliff House on Saturday afternoon, as he had been invited to do, he hoped to have a little talk with Clement before presenting himself at Mrs Kane's tea table. Clement agreed, vaguely thankful that he would be able to make his position clear to Roberts without having to encounter at the same time arguments, and possibly recriminations, from his two partners.

"He's going to turn it down," Paul said.

"I'm afraid so. I'm afraid so," Joe Mansell replied. "I would never have thought it of him. Never."

Paul smiled rather unpleasantly but said nothing.

"Roberts may manage to persuade him," Joe said, but without much hope.

"Why should he?" Paul shrugged. "Plenty of other firms who'd jump at his proposition if we pass it up."

"No doubt, but there's only one Kane and Mansell," said Joe. "I fancy we stand alone."

"He won't care about that," Paul said. "He wants the best if he can get it, but if he can't the next best will do very well. You'll see."

"I have half a mind to call at Cliff House on Saturday myself," said Joe. "After all, I am much older than Clement, and if he listens to anyone it will be to me. I can quite well go to see the old lady. In fact, I ought to pay her a visit. I haven't been there since Silas died."

Emily, had he but known it, counted this a gain and would certainly have elected to stay in her own room on Saturday if she had had warning of his fell design. Since Clement's arrival at Cliff House she had segregated herself as much as was possible. On fine mornings she drove out for an hour in a landaulette Daimler of antique design which she obstinately refused to part with, but she usually lunched upstairs and rarely came down afterwards. Rosemary, who was expecting Trevor Dermott, thought that sheer perversity prompted Emily to elect to be wheeled into the garden at three o'clock on Saturday afternoon. She was convinced that Emily knew of Dermott's impending visit and wished to spy upon her, and complained bitterly to Patricia that when the disconcerting old lady was at large you were never safe, because for all her pretence of having to be wheeled about she could move perfectly well on her own feet and very often did so.

Patricia, who had more than once been surprised at Emily's mobility, could not help laughing at Rosemary's injured expression. She suspected shrewdly that it amused Emily to startle her family by sudden spurts of energy, but she knew that her unaided excursions tired her more than she would admit. She quite agreed that it would be impolitic to present Trevor Dermott to Emily and managed by the exercise of considerable tact to settle her comfortably on the south side of the house, out of range of the front avenue. Here Jim joined her, a circumstance which made it possible for Miss Allison to slip away into the house to make up the weekly accounts which formed a part of her duties.

Rosemary, aware that a highly dramatic and possibly violent scene lay before her, armed herself for it by putting on a dove-grey frock and an appealing picture hat. The facts that Emily was seated within earshot of the drawing room, that Clement was working in the study, and that Timothy showed a disposition to drift in and out of the house made her decide to conduct her interview with Dermott elsewhere. Accordingly she strolled out of the house and down the avenue to meet him, naïvely informing Miss Allison that she thought it would really be better if Clement did not see that provocative touring car drive up to the door.

Miss Allison quite agreed with her. She watched her compose her face into an expression of wistful saintliness, enjoyed a private laugh at her expense, and retired to wrestle with accounts in the little room she used as an office.

These did not take her long, and by half-past three she had finished. She picked up the detailed list for Clement and was about to take it to his study when she heard a bell ring faintly in the distance and, going out into the hall, encountered Pritchard on his way to the front door.

He opened it, and Oscar Roberts stepped over the

threshold, saying pleasantly: "Good afternoon. I fancy Mr Kane's expecting me."

"Yes sir. Will you come this way?" said Pritchard, relieving him of his hat and cane.

Oscar Roberts smiled at Miss Allison and was about to follow the butler when a sudden report, as from a gun, startled them all into immobility. For an instant no one moved. Then Pritchard muttered: "My God, what's that?" and almost ran to the study door and flung it open.

Clement Kane lay crumpled across his desk, one arm hanging limply at his side, the other crooked under his fallen head.

CHAPTER FIVE

MISS ALLISON did not scream, because she was not in the habit of relieving her feelings by a display of hysterics, but her knees felt suddenly weak, and she grasped a chair back instinctively.

Pritchard, after one instant's shocked recoil, had started forward to his master's side. Miss Allison heard him say in a shaken voice: "My God, he's been shot through the head! Oh, my God!"

Oscar Roberts, with a murmured word of apology, put Miss Allison out of his way and strode into the study. He wasted no time in verifying Pritchard's statement but after a quick glance round the room leapt for the open window, threw a leg over the sill, and the next instant had plunged into the shrubbery on the other side of the narrow gravel path.

Miss Allison set her teeth and walked into the study. The butler was looking very white and made a sign to her not to come near his master's desk. "Don't, miss! I wouldn't . . ." he said, wiping his face with his handkerchief.

"The police. We must telephone to the police," Miss Allison said in an unnaturally calm voice and picked up the receiver from the instrument on the desk, keeping her eyes carefully averted from Clement's huddled body.

A quick footstep sounded in the hall, and the next moment Jim Kane came into the room. "What was that?" he demanded. "I could have sworn I heard a——" He broke off. "Good God!" he said and went at once to the desk and bent over Clement. He straightened himself almost at once, nearly as white as Pritchard. "Who did it?" he said curtly.

The butler shook his head. Miss Allison, connected with the police station, said baldly: "I am speaking from Cliff House. Mr Clement Kane has been shot. Will you please send someone at once?"

Oscar Roberts, rather dishevelled and out of breath, reappeared at the window and climbed into the room again. "Those gosh-darned rhododendrons!" he said. "He's gotten away, the skunk!"

"Who?" said Jim sharply. "Do you know who did this? Did you see him?"

"Not to say saw," Roberts replied. "I kind of heard a rustle amongst those bushes and made for it, but it's like a jungle out there, and he had the start of me. The way I figure it he was making for the front drive. You've got all of a twenty-foot bank of those rhododendrons right the way up the drive. It was a cinch for that guy! Through that darned shrubbery to the drive, across it into the rhododendrons. Surest thing you know, he was over the wall with a clean getaway before I reached the drive. Say, did you ring up the police?"

Miss Allison nodded. Jim said: "Look here, do you know who did this?"

Roberts bent to brush the leaf mould from his trousers. "If I knew who did it I wouldn't be standing here waiting for your comic police, Mr Kane," he replied enigmatically.

Jim stared at him, his brows knit. "Any ideas on the subject?" he said.

"That's a large question, Mr Kane. Guess we can all of us have ideas, but believe me, there's more harm done spreading them about than by keeping them to yourself." His deep-set eyes fell on Miss Allison. He said significantly: "Maybe you'd like to take Miss Allison out of this."

"I'm all right," said Patricia, pressing her handkerchief to her lips.

Timothy's voice was heard in the garden. "I say, what's up?" he panted. "I swear I heard a shot!"

Oscar Roberts moved swiftly to the window, to block the view, just as young Mr Harte came plunging out onto the path from the shrubbery.

"Hullo, Mr Roberts!" said Timothy. "Who's shooting around here?"

Roberts said quickly: "Hullo, son! Whereabouts have you been?"

"Well, I went down to the lodge to meet you, but——"

"That's fine. Look, now! Did you see anyone?"

Timothy stared. "No, only Mr Dermott. I say, what on earth . . ."

Miss Allison gave a start and groped for a chair. "Jim! He couldn't have——"

"Shut up, of course not!" said Jim roughly. "Keep calm!"

"Mr Dermott?" repeated Roberts in his drawling voice. "I get you. And what was he doing?"

"I don't know. He looked like nothing on earth. He simply bolted for his car and went off at about a hundred miles an hour. Has he had a row with Clement, or something?"

Jim removed his hand from Miss Allison's grasp and joined Roberts at the window. "I say, Timothy, push off, will you, and keep your mouth shut? There's been ——an accident or something. Clement's been shot."

Timothy's eyes grew round; speechless, he stared at his stepbrother. Jim said: "Go and keep Aunt Emily company, old thing. Do you mind?"

"Gosh!" gasped Timothy and, ducking under Jim's arm, thrust his head and shoulders into the room. A moment later he withdrew them, started to say something, and ended by vanishing discreetly into the shrubbery. When he reappeared he was rather wan of countenance and made no further attempt to look into the study. "Sorry!" he said jerkily. "Ate something that disagreed with me. Who—who did it?"

"We don't know. Clear out, and keep Aunt Emily away. See?"

Mr Harte, unusually subdued, said that he did and departed.

Jim turned back into the room. "Come on, Pat; you can't do anything here. As far as I can see, there's nothing to be done till the police turn up. Suppose you clear out?"

"Yes," she agreed, getting up. "Of course. I'll go to Mrs Kane. Do you want me to tell her—or—or what?"

"I should think you'd be the best person. Feel all right?"

"Perfectly, thanks." She moved to the still-open door and went out and through the drawing room to the south side of the house, where she had left Emily.

Emily was standing by her chair, leaning on her ebony cane, with her other hand on Timothy's arm. Ogle was engaged in spreading her rug over the chair for her to sit on, fussily scolding.

"That'll do!" said Emily snappishly. "I suppose I can stretch my legs if I choose? Anyone would think I was decrepit. I've had a little stroll, and I feel the better for it." She sank down into her chair, rather out of breath, and allowed Ogle to fold the ends of the rug over her knees. "You can tell Jim that Ogle brought the rug," she informed Miss Allison.

Ogle, on her knees and tucking Emily's feet up tenderly, raised her head and said pugnaciously: "I knew she'd feel the wind chilly. I didn't want telling to fetch her rug. Left alone like she was!"

A phantasmagoria of nightmarish conjecture for an instant possessed Miss Allison's brain. She looked from the maid's dark countenance, upturned to hers, to Emily's wrinkled one, with the clenched jaw and the remote eyes staring straight ahead. She said hurriedly: "Mrs Kane, there is something I've got to tell you. It's very bad news."

Emily's grim mouth twitched sardonically. She glanced up. "I dare say I can stand it. What's the matter now?"

"Mr Clement has been shot," said Miss Allison baldly.

There was a long pause. Ogle's head was bent over her task; her hands arranged the rug mechanically. "What do you mean by that?" said Emily at last. "Is he dead?"

"Yes, Mrs Kane."

"Murdered!" said Timothy.

The old eyes snapped at him. "I didn't suppose it was suicide!" said Emily sharply.

"Didn't you hear the shot? I did!"

"No, I did not," said Emily. Her hands folded themselves together in her lap. "So Clement's dead!" she said. "He's no loss."

Miss Allison saw Rosemary coming towards them from the direction of the lake and realized that she had been forgotten by them all. She said: "Oh, good heavens! Mrs Clement! . . ."

Emily looked contemptuous. "Well, she won't break her heart over it." She watched Rosemary's slow approach. "Where's that Dermott?" she asked abruptly.

"He's gone," Patricia answered before Timothy could speak.

"H'm!"

"I think, if you don't mind," said Timothy, "that I'll go and see what's happening indoors."

"I don't think they really want you," said Patricia, sympathizing with his evident desire to escape from what promised to be a highly emotional scene.

"I like their darned cheek!" Timothy said indignantly. "Who was it who said all along it was murder? You know jolly well it was me! I bet some people are feeling pretty silly now, that's all!"

"He's probably right," said Emily as he disappeared into the house. "*I* don't know where he gets his wits from. His mother never had any, and his father always seems to me a fool. You needn't stand about, Ogle; I don't want you."

"You don't—surely you don't connect this with Mr Kane's death?" said Patricia.

"I never said so, did I?" retorted Emily. She waited for Rosemary to mount the shallow steps onto the terrace and then nodded an imperious summons to her. Rosemary, whose air of wistful renunciation proclaimed unmistakably to those who knew the circumstances that she had given Trevor Dermott his congee came up to her and said: "Do you want me, Aunt Emily? I was just going up to my room. I want to be alone just for a little while."

This speech clearly invited question, but Emily replied in her flattest tone: "You'd better know before you go any farther that your husband's been shot."

Rosemary looked blankly down at her. "My husband? *Clement?*"

"You've only one as far as I know," said Emily testily.

Under her delicate make-up Rosemary had turned very pale. There was fright in her eyes, fixed painfully on Emily's face. She faltered: "When?"

"Just now—or so I imagine," replied Emily. She looked up over her shoulder at Patricia. "Wasn't it?"

"Yes. About twenty minutes ago, I suppose. Will you sit down, Mrs—I mean Rosemary?"

Rosemary shook her head, moistening her lips. "No, I'm all right. I don't seem able to grasp it, quite. My mind feels numb. It's the oddest sensation. As though——"

Emily interrupted with her usual ruthlessness: "There's no need to tell me what you feel like. I've never been interested in your sensations yet, and I never shall be, what's more."

"It's too terrible, too ghastly!" Rosemary said. "How—how did it happen?"

She looked at Patricia, but it was Emily who replied: "That's for the police to discover."

Rosemary looked as though she were going to faint. Patricia moved quickly to her side and took her arm. "I'll take you up to your room," she said. "It's a dreadful shock for you."

Rosemary made a vague gesture. "Everything seems *black!* I can't realize it. I simply don't seem to be able to take it in."

Emily gave a short laugh under her breath but said nothing more. Miss Allison led Rosemary in through the drawing room to the hall. Here they were checked by the sight of a uniformed police-sergeant and a man in plain clothes who was speaking to Oscar Roberts.

Rosemary gave an uncontrollable start; her long pointed fingernails dug into Miss Allison's arm; Patricia heard the quick intake of her breath and gave her hand a reassuring squeeze.

Jim Kane turned. "Oh! . . . Just a moment, Rosemary. Take her into the morning room, Pat. The inspector wants to ask her one or two questions."

Miss Allison could not help thinking that he seemed to have changed from the man she knew into a rather forbidding stranger. He gave her a brief hint of a smile and walked across the hall to open the door into the morning room.

"I don't know anything!" Rosemary said rather too loudly. "I feel utterly dazed. I can't *think!* For God's sake don't leave me, Patricia!"

"It's all right; I won't go," Patricia said soothingly.

Jim shut the door on them. Rosemary sank into a

chair, shivering. "Oh God, I feel most frightfully sick!" she said, pressing her hands to her temples. "What does he want to see me for? I wasn't even in the house. I can't tell him anything. I don't *know* anything. Where are you going?" Her voice rose on a note of panic.

"Only to get you something to help you pull yourself together. I won't be a minute."

"No, no, don't! I simply can't bear it. He might come in at any moment!"

Patricia came back to her side but said sensibly: "Well, you must try to calm yourself. The inspector won't eat you. Don't you see that you're one of the first people he's bound to want to talk to? Honestly, there's nothing to be afraid of."

"Oh, I know, but when one's nerves have had a frightful shock, one simply isn't oneself. I really do feel as though I were going to be sick, or faint, or something."

At this moment Jim came into the room with a glass in his hand. Rosemary was rocking herself slightly, giving little dry sobs. He went to her and, putting his arm round her shoulders, held the glass to her lips. "It's only brandy . . . Come along!"

Her teeth chattered against the glass, but she swallowed the spirit and said chokingly: "Thanks. What does that awful man want with me?"

"He isn't awful. Quite human," Jim replied.

"There's something about policemen that makes one's inside turn upside down," said Rosemary. "I can't help it. I shall be all right in a minute."

"Have they found out anything, Jim?" asked Miss Allison in a low voice.

Over Rosemary's head his eyes met hers for a moment. "No. Not yet."

"What's going to happen?"

"I don't know. Looks like a nasty mess. Do you feel fit enough to see Inspector Carlton now, Rosemary?"

"As long as he doesn't expect me to *think!*" said Rosemary unpromisingly.

Jim went out again, and in a few minutes the inspector came into the room.

His initial speech of sympathy for the murdered man's widow and his apology for being obliged to disturb her at such a time did much to restore Rosemary's poise. She stopped rocking herself to and fro and achieving a wan smile explained that she was one of those excessively highly strung people whose nerves were simply unequal to the task of bearing her up in the face of disaster.

The inspector said that he quite understood.

"Everything seems to be a blank," added Rosemary, passing a hand across her eyes.

"I am sure no one could be surprised that you should feel like that, madam. It must be a terrible shock. I understand you were not in the house when it happened."

"Thank God, no!" answered Rosemary with a strong shudder. "I think I should have gone quite, quite mad."

"Yes indeed, madam. I wonder if you would mind telling me just where you were at the time?"

"I think I must have been down by the lake. I went there—oh, at about three, I should think. Miss Allison saw me go, didn't you, Patricia?"

Miss Allison corroborated this and found herself favoured by the inspector with a long searching look. "Miss Allison?" he said.

"Yes."

"You are Mrs John Kane's secretary, I understand?"

"Yes."

"You were in the house at the time of the murder?"

"Yes. I was in the room next to this."

"Thank you," said the inspector, making an entry in his notebook. He glanced at Rosemary again. "Was anyone with you in the garden this afternoon, madam?"

"Oh yes!" replied Rosemary nervously. "A friend of

ours called. I was sitting talking to him by the lake for quite some time."

"His name?" asked the inspector, pencil poised.

"Dermott—Mr Trevor Dermott. A very old friend of ours."

The inspector looked up. "Is Mr Dermott on the premises now?"

"No, oh no! He left some time ago. I mean, before I'd the least idea of this frightful thing having happened."

"Mr Dermott did not, to your knowledge, see your husband this afternoon, madam?"

"No, I know he didn't. He never came up to the house at all. My husband had a business appointment, and I walked down the drive to meet Mr Dermott. He simply left his car down the drive, and we sat by the lake till he had to go."

The inspector looked at her. "You were expecting Mr Dermott this afternoon?"

"Well, yes, in a way I was. I mean, he said he might look me up today if he got back from town."

"I see." The inspector closed his notebook. "Had your husband, to your knowlege, any enemies, madam?"

Rosemary did not answer for a moment. Miss Allison watched her with misgiving. Rosemary raised her eyes to the inspector's face and said hesitantly: "I hardly know what to say. As a matter of fact, I do happen to know that he was having a good deal of trouble at the office with his partners. I don't really understand business—I simply don't pretend to—but I know his partners were absolutely set on doing something my husband wouldn't agree to."

"Mr Clement Kane was, I understand, the senior partner in the firm?"

"Yes, he was; that's just it."

"You don't know of any private quarrel Mr Kane may have had?"

"N-no," Rosemary answered. "Not exactly a *quarrel*. Of course, I know his great-aunt resented his inheriting all Silas Kane's property and loathed us being here, but they didn't quarrel. I simply hate having to tell you this, but I do feel it's my duty not to keep anything back. And actually it's no secret that his great-aunt hated Clement. Everyone knows that James Kane is the one she'd like to have here."

Miss Allison fixed her gaze upon the prospect outside and thought of all the painful ways there might be of killing Mrs Clement Kane. Rosemary's voice flowed on, but at last the inspector went away, and Miss Allison was able to favour Rosemary with a pithy résumé of her own character as seen through the eyes of Mr James Kane's affianced wife.

Her remarks, however, glanced off the armour of Rosemary's superb egotism. Rosemary was grieved to think that anyone could so misjudge the purity of her motives. She explained earnestly that she had gone through the familiar processes known to her as Asking Herself What She Ought to Do. Miss Allison, who knew that Rosemary's mysterious Self, so often appealed to, so invariably in agreement with Rosemary, was divinely guided, at this point abandoned the argument and left the room.

The inspector, meanwhile, encountering James Kane in the hall, had requested him to accompany him to the study, whence Clement's body had by this time been removed for the purpose of answering a few questions on his own movements during the course of the afternoon.

"You state that you were seated on the terrace in the company of the elder Mrs Kane until about half-past three, when the shot was fired?"

"Yes," agreed Jim.

"When you left Mrs Kane, where did you go, sir?"

"Up to her rooms on the first floor. She wanted her garden rug, and I went to ask her personal maid for it."

"I understand the maid was not in Mrs Kane's rooms at the time?"

"No."

"So what did you do, sir?"

"I looked round for the rug but couldn't see it. I then came downstairs again and went into the garden hall, thinking it might be kept there."

"The garden hall? That is the room on the same side of the house as this?"

"Correct."

"With a way into the garden, I think?"

"Of course. I'll show you."

"You were, I think you said, in this garden room when you heard the shot fired?"

"I was, yes."

"Did you form any idea of the direction from which the sound came?"

"I thought it came from just outside."

"What did you do, sir?"

"I went out at once through the door onto the path that runs down the side of the house and looked round."

"And you saw no one, Mr Kane?"

"Not a sign of anyone."

The inspector moved to the window and looked out. Then he drew his head in again. "You stated a little while ago that you went out *immediately* you heard the shot. If that is so, it seems very strange that you should not have caught a glimpse of anyone on this side of the house. There does not seem to be any room for doubt that your cousin was shot from the window."

Jim frowned a little. "Yes, it does," he admitted. "Damned odd. I can only suppose that whoever it was must have managed to get to cover in the shrubbery before I came out. I shouldn't have thought he had time. He must have been darned nippy."

The inspector's eyes measured the distance from the path to the shrubbery. Then he looked at Jim again and said: "When you failed to see anyone, did you make any sort of search in the shrubbery, sir?"

"No. I waited for a moment or two and then came into the house again. Then I saw this door standing open and heard the butler and Miss Allison talking."

"You waited for a moment or two? Why did you do that, sir?"

Jim smiled. "Well, to tell you the truth, I thought it might be my young stepbrother up to mischief. I shouted at him, but he answered me from quite some way off, and I realized it couldn't have had anything to do with him."

The inspector made a lengthy note in his book and after an appreciable pause said: "Mr Clement Kane had recently inherited a considerable property. I understand you are the present heir, are you not, sir?"

"I?" said Jim. "No, you've been misinformed there. I belong to the youngest branch of the family. After my cousin Clement, it would go to the Australian branch."

"Indeed, sir, is that so?" The inspector seemed interested. "Would you mind giving me the name of the present heir?"

"Sorry, I'm afraid I can't. My great-aunt would probably know, though. I think it's a female—but I'm not entirely sure. Perhaps you'd like to see Mrs Kane yourself?"

"If you please, sir," said the inspector, standing aside for Jim to go before him out of the room.

In the hall Jim stopped, for Pritchard was standing by the open front door, speaking in a low voice to Joseph Mansell.

Joseph caught sight of Jim and came forward at once. "Jim! This—this appalling—— Pon my word, I don't know what to say! I came round to pay a call on Mrs Kane and was met by this shocking news. I—really, I'm so overwhelmed by it—so upset! . . . Good God, it's incredible, utterly incredible!" He wiped his face with his handkerchief as he spoke, and Jim saw that his hand was shaking a little. "Pritchard tells me he was shot in his study. I suppose you have no idea who can have done such a dastardly thing?"

"None at all, sir."

"No, no, naturally not!" Joe said. "It's inexplicable! I shouldn't have said he had an enemy in the world.

Poor fellow, poor fellow!" He became aware of Inspector Carlton at Jim's elbow and gave him a nod of recognition. "This is a terrible business, Inspector. It doesn't bear thinking of. The loss to the firm too! A most able fellow, a splendid man to work with, just like his cousin before him! What a tragedy!" He shook his head and, fetching one of his gusty sighs, said: "I had better go now. I wouldn't dream of worrying Mrs Kane at such a moment." He glanced uncertainly at Carlton and added: "If there's anything I can do, or—or if you want me, Inspector, you know where you can find me, don't you?"

"Yes sir. I shall be wanting to ask you one or two questions."

"Certainly, certainly! Anything I can tell you—only too anxious to be of assistance!" Joe assured him.

"If you'll wait a minute I'll find out if my great-aunt can see you, Inspector," said Jim.

The inspector bowed and walked over to study a somewhat gloomy seascape hanging by the front door. Jim went into the drawing room, where he found not only Emily, but Oscar Roberts, and Timothy, and Miss Allison as well.

Emily, having said that she saw no reason why tea should not be served as usual, was seated in her particular chair, eating a slice of bread and butter. Miss Allison, behind the tea table, did not seem to be hungry, but Timothy and Mr Roberts were following Emily's example.

"Well?" said Emily, glancing up at her favourite great-nephew. "Have they done yet? Your tea will be cold."

"Just a moment, Aunt. The inspector wants to ask you a question. May I show him in?"

Emily said in her most disagreeable voice: "I don't know what he thinks I can tell him. You can show him in if you want to."

"It's only about the Australian cousin," explained Jim. "He wants to know her name. It is a she, isn't it?"

"What's that Australian lot got to do with him?"

said Emily, opening her eyes to their widest extent.

"I suppose he feels he must check up on every-body," replied Jim. He opened the door again and turned. "Will you come in, Inspector? Mrs Kane will see you."

The inspector, in asking to question Mrs Kane, was doing no more than his duty, but he came rather diffi-dently into the room and, confronted by the old lady seated so upright in her chair and holding in her hand a cup and saucer, at once apologized for intruding upon her. Emily nodded at him and stared in a way calculated to upset the coolest nerves.

"Very sorry to disturb you, madam, I'm sure. If you would just be good enough to confirm that you were seated upon the terrace with Mr—er—Mr James Kane up till, approximately, three-thirty this afternoon——"

"Yes, I was," said Emily.

"I understand you asked Mr Kane to fetch a rug at about the time of the murder?"

"I dare say," said Emily. "Not that I know when the murder was committed, for I don't."

"You did not hear the shot, madam?"

"No, I did not," said Emily. "If I'd heard the shot I should have said so."

"Yes madam—I'm sure." The inspector coughed and added tentatively: "I beg pardon, but are you at all deaf, madam—if I may ask?"

Emily, who, in common with most people afflicted by slight deafness, strongly resented such an implica-tion being made, glared at him and said angrily: "There's nothing wrong with my hearing at all! I hear very well indeed—as long as people don't mumble at me!"

The inspector recognized this bitter rider. He had heard it from his own father many times. He made haste to assure Emily that he quite understood.

"If I didn't hear the shot it was because I wasn't near enough," said Emily. "I went for a little walk while my great-nephew was looking for the rug."

The inspector looked consideringly at her. She was a

very old lady, he knew, and there was a cane leaning against the arm of her chair.

"Is there anything more you want to know?" demanded Emily.

"Just one point, if you please, madam. Might I have the name and address of the present heir to the property?"

There was a pause. Emily was still staring at the inspector as though at some irrelevant intruder. She said at last: "I don't know what you're talking about."

Jim said helpfully: "The Australian lot, Aunt Emily. Isn't there a cousin, or something?"

Emily transferred her gaze slowly to his face. "What about her?"

"Well, she must be the heir," Jim pointed out.

"Rubbish!" said Emily scornfully. "She's no such thing. You're the heir."

Her words produced something in the nature of a sensation. Even Oscar Roberts, who had been tactfully gazing into his teacup, looked up. Miss Allison gave a gasp, and Timothy summed up the situation by saying in an awed voice: "Gosh!"

Jim blinked. "But hang it all, Aunt, I can't be! My grandfather was the youngest son, surely? This Australian woman must be senior to me!"

Emily drank her tea and set the cup and saucer down on a small table at her elbow. "If you'd ever taken the trouble to read your great-grandfather's will, which I've no doubt you didn't, you'd know that while there's a male heir living the property can't descend to a female," she said.

"Good God!" said Jim blankly. "Do you mean Matthew Kane entailed it?"

"It's no use talking to me about entails: I don't know anything about them. But the property doesn't go to a woman while there's a male Kane living—that I do know."

An astonished silence fell. Oscar Roberts broke it, saying: "Well, I'll say that beats all! Imagine you not so much as suspecting you stood next in the line of succession, Mr Kane!"

"I'd no idea," said Jim. "I never even thought about it!"

"Why should he?" demanded Emily with a fierce look at Roberts. *"He* couldn't expect both his cousins to die within a month of each other, could he?"

"I'll say not, Mrs. Kane," replied Roberts, smiling. "But to find yourself heir to a fortune without having had the least suspicion of it coming your way—say, that certainly is ro-mance!"

CHAPTER SIX

"AND SO, Superintendent, I felt—all things being considered—that the case would be better in the hands of Scotland Yard," said the chief constable, half wishing that he had someone of real brilliance amongst his own men, half glad to be getting rid of a case that looked like being not only very unpleasant but very difficult to handle into the bargain.

Detective Superintendent Hannasyde, of the C.I.D., nodded understandingly and glanced from the chief constable to Inspector Carlton.

"Local bigwigs, you know," said Colonel Maurice. "Not that that makes any difference, of course; but you know how it is."

Superintendent Hannasyde did know and said so in his deep, pleasant voice.

"Well . . ." said the colonel. "You've read the inspector's notes on the case. If you'd like to talk it over with us . . ."

"I should, sir, very much." Hannasyde directed a brief smile up at the inspector, standing at the colonel's elbow. "You've got the advantage of me in knowing the various people concerned, Inspector. I'll be very glad of your help."

"Of course, the Inspector is absolutely at your orders, Superintendent. Pull up a chair, Carlton, and sit down."

While the inspector complied with this order Hannasyde laid a folder down on the table and began to glance through the typewritten pages.

The chief constable started to fill a pipe. "I think it's all there," he said.

"Yes sir; it's perfectly clear. Clement Kane was shot with a 38 bullet, at a range of not less than six feet, the bullet entering the skull—yes . . ." He flicked over a couple of pages and folded the sheets open at a neat plan. "The inference being that the murderer shot him from outside the window." He laid a square forefinger on the plan and glanced up.

"There doesn't seem to be any room for doubt on that point, eh, Carlton?"

"No sir. The desk is set at an angle, a matter of a few feet from the window. Mr Clement Kane was seated at it, as you see, Superintendent, with his left side to the window, and the bullet entered the left temple. There's no other way out of the room beyond the door into the hall. When the shot was heard the butler and Mrs Kane's secretary and Mr Robérts were in the hall, so that no one could have come out of the study by the door without they'd have seen him. According to their stories, the butler and Mr Roberts ran into the room directly they heard the shot, or, at the most, half a minute later. The butler went straight to the corpse, but Mr Roberts had the sense to make a dash for the window. He was too late, but his story is that he distinctly heard someone moving amongst the bushes in the shrubbery. You'll see by the plan, Superintendent, that there's a regular thicket of rhododendrons and the like not ten feet from the path by the house. By my reckoning anyone standing outside the study could have got to cover before Mr Roberts had time to reach

the window, coming from the hall as he did." He
paused and frowned down at the plan. "What I don't
see myself is how it was that Mr James Kane, coming
out of that garden hall immediately, as he stands to it
he did, didn't catch so much as a glimpse of anyone."

Hannasyde's finger travelled to the plan of the garden hall, separated from the study only by a lavatory
opening out of it. "Mr James Kane stated that he went
out immediately? People sometimes say immediately
when they mean within half a minute, you know."

The inspector shook his head. "I thought that myself, Superintendent; but he won't have it that he
wasted as much as thirty seconds. Come to think of it,
if his story's true, the gun was fired near enough to
startle him so much he'd be pretty certain to run out
just as he says he did." He rubbed his chin reflectively,
eyeing the plan. "But if it all happened like he says,
I'm bound to say I don't see how he can have failed to
have seen, or at least *heard*, something."

Hannasyde glanced back through the typescript to
refresh his memory. "James Kane—he's the heir, is
he?"

"Yes," said the inspector slowly. "He is—and that's
another queer point, Superintendent. What we're asked
to believe is that he didn't know he was. Well, I was
present when old Mrs Kane came out with it, and in
fairness to him I must say that if he was acting he took
me in. He looked as dumbfounded as anyone would,
coming into close on a quarter of a million without a
word of warning, as you might say. But—well, I ask
you, Superintendent! Does it seem to you reasonable
he shouldn't have had the least idea he stood next to
his cousin?"

"I don't think that's quite fair, Carlton," interposed
the colonel. "You must remember that a month ago
his chance of inheriting the Kane fortune was very remote. It's true Silas Kane was a bachelor, but Clement
wasn't. Moreover, Clement was quite a young man and
might very reasonably have been expected to have sons
of his own. He hadn't been married so very long—let

me see, when was Clement's wedding? I think it was about four years ago. Lots of married couples nowadays don't seem to be in a hurry to start their nurseries. No reason to think there would never be one. Moreover, that will of old Matthew Kane's is a very odd affair. I take it you've read it, Superintendent?"

"Yes sir."

"Well, there's no doubt none of the younger generation was at all familiar with its details. Of course, I don't know about Clement. He may have known, but I don't suppose it would strike him as being particularly important. The clause excluding all female heirs while a male heir was living wouldn't concern him; as far as Jim Kane was concerned, I should doubt very much whether he'd even know that his great-grandfather tied the estate up in the way he did."

"Could you tell me anything about Mr James Kane, sir?" asked Hannasyde. "I see he works at the Treasury and seems to be in comfortable circumstances. Nothing known of any debts?"

The colonel jabbed a dead match into the dottle of a pipe in the ash tray beside him. "I've known Jim Kane since he was a boy," he said. "Matter of fact, he was at school with my youngest boy. I should have said he'd be the last person in the world to commit a murder."

Hannasyde nodded, as though satisfied, and turned back to the typescript under his hand. His finger travelled down a list on one page and stopped. "Trevor Dermott," he read out and looked up inquiringly.

The colonel pursed his lips and glanced at the inspector. "Yes," said the inspector. "That's a queer-looking business all right, Superintendent. There's more to it than comes out in the evidence, if you understand what I mean. He don't admit it, and she don't either, but there's plenty of people in this town to tell you how things were between Mr Trevor Dermott and Mrs Clement Kane."

The colonel removed his horn-rimmed spectacles and polished them with his handkerchief. "I don't listen to scandal; but there's no doubt there's been a lot of talk about Mrs Clement and Dermott. May be nothing in it; don't know the fellow myself; he's not a Portlaw man. Big handsome chap, the sort of brute some women fall for. I can only tell you he's been living pretty well in Mrs Clement's pocket for the past three months."

"Well, sir, but there's a bit more to it than that, isn't there?" said the inspector. "By what Mrs Clement's servants say she'd have run off with Dermott if it hadn't been for Clement Kane coming into the property."

"Don't know that I set much store by servants' gossip," said the colonel. "Both under notice too. But I'm not saying that Dermott isn't badly hit where Mrs Clement's concerned. I should say he was head over ears in love with her. She's a remarkably beautiful young woman. Mercenary, of course, but I dare say a man like Dermott wouldn't see that. You couldn't picture Rosemary Kane giving up a fortune for the sake of a *grande passion*."

"No sir," agreed the inspector. "What's more, his actions on the day of the murder make it look very much as if Mrs Clement had told him she wouldn't, down there by the lake. I mean to say, when a man goes off to his hotel and drinks himself silly, and then drives off into the blue and gets pinched for driving a car under the influence of drink at five o'clock in the afternoon, it looks as though he's had a bit of a facer, doesn't it?"

"Yes, I certainly think we want to go rather carefully into Trevor Dermott's movements that afternoon," said Hannasyde. "I see here that Mrs Clement Kane appeared to be anxious to convey the impression that he was an old friend of hers and of her husband."

"Which I'm ready to swear he was not, Superintendent. He may have known Mrs Clement before he started coming down here to see her—that I can't say; but he was no friend of Mr Kane, either old or new."

"Does anyone corroborate this story of the schoolboy's about him driving off at a—oh yes, I see the head gardener's wife at the lodge also saw him. He seemed in a great hurry and looked ever so queer." Hannasyde smiled slightly. "Yes, that looks to me like someone being wise after the event. If he was driving at a reckless speed I doubt whether the gardener's wife would have had time to notice what he looked like."

"No, I don't suppose she did have," said the inspector. "But the boy, Timothy Harte, met him on foot, making for his car, and told Mr Roberts he looked like 'nothing on earth' before he even knew of his cousin having been murdered."

"What about this boy?" inquired Hannasyde. "Fourteen—seem to you reliable?"

The inspector grinned. "Well, I couldn't say, Superintendent, not for certain. He's as sharp as a sackful of monkeys, but by the way he talks he's got crime on the brain. American gangster stuff, you know. It seems he would have it all along that Mr Silas Kane was murdered."

"Mm, yes," said Hannasyde. "I'd very much like to look over the police record of that case if I may. Accidental death, wasn't it?"

"That's what it was brought in," replied the inspector rather guardedly. "There wasn't any evidence— nothing to make a case on. He was an old man, and not a good life, either. If he was murdered, the likeliest person to have done him in was Clement Kane—you might say the only person who had what you could call a real motive. But we established the fact that Clement drove from Cliff House to his own home that night, and he could hardly have got back to Cliff House in time to catch Mr Kane on his walk. But I'm bound to say that that case looks different in the light of this fresh one. I'll send for the records."

While these were being fetched Hannasyde continued to run down the list of suspected persons. He said after a moment: "I see you've put a query against Jane Ogle's name. She's the old lady's maid, isn't she?"

"That's right," said the inspector. "She's been in service up at Cliff House for a matter of forty years. She fair dotes on Mrs Kane. You know the style, I dare say. Well, it's hard to know how to take her. She's one of those who can't answer a simple question without thinking you're trying to trap her into saying something she doesn't mean to. On the face of it, her way of carrying on is highly suspicious, but at the same time I know she's an eccentric old maid, and it doesn't do to set too much store by the silly way she acts. You'll see by my notes she was in the garden at the time of the murder. According to what I've been able to get out of her, she thought the old lady ought to have her rug and took it down to her before ever Mr James Kane went to ask her for it. She says she carried a tray down to the pantry at the same time, thus accounting for having gone out into the garden by way of the back door. By the time she reached the terrace, where Mrs Kane should have been sitting, James Kane had gone into the house after the rug, and there was no sign of the old lady."

Hannasyde looked up. "I thought Mrs Kane was supposed to be very infirm?"

The inspector smiled wryly. "Well, she is and she isn't, Superintendent, if you take my meaning. Some days she'll be carried pretty well everywhere, or at the best creep about with a stick and someone's arm to lean on, and others she'll get taken with a fit of energy and move without anyone's help. She says she went for a stroll towards the lake, and I'm bound to admit I shouldn't be surprised if she did. The way she has it in for Mrs Clement it's quite likely she'd go to spy out what young Madam was up to with her fancy boy. What's more, if her story's true, she'd be out of sight of the terrace in about three minutes, even walking at her pace. She'd go through the rose garden, and that's surrounded by a big yew hedge, as you'll see when you go up to Cliff House."

"And the maid went to look for her through the gardens?"

"She says she did. She says she found her, beyond

the rose garden, by the potting-shed and the glass-houses. Well, that's certainly on the east side of the house, same as the shrubbery—call it southeast—but it's far enough away from the study for a deaf person not to have heard the shot. But it's only their word for it that we've got, Superintendent. By the time anyone else got out to the terrace Mrs Kane had got back there. Mind, I don't say her story isn't true; but what I do say is that it wouldn't make a bit of difference to Jane Ogle if it wasn't. She'd lie herself black in the face to protect the old lady, and the impression she gives me is that that's just what she is doing. That, or she was up to something herself."

"Oh!" Hannasyde considered for a moment. "A bit far-fetched, isn't it?"

"Exactly what I say," nodded the colonel. "I'm ready to admit Emily Kane's a ruthless old woman—to tell you the truth, I'm scared stiff of her!—and she never made any secret of the fact that she detested Clement. But somehow I don't see an old lady of eighty being able to commit that murder, get to cover before Jim Kane could see her——"

"If we are going to consider the possibility of Mrs Kane's having committed the murder, sir, mustn't we also take into consideration that James Kane would be very unlikely to give his great-aunt away?" interposed Hannasyde.

The colonel was silent for a frowning moment. "Yes, I suppose you're right there. But damn it all, the idea's preposterous!"

"Yes sir; I can't get round to it myself that it was the old lady," agreed the inspector. "My idea is the maid might have shot Clement Kane, either with Mrs Kane's knowledge or without it." He saw a sceptical look in Hannasyde's eye and added: "I'm not saying it doesn't sound crazy, Superintendent, but the point is, Jane Ogle is crazy where her mistress is concerned. Ever since Clement Kane came into the fortune, and Miss Allison got herself engaged to young Kane, she's been going about saying how there's no one cares about the old lady but her, and a lot of silly talk about her seeing to it no one should make her mistress's last days a misery to her."

"What about the gun?" asked Hannasyde. "I see the bullet was a 38. Any line on it?"

"Yes, Superintendent, there is a line on it. We've established the fact that old John Kane—that's Emily Kane's husband that was—once owned a 38 Smith and Wesson."

"That's interesting," Hannasyde said. "Has that gun been produced?"

"No, it hasn't, sir; and it doesn't look as though it will be. No one's seen it for years, according to the evidence. I've asked for it to be found, but you know what a big household like that is. If the gun's really lost, it would take anyone a month of Sundays to look for it through all the chests, and lumber rooms, and cupboards full of junk, that there are in the place. But if it wasn't lost, anyone living in the house—and James Kane, too. for that matter—might have known where to put their hands on it any time they wanted."

"I see." Again Hannasyde seemed to be considering the point. He glanced down at the typescript and said after a slight pause: "Some dissension in the firm of Kane and Mansell, apparently. Can you give me any line on these Mansells?"

The inspector glanced at Colonel Maurice. "Nothing known against them, is there, sir? They do say Paul Mansell's a bit sharp, but you might say the same about a lot of businessmen. Mr Mansell's well spoken of, but people don't like the young one much. Bit of scandal there, on account of him being divorced. Nothing relevant to the case."

"Paul Mansell's a flashy young bounder," stated the colonel suddenly. "Old Mansell's all right, but I don't like what I know of his son. I don't see Joe murdering his partner for the sake of putting through a deal that would ease his finances; but, frankly, I wouldn't put it above Paul—if he had the courage to do it. Mind, that's nothing but prejudice on my part."

Hannasyde nodded. "This man, Oscar Roberts—he's representing the agency in Australia?"

"That's right. By what I can make out," said the inspector, "he was very anxious to come to terms with the firm. Of course, they've got a name."

Hannasyde wrinkled his brow. "Yes, but so have several other firms. I can't see that he had the least motive."

"No sir, nor me. What's more, even though he might have murdered Silas Kane—if he was murdered, that is—we know he couldn't have murdered Clement. He was in the hall with the butler and Miss Allison when the shot was heard."

"Oh yes, I wasn't seriously considering him," Hannasyde replied.

He looked up as the door opened to admit a constable who came in with a folder which he laid on the desk at the inspector's elbow. The inspector picked it up and handed it to Hannasyde. "You'll find all the facts concerning Silas Kane's death there, Superintendent."

Hannasyde took the folder and opened it. While he read through the notes on the case the colonel and the inspector sat in silence, waiting for him to finish. When he at length laid the folder down the colonel said: "Well, Superintendent, what do you make of it?"

"I should like to go into it again, sir."

"Yes. Yes, I suppose so. Now Clement's been murdered, it does look suspicious. You think the two deaths hang together?"

"There's a big fortune at stake, sir. At the same time the methods employed—assuming Silas Kane's death was contrived—are very different. In the first instance, you have the murder made to look like an accident; in the second, there's no attempt at camouflage. One point strikes me: I see that James Kane was present at Silas' birthday-party and left shortly after eleven o'clock to motor back to London."

"Well?" said the colonel rather curtly.

Hannasyde looked at him. "Doesn't it seem rather a long way to come, just to attend a dinner party, sir?"

"Oh, Jim wouldn't make anything of a three-hour motor run! Besides, he didn't come only to see Silas. He brought his stepbrother down—Timothy Harte. Really, I don't think there's anything in that, Superintendent."

"You know him, of course, sir," said Hannasyde in a noncommittal voice. "The rest of the servants—and Miss Allison: nothing there?"

"No possible motive," said the inspector. "Of course, I suppose you could say that Miss Allison had a motive, since she's engaged to be married to James Kane; but she was with Mrs Kane at the time Silas must have met his death, and in the hall along with Roberts and the butler when Clement was shot." He paused and added hopefully: "Do you get any sort of line on it, Superintendent?"

"Well, no, not at present," replied Hannasyde. "One or two points seem to stand out. I'd like to keep the notes on Silas Kane's death, if I may. I'll go up to Cliff House and take a look round and have a talk with all these people."

"I don't know about the rest of them, but you can be sure of getting a welcome from Master Timothy Harte," said the inspector with a grin.

This prophecy was fulfilled. From the moment of hearing that a superintendent from Scotland Yard had taken charge of the case, Mr Harte's spirits, a little quenched by this first sight of violent death, rose to dizzy heights. His elders might look upon the affair with anxiety, but Mr Harte anticipated nothing but the keenest enjoyment to be derived from association with a member of the C.I.D. Superintendent Hannasyde, who was a large thick-set man with a square, good-humoured countenance and little conversation, he regarded with awe, not altogether unmixed with disappointment; but the superintendent's satellite, a birdlike sergeant, with bright eyes and a flow of small talk, at once took his fancy. Realizing instinctively that there was little to be got from Hannasyde (who annoyed him by regarding him with a palpable twinkle in his eye), he attached himself firmly to Sergeant Hemingway, while the superintendent pursued his investigations in peace.

Finding his footsteps dogged by Mr Harte, the sergeant suggested that he would be better employed in the pursuit of his usual avocations. Timothy said simply: "I'd rather watch you, thanks."

"Oh!" said the sergeant. "You would, would you? You take care I don't have you up for obstructing me in the execution of my duty."

This piece of facetiousness did not please. Timothy said somewhat severely: "You must think I'm a pretty good ass to swallow that. Besides, I'm not obstructing. I bet I can help you a lot more than you know."

"Well, what I don't know I shan't grieve over, see?"

"All right!" said Timothy with an air of veiled menace and left him.

Twenty minutes later the sergeant, pursuing investigations in the shrubbery, discovered that Mr Harte was once more with him.

"Say, Sarge," quoth Mr Harte cheerfully, "if you're looking for the gat I reckon you've got another guess coming to you."

The sergeant looked at him with assumed ferocity. "Scram!" he said.

"Nothing doing," replied Mr Harte. "Whose garden is this, anyway?"

"Well, if it's yours, it's the first I've heard of it," said the sergeant, allowing himself to be led into argument.

"It isn't. As a matter of fact, it belongs to my stepbrother now, so it's all the same. Besides, he told me to come out here."

"Told you to come out and pester me?" demanded the sergeant, revising his first favourable impressions of Mr James Kane's character.

"No, of course not!" said Mr Harte impatiently. "He said I was to clear out into the garden, and I have."

"I don't blame him," said the sergeant.

"Well, can't I help?" said Timothy, suddenly adopting an ingratiating tone. "Honestly, I won't bother you; but I do most frightfully want to see how a real detective works!"

Sergeant Hemingway met the appeal in the worshipful blue eyes upturned to his and felt himself weakening. He explained afterwards to his superior that he had always been a softy with kids. "I don't mind you trotting round after me as long as you don't get in my way," he conceded. "But mind, now, if I tell you to scram, you scram double-quick!"

"All right, it's a deal," said Timothy, promptly abandoning his wistful expression.

"And you're not to talk me silly!" added Hemingway.

"No, rather not. I say, do you wear a badge, like American policemen?"

"No," replied the sergeant.

"Oh! Rather rotten. It's great when the detective suddenly turns up the lapel of his coat, and there's his badge. What do you do?"

"Hand in my card. Know what I think would be a good idea?"

Timothy eyed him rather suspiciously. "No?"

"If you'd give over wasting my time with asking me silly questions."

"Well, I wanted to know. Besides, you're wasting your time, anyway. I told you the gat wasn't here, only you wouldn't listen. I looked for it myself, ages ago, because I thought probably the murderer would be pretty likely to hide it amongst the bushes. Well, he didn't, and I don't think it's in the bushes on the other side of the drive either. I haven't actually *combed* them, but I've got a theory about it. I'll tell you what it is, if you like."

"The way I look at it is, you'll tell me whether I like it or not," said the sergeant. "Go on; what is it?"

"Well, look here!" said Timothy eagerly; "I know we haven't proved anything yet, but suppose it *was* Mr Dermott who did it?"

"All right, I'm supposing it."

"He had a row with Cousin Rosemary down by the lake—at least, not exactly a row, but a Big Scene, with her turning him down, and him realizing that while Cousin Clement was alive he would never see her again——"

"Look here, where did you get all this from?" demanded the sergeant, shocked. "Nice thing for a boy of your age to be talking about!"

"Oh, can it!" begged Timothy. "All the skivvies say Cousin Rosemary would have got a divorce if it hadn't been for Cousin Clement inheriting a fortune. Besides, I've seen lots of films where things happen just like that. Only now I come to think of it," he added, frowning, "it isn't ever that man who actually did the murder. You simply see him absolutely livid, and stiff with motives, just to put you off the scent. Still, I dare say it's different when it really happens. Suppose it was Mr Dermott."

"I've been supposing it for five minutes," said the sergeant.

"All right. He parts from Cousin Rosemary in a complete flat spin, gets his gun out of the car, which he left halfway down the drive, and bursts up through the shrubbery to the study window, shoots Cousin Clement, bunks into the shrubbery again, and instead of making for the wall beyond the bushes on the other side of the drive, as Mr Roberts thinks he did, goes back to the lake, chucks the gun in, and makes for his car. When I met him he was definitely coming from the lake, and he looked absolutely batty. I've worked it all out, and he could easily have done it. What's more, the only person who could have seen him was Cousin Rosemary, and naturally she wouldn't split on him."

"Sir," said the sergeant, shaking his head, "it's lucky for the rest of us you're not in the Force. We'd be nowhere."

"No, but really," protested Timothy, "don't you think there might be something in my theory?"

"There's a lot in it," replied the sergeant gravely. "But it's got a weak spot. That's what you must learn to do if you're going to be a detective: find the weak spots in your own theories."

"Well, I'm not going to be a detective. My mother wants me to be an explorer. Actually, I expect I shall be a barrister, because if you're an explorer you seem to me to go to the most lousy places and muck about with camels and things. I like cars. Oh, I say, what is the weak spot in my theory?"

"Eh?" said the sergeant, who had not been attending very closely. "Oh, the weak spot! The gun, sir, the gun! People don't generally carry guns about in their cars just on the offchance they might need them—not in my experience, they don't."

"That's just where you're wrong!" said Timothy triumphantly. "I don't absolutely know that Mr Dermott carries one now, but he used to, because he told Cousin Rosemary he always had a gun in his car when all those motor bandits kept on holding people up! So *now* will you let me show you how he could have got back to the lake without anyone seeing him?"

"All right," said the sergeant. "You show me!"

An hour later, when he left Cliff House in company with his superior, Timothy bade him a regretful farewell, addressing him as Sarge, and prophesying that he would be seeing him.

"You seem to have made a hit with that youth," remarked Hannasyde as they walked down the drive. "Has he been a nuisance?"

"Taking it by and large, Super, no," replied Hemingway. "I don't deny he'd pretty well talk the hind leg off a donkey, but one way and another I've gleaned a good bit from him. This Dashing Dermott, for instance. He'll bear looking into. Well, I ask you, Chief! If it's such common talk Mrs Clement Kane was as near as a toucher to going off with him that a kid of fourteen knows all about it, you may bet your life there's something in it."

"There is something in it," said Hannasyde. "That young woman is badly scared. When she isn't engaged on describing her mental reactions to me, she's trying to throw suspicion on every other member of the household."

The sergeant nodded sapiently and made a pronouncement. "There are two kinds of witnesses I've got it in for. There's the one that says too little and the one that says too much. You don't get any forrader with the first, and you get too far with the second."

"Then you won't like this case," said Hannasyde. "We've got both." He smiled a little. "The old lady says she supposes I don't need her to help me solve the problem."

The sergeant looked sympathetic. "Bit of a tartar, so I hear. What did you make of her, Chief?"

Hannasyde shook his head. "I don't know. Impossible to say."

"Ah!" said Hemingway. "That's where psychology comes in."

"You should be a soul mate of Mrs Clement Kane," said Hannasyde. "Did you pick up anything?"

"Characters of the dramatis personæ, that's about all," replied Hemingway, whose forte lay in his ability to cajole his fellow men into talking. "Very superior line of servants: stock parts, most of them. They all liked the late Silas, and they all like young James. The late Clement didn't cut any ice with any of 'em, and as for Mrs Clement—well, what they say about her in the servants' hall I wouldn't like to repeat. You can take it from me she doesn't fit in with the general décor, Chief. As for Dashing Dermott, if the half of what Mrs Clement's old cook told me is true, he's a three-act drama in himself. Talk about passion! Well, Romeo wasn't in it with him. Up at the house now, isn't he? What did you make of him?"

"Oh, he could have done it all right!" Hannasyde answered. "He strikes me as being a man who invariably flies to extremes. But I'm not at all sure that he did do it."

The sergeant cocked an eye at him. "What's on your mind, Super?"

"The first death," said Hannasyde.

CHAPTER SEVEN

SUPERINTENDENT HANNASYDE'S visit left everyone but Mrs Kane and Timothy feeling anxious and rather alarmed. Lunch was not a comfortable meal, nor was it made more pleasant by Emily's refusal to treat Mr Trevor Dermott with common civility. When asked by Rosemary in his presence whether she minded his staying to lunch, she said that since he would have to pay for it at his hotel, anyway, it was a pity he didn't eat it there. Dermott, whose method of dealing with old ladies was to assume the jolly air he used with children, laughed heartily and said: "Aha, Mrs Kane, that sounds to me as though you must have Scotch blood in your veins!"

Emily glared at him for one moment and thereafter ignored him. Miss Allison, who knew that it was not one of Emily's good days, slipped out of the room to tell Pritchard on no account to put Mr Dermott near her at the lunch table.

She herself felt a trifle jaded. She had had a trying morning with her employer, for Emily had got up in a bad temper and had been further incensed by receiving a letter of condolence on Silas' death from her great-niece in Australia.

Emily's most common reaction to the sight of a familiar handwriting on an envelope addressed to herself was to regard it with bitter suspicion and to say in her most disagreeable voice: "I wonder what *she* wants." In this instance she added a rider, remarking, as she slit open the envelope: "Well, she won't get anything out of me." The fact that Maud Leighton, née Kane, did not want anything, but wrote merely to express her sympathy for what her great-aunt must be feeling, did nothing to soothe her annoyance. She said she thought it a very extraordinary thing in Maud to have written, considering she had only laid eyes on her once in her life, and that when she was a baby; and further expressed a desire to know who had been officious enough to send the news to "that Australian lot", anyway. Miss Allison rather unwisely advanced the suggestion that Clement had probably had the notice of Silas' death published in the colonial papers. There was no reason why Emily should object to the colonial papers publishing it, except her dislike of Clement and all his works, but she said angrily that she had never heard anything to equal it.

Having unburdened herself of various ill-natured remarks about Maud Leighton at intervals during the course of the morning, she chose the luncheon hour as a suitable time for the recountal to Jim of the whole affair of the letter, leading off with the snappish remark that she should have thought Maud could have found a better use for her money than to squander it sending letters by air mail.

"That lot never could keep twopence to rub together in their pockets," she said.

Jim, seated at the head of the table, was being told by Rosemary, on his right, that the visit of Superintendent Hannasyde had shattered the last threads of her nervous resistance. He said bracingly: "Oh, I don't think you need feel like that about it," and transferred his attention to his great-aunt at the the other end of the long table. "Sorry, Aunt Emily, something about the Australian cousin?"

"I remember her parents bringing her here when she was a baby. Of course, they always liked coming here

when they were in England. It saved them having to
pay hotel bills," said Emily.

Miss Allison, having a shrewd suspicion that this remark was levelled at Dermott, created a diversion by
asking Timothy how he had spent the morning. His
answer, that he had been helping Sergeant Hemingway
to hunt for clues, had the effect of making Dermott
break into a diatribe against dunderheaded fellows who
had the impudence to call themselves detectives.
"Really, their methods are laughable!" he said.

"I bet some people won't do much laughing by the
time the superintendent's through!" retorted Mr Harte.

"Shut up, Timothy!" said Jim.

Mr Harte muttered: "Well, I bet they *won't,* that's
all."

"Your Cousin Silas sent her a very handsome present when she got married," pursued Emily. "Far too
generous, in my opinion. Leighton was no good at all.
I told your cousin I didn't want to be mixed up with
any of them. Encroaching lot!"

"I've got such a feeling that it was one of the Mansells," said Rosemary, gazing straight in front of her
with the slightly narrowed eyes of one seeking to see
through a fog. "I can't shake it off."

Jim, who did not think that she had tried to, said
bluntly: "If you're wise, you won't say so. You've
nothing to go on, and that kind of remark's likely to
lead to trouble."

"I'm afraid it's too late to try and change my whole
nature," replied Rosemary with a faint smile. "I've always been honest—perhaps disastrously so. I must say
what I think. I dare say I should find life much easier
if I didn't see things so terribly clearly. I seem to be
able to detach myself in the most extraordinary way. I
mean, I'm perfectly calm now, the inside me—just as
though a part of me was utterly aloof from everything
that's happened. I don't say I feel it was one of the
Mansells from spite or any emotional impulse whatsoever. It's just as though a voice was saying in my
brain——"

"I see she's living in Melbourne now," said Emily, who had not been paying the least attention to this speech. "They used to live in Sydney. I dare say it's much the same thing."

No one but Trevor Dermott felt any inclination to argue this point. He was always rather pleased when a woman made an irrational remark, because he could then correct her folly, not unkindly, but with an indulgent laugh at the limitations of the female brain. He began to tell Emily how wrong she was in her conception of Australia.

"Most people talk about having intuitions when they simply don't know the meaning of the word," continued Rosemary; "I'm not a bit like that. In fact, I think I usually mistrust my instinct. I've got a much more logical mind than most women—I'm not patting myself on the back about it; it just happens to be so. I can always see all round a question. But just occasionally—probably because I'm rather the spiritual type, if you know what I mean—I get an intuition that's like a blinding flash of light. And," she concluded impressively, "when it happens like that, it's nearly always right."

"Sez you!" murmured Mr Harte to his plate.

"I don't suppose you know what it's like. I don't think men ever get it," said Rosemary, looking pitifully at her host.

"For God's sake stop talking about it!" said Jim. "I never heard such drivel in my life!" He pulled himself up and added: "Sorry, but I really can't do with a lot of—of . . ."

"Boloney," supplied Mr Harte helpfully.

". . . on top of everything else!" ended Jim, apparently accepting this suggestion.

"But don't you see, Jim, that if the Mansells didn't do it, there's only you left?" asked Rosemary.

"Not quite, I think!" struck in Miss Allison, showing her claws.

Mr Harte looked up approvingly. "Attababy!" he applauded.

Emily, who had been sitting in somewhat toadlike immobility, staring before her, while Trevor Dermott lectured her on the size of Australia, chose at this point to demonstrate her deafness by demanding of Miss Allison what Timothy had said.

"I said Attababy, and what's more I meant it!" announced Timothy with a hostile glance at Rosemary. "Considering everything, I think it's a bit thick of Cousin Rosemary to go about saying no one but the Mansells or Jim could have murdered Cousin Clement! I can jolly well think of *two* other people who could have done it, and if you like I'll tell you who they are!"

"Shut up!" said Jim sharply.

"Leave the boy alone!" commanded Emily.

"Of course, I quite understand how you feel about it," said Rosemary. "But one has to face facts, you know. You mustn't think I believe it was Jim just because my reason tells me that it might have been. I'm only pointing out——"

"Really, you know—really, I wouldn't," put in Dermott uneasily. "Case of 'least said soonest mended', what?"

She turned her wide gaze upon him. "But don't you see that it's important, Trevor? I'm trying to be absolutely dispassionate. I want to know the *truth*. I can't bear pretence! Let us, for God's sake, be honest with each other!"

This impassioned plea drew a response only from Mr Harte, who said: "I bet you'd be pretty sick if we were."

"*Will* you shut up?" said Jim.

"I don't think anyone could seriously accuse me of shrinking from facts," said Rosemary. "You none of you understand how I feel about things. I don't deny I care for Trevor; I don't deny that Clement's death hasn't touched the Essential Me. I can even see that people who don't know him might think Trevor could have done it. Only I *know,* inside me, that he didn't."

Trevor Dermott turned a dark red. There was an

awful pause. Emily's voice broke the silence. "Very nice," she said dryly. "I'll thank you to ring the bell for my chair, Miss Allison."

It was generally felt that this request had relieved the situation. Everyone rose from the table, and Trevor Dermott was heard to draw a sigh of thanksgiving. When Emily had left the room he and Rosemary went out into the garden. He said: "Darling, I know how frank you always are—damn it, I love you for it—but you shouldn't have said that."

"It's true," replied Rosemary. *"I* am not ashamed to own it."

"No, no, that's not the point! Look here! We're in a damned tight corner, and the least said about—well, about our caring for each other, the better. You dealt me a knockout on Saturday. I'm not blaming you; I do understand how you felt, and, anyway, that's all over and done with now. But don't talk about us being in love! Do you see?"

"I'm afraid I don't," said Rosemary. "I believe in being honest, and as everyone knows——"

His face darkened again; he seized her by the shoulders and gave her a shake. "Don't be such a little fool!" he said in a low, angry voice. "Do you want to get me arrested for murder?"

"Of course not. But I absolutely believe in you. Something tells me you didn't do it."

"Oh, to hell with that rubbish!" he said. "Keep your mouth shut, that's all I ask of you!"

She said in a voice of ice: "Indeed! Well, that's interesting, at all events."

"I didn't mean that!" he answered quickly, releasing her. "But it seems to me you don't realize how serious this is. Of course I didn't do it—naturally I didn't!—but when I left you I went back to the Royal and had one or two, and like a fool started to drive up to town. Got pinched about ten miles from here. You see how suspicious it looks? Then there's that little swine, Timothy, yapping to the police about having seen me drive off from here in a flat spin. All lies, of course, and so I told that thickheaded superintendent."

"Why do you say that to me?" asked Rosemary calmly. "You were quite beside yourself. I don't blame you, but it's quite useless to tell me that you were——"

"All right, go and tell the police I was crazy with the shock of having lost you! Go on, tell them, if you're so damned keen on the truth!"

"Whatever else I am," said Rosemary, "I *am* loyal."

Miss Allison would have enjoyed the unconscious humour in this remark, but Dermott saw nothing absurd in it and replied at once: "I know, I know! Fact of the matter is, the whole thing's a bit on top of me. You must be guided by me." He gave an unconvincing laugh. "That pretty little head of yours wasn't made for all this brainwork, darling. Just do as I say, and everything will be all right."

He left her, and after vainly trying to engage Miss Allison in a discussion on the affair, with particular reference to her own spiritual reactions, Rosemary rang up Mrs Pemble and begged her to come to tea. "I feel stifled here!" she announced. "There's no one I can talk to. I feel if I have to bottle it all up much longer I shall go out of my mind."

Betty was suitably flattered by this invitation and made haste to assure Rosemary how well she understood what she meant. "The only thing is, it's Nanny's afternoon off, and I can't leave the children," she said.

Rosemary was not very fond of children, but the prospect of acquiring a sympathetic listener was too enticing to be foregone. She at once included Jennifer and Peter in her invitation, consoling herself with the thought that Timothy could quite well amuse them.

Timothy, however, did not see the matter in the same light and said so with more frankness than civility. Rosemary somewhat unwisely retorted that he would do as he was told, whereupon Timothy went off immediately in search of his stepbrother, whom he found in the library with Miss Allison, and enlisted his support.

Jim was sufficiently annoyed to hear that Rosemary had invited a comparative stranger to tea at such a time to uphold Timothy. Miss Allison went farther and said darkly that one of these days Rosemary would get what was coming to her. At this point Rosemary came in, also to enlist Jim's support. Jim said in a rather cold voice that he wanted Timothy to go on an errand to Portlaw. This led to a spirited and slightly acrimonious dialogue, during the course of which Jim requested Rosemary to remember that this was hardly the moment to invite strangers to tea, Miss Allison advised her not to indulge in any indiscreet conversation with a garrulous woman like Betty, and Rosemary supposed, viciously, that she ought to have asked Jim's permission to invite anyone to his house.

Before he could reply, Pritchard came into the room to tell him that Mr Paul Mansell wished to speak to him on the telephone. He said: "All right; I'll come"; and to Rosemary: "Aunt Emily's permission is the one you should have asked."

"I think," said Rosemary as he went out, "that as Clement's widow I am entitled to *some* consideration!"

"Considering you have just informed us all that you are in love with Mr Dermott, I think the less you say about being Clement's widow the better it will be!" retorted Miss Allison.

Rosemary looked at her. "You don't understand me a bit, do you?" she said. "I've always had the feeling that you disliked me."

Miss Allison deigned no response to this, so Rosemary went away.

"Say, sister!" quoth Mr Harte; "you're a peach!"

Miss Allison laughed. "Oh, Timothy, I'm afraid I'm merely a cat. I suppose you couldn't take those ghastly children down to the lake and push them in?"

"Nope!" said Mr Harte. "I don't want the cops to have the drop on me."

"I expect you're right," agreed Miss Allison.

Jim came back into the room. "Can you lose yourself, or do you want me to give you a real errand?" he inquired of his stepbrother.

"I'm going to Portlaw to see James Cagney's new film," replied Timothy. "You can give me an errand if you like."

"Well, buy me a box of matches, or a local paper or something," said Jim. Mr Harte said that he would if he remembered, and vanished.

"What did Paul Mansell want?" asked Patricia.

"He's coming up to see me—to talk things over. I told him I really hadn't had time to get my bearings, but that didn't seem to deter him."

"The Australian business," she said. She raised her eyes to his face. "Jim, let them do what they want!"

"My dear good child, I can't decide on a matter like that at a moment's notice!" he replied. "I haven't gone into it. All I know is that Silas and Clement were dead against it!"

"Jim!" She laid a hand on his and clasped it. "Never mind that! It can't matter to you how much money you have to put up for it. Let them do as they like!"

He looked down at her, half smiling. "I thought you wanted to marry a very rich man?"

"Don't be silly. I'm serious, Jim. Let the Mansells have it as they want! You'll still be a very rich man."

"True, my love; but that isn't quite the point. I'm not a bit interested in Kane and Mansell's nets, but Silas and Clement were, and I shouldn't like to let them down. I can't possibly decide a question of that size offhand."

"Jim, couldn't you get out of having anything to do with the firm?"

"Yes; what I rather think I should like to do, if the Mansells would consent, is to turn the whole thing into a public company."

"Would they like that?"

"Depends on who had control. They might."

"Then do it. I—Jim, I'm frightened!"

"Pat, you cuckoo!"

"I know. But I'm still frightened. I don't want to sound like Rosemary, but there's some awful feeling of —of danger hanging over this place. You can say I'm overwrought if you like, and perhaps I am. I've tried to shake it off, but I can't. I tell you, Jim, I can hardly bear to let you out of my sight for fear something may happen to you."

He put his arm round her comfortingly. "My sweet, you've let this get on top of you."

"Yes. I know. But don't tell Paul Mansell you won't consent to the Australian scheme! *Please* don't, Jim!"

"No, of course I shan't. I don't propose to commit myself in any way till I've had time to look into it."

"They want an answer at once. Jim, don't you realize that there's someone utterly ruthless at work?"

His arm slackened about her. The smile faded from his face. "Go on. What are you getting at?"

"First Mr Kane and now Clement," she said, nervously rolling her handkerchief between her hands. "It sounds fantastic—I *know* it sounds fantastic; but that Scotland Yard man thinks Mr Kane's death was murder. He asked me question after question."

"Are you seriously suggesting that the Mansells did away with Silas and Clement all because of a split on a matter of business policy?"

"Not old Mr Mansell, no. But Paul could. You don't know him, Jim. He's horrible."

"I don't want to be rude, darling, but have you been consorting much with Timothy of late?"

"Oh, Jim, don't laugh! I'm so sure it's serious!"

"Well, I promise I won't turn down the Australian scheme today. Will that do?"

"I wish you'd consent to it."

"Not really, Pat."

She reflected. "No, I suppose not. Sorry. Do as you think best. I've gone a trifle over at the knees."

"What you want is a good stiff blow," said Jim. "How would you like one in the Seamew? I rather thought of having her out tomorrow."

"I should probably be scared white," replied Miss

Allison candidly. "However, I quite see that if I mean to go through with this marriage I shall have to get used to racing cars and speedboats. I'll go with you if Mrs Kane doesn't want me."

Shortly after three o'clock Paul Mansell arrived at Cliff House, bringing with him his sister and her two children. Betty Pemble had been inspired to array her offspring in their best clothes, undeterred by any consideration of the unsuitability of jade-green silk for garden wear. Peter, who was a strong-minded-looking child of three, wore in addition to his jade knickers a frilled shirt of primrose yellow. Judging from his expression, which was forbidding, he did not regard his gala raiment with favour. Jennifer, on the other hand, who was three years his senior, was looking pleased and rather smug. She had beguiled the tedium of the drive out from Portlaw with a flow of innocent prattle which made her uncle wonder savagely why no one had had the sense to stifle her at birth. Upon arrival at Cliff House she skipped out of the car and offered to embrace her hostess. "How do you do, Mrs Kane? Look, Mrs Kane, I've got my party frock on! Do you know, Peter was awfully naughty, Mrs Kane, and he screamed because he didn't want to have his clothes changed? I wasn't naughty. I'm three years older than Peter, Mrs Kane. He's only a silly baby."

"Hush, darling!" said her mother fondly. "Give Auntie Rosemary a nice kiss, Peter dear."

"No," said Peter, with a lowering look at Rosemary. "Don't want to."

Betty bent over him and said in a coaxing voice: "Darling, you know you promised Mummy you'd be a good boy. You love Auntie Rosemary, don't you?"

Master Pemble, exasperated, thrust her off with one fat clenched fist. "I don't *want* to!" he repeated loudly.

"Oh, please don't worry about it!" begged Rosemary. "I can never see why children should be expected to kiss everyone. Really, I don't in the least want him to!"

"No, Peter must do what he's told," said Betty

firmly. "I always insist on them obeying me, you know: it's the only way. Now, darling, listen! You wouldn't like Mummy to take you home again, would you?"

"I want to go home!" replied Master Pemble. "I want to go home now! *I do* want to go home! I *do!*"

His mother interrupted this steady crescendo, saying: "Oh, *Peter!* Don't you know how sad it makes Mummy when you behave like this?"

"*I'm* not naughty, Mummy, am I?" asked Jennifer, jumping from one foot to the other with more energy than grace. "*I* kissed Mrs Kane without being *told* to, didn't I, Mummy?"

"Yes, darling; but don't jump about like that! You'll get so hot."

Master Pemble, pardonably annoyed, saw fit at this point to deal his ecstatic sister a shrewd blow in the ribs. Jennifer at once complained of his brutality in a whining voice, and by the time Betty had reminded her that Peter was only a very little boy, after all, and told Peter that boys never, never hit girls, the original cause of the dispute had been forgotten. Rosemary, who by no means enjoyed the unenviable role of one waiting to be embraced by a reluctant child, made haste to conduct the party on to the south lawn below the terrace.

"You don't know how glad I am to see you!" she told Betty. "Honestly, if you hadn't come I think I should have gone mad!"

"My dear, I was only too pleased to come. I know so well what you must be—no, Peter dear, you mustn't pick the pretty flowers! Just look at them, but not *touch!* Aren't they lovely? I'm sure Auntie Rosemary wouldn't mind you smelling them. Jennifer darling, you show Peter how to smell the pretty flowers." She turned to Rosemary. "Jennifer's got the most extraordinary love of beauty. Of course, it's just heaven to her to be in this perfect garden. She'll talk of nothing else for weeks. I do so believe in bringing them up to have only beautiful thoughts, don't you?"

"I don't know," said Rosemary impatiently. "I don't know anything about children. I suppose they'll be all right playing about by themselves, won't they?"

"Oh, perfectly!" Betty assured her, sitting down in one of the deck chairs under a large cedar. "As long as they don't go out of sight, or anything. Run along, darlings, and play quietly together."

"There isn't anything to play with, Mummy," objected Jennifer.

"Never mind, darling; just run along and amuse yourselves! Mummy wants to talk to Auntie Rosemary."

"But, Mummy——"

"Pussy!" suddenly exclaimed Master Pemble as the kitchen cat crossed the lawn. "I want the pussy!"

Both children immediately launched themselves in the direction of the cat, screaming: "It's my pussy! I saw it first. You're not to have it." A fight to the death seemed inevitable; but the cat, after one horrified look, made for the shelter of the nearest hedge like a streak of lightning. The children, after vainly trying to lure it out again, returned disconsolately to their elders, and Peter informed Rosemary that he had had a pussy once.

"Yes, and do you know what happened to him, Auntie Rosemary?" asked Jennifer eagerly. "He got out on to the road, and a motorcar came and killed him *flat!*"

"He was squashed!" corroborated Peter with enthusiasm.

"I can't think who told them that!" said Betty in an annoyed voice. "I mean, I've always been so careful not to let them know anything about Death and that sort of thing."

For the next quarter of an hour all conversation between the two ladies was punctuated by admonitions from Betty to her children and answering whines from them that there was nothing to do. Fortunately for Rosemary's temper she caught sight of one of the gardeners and had the happy thought of consigning the children to his care. They went off with him, followed by a fire of affectionate reminders not to get hot, or cold, or overtired, or dirty, and were not seen again until tea-time, the entertainment offered by the gardener being of a high order, namely, the plucking and drawing of a fowl killed that morning.

While Rosemary was unburdening herself to Betty Pemble in the garden, Jim Kane was confronting Paul Mansell in the library and thinking privately that he was a fairly nasty piece of work.

Upon arrival at Cliff House Paul had stayed only to greet Rosemary before going into the house. Pritchard had shown him into the library, where Jim presently joined him, and after a slight interchange of civilities he had broached the object of his talk. His father and he, though averse from obtruding the matter so soon, were anxious to know what the chief shareholder's pol-icy was to be.

Jim laughed and shook his head. "No use asking me that yet, Mansell. I haven't had time to find my feet. Nets aren't much in my line, you know."

"Quite. We quite appreciate that," smiled Paul, crossing one leg over the other and gently swinging a suède-clad foot. "I expect it would suit you best to let Dad buy you out. You don't want to be bothered by business. I know I wouldn't touch it if I were in your place."

This was the conclusion Jim had already reached, but he now felt an irrational disinclination to leave the business in the Mansells' hands. He said: "No, I don't think I want to be bought out, thanks. How would you and your father feel about turning it into a public com-pany?"

Paul Mansell put up his brows. "Rather a large question to answer offhand, isn't it? I don't know that I think Dad would quite cotton on to the idea. I really haven't considered it. What I came about—assuming that you don't wish to get out of having anything to do with the business—was to talk over the new venture with you. I don't know whether you've been told anything about our Australian scheme?"

"A certain amount," replied Jim.

"Ah, perhaps I had better explain it to you!" Paul said languidly.

Jim heard the explanation out, merely interrupting once or twice to put a question. His questions were so pertinent that Paul began to realize that this big cheerful young man was not the fool he had supposed him to be. His eyes narrowed a little; his voice grew more suave.

"On the face of it, it looks good," Jim admitted when Paul Mansell had done. "At the same time, I know next to nothing about the business, and I want to go into things before I start making any decisions. I take it you don't expect me to give you an answer offhand?"

"I think," said Paul gently, "that it would be wisest for you to allow yourself to be guided by us."

All trace of his smile left Jim's face. The muscles about his mouth hardened, giving him a slightly pugnacious expression. He looked steadily into Paul's eyes and said with deliberation: "Do you?"

Paul made a graceful gesture with one hand. "My dear fellow, haven't you just said that you know nothing about the business?"

"Next to nothing," said Jim.

Paul smiled. "I stand corrected. There isn't really much difference, is there?"

"Not much," replied Jim. "Just that I am aware that Silas and Clement, whether rightly or wrongly, disliked the scheme."

"Your cousin Silas," countered Paul, "was an old man with strong prejudices, and your cousin Clement, if I may say so, was handicapped by a wife who could never get enough money to spend. Do forgive me if I am being too frank!"

"Not at all," said Jim with equal courtesy. "You may very likely be right in all you say of this scheme.

But I'm sure you'll realize that, in the face of my cousins' known dislike of it, I should have to be a thundering fool to go into it without knowing anything more about it than what you've told me."

"You are as cautious as your cousins, I see. May I point out to you that while you are—er—acquiring a knowledge of the business, the opportunity to expand it will have gone? Roberts has been very patient, but he is not acting for himself and cannot be expected to wait for ever."

"Certainly," said Jim. "But may I in my turn remind you that I came into this inheritance without the least warning only two days ago? From what I've seen of Roberts, I should say he would be the last person to want to hustle me into the affair without going into it thoroughly first."

Paul Mansell uncrossed his legs and rose. "Then I am to tell my father that the matter must still rest in abeyance?"

"That's about the size of it," said Jim. "I shall hope to see Mr Mansell in a day or two. There's more than this point to be discussed. You'll stay to tea, won't you?"

"I'm afraid I must get back to the office, thanks. My brother-in-law will no doubt call for his family on his way home from the golf course." He paused, and his eyes glinted a little. "By the way, I understand that I have to congratulate you on becoming engaged to Patricia Allison?"

"Thanks very much, yes," said Jim.

"You are fortunate," smiled Paul. "A charming girl —so sensible too! Do offer her my congratulations! One ought not to congratulate the lady, I believe, but in this case I really think congratulations are due to her."

"You almost overwhelm me," said Jim pleasantly and held the door open for him to pass out into the hall.

He went out into the porch to see his visitor drive away and was about to go back into the house when a taxi drove up the avenue and set down a middle-aged gentleman of lean proportions and expensive tailoring, who said placidly: "Ah, there you are! I fancy I must have forgotten to let you know I was coming."

"Hullo, Adrian!" said Jim, stepping forward to greet the newcomer. "Where on earth did you spring from? I thought you were in Scotland!"

CHAPTER EIGHT

SIR ADRIAN HARTE paid the taxi driver, saw his suitcases safely in the hands of Pritchard, who had appeared as if by magic at the sound of an approaching car, and walked into the house beside his stepson. "My dear boy, in this weather?" he asked plaintively.

Jim, no fisherman, apologized. "I forgot. When did you get back to town?"

"Yesterday evening," replied Sir Adrian. "I thought I had better come down and see what was happening here." He put his monocle into his eye and glanced at Jim with a pained, faintly inquiring expression. "Rather unusual, isn't it?"

"It is a bit, sir," said Jim. "Not altogether pleasant, either."

"Ah no, I dare say not," agreed Sir Adrian. "I have never been mixed up in a murder case myself, but I imagine the situation must be very disagreeable. A pity you should have been here at the time. I don't know what your mother will say."

"How is Mother?" asked Jim. "Have you had any news of her?"

"No," said Sir Adrian, preceding him into the library, "not a word. I wondered whether you might not have had a letter."

"Nothing since the card she sent from that illegible address. What do you suppose can have happened to her?"

"I've no idea," replied Sir Adrian. "If your mother were not such an erratic letter writer, I should consider it really rather disturbing. However, I've no doubt there is some perfectly ordinary explanation for her silence." He sank into a chair. "Well, my dear boy, you had better tell me all about it. I imagine you are not, at the moment, in a very enviable position."

"No, not entirely," said Jim. "The evidence all seems to point my way. I don't think the police can bring themselves to believe that I really had no idea I was the next heir."

"I confess I was rather surprised that you were apparently ignorant of the fact," remarked Sir Adrian.

"Did you know, sir?"

"Oh yes; I'm sure your mother told me the rights of it years ago. If it is not a vulgar question, how much do you inherit?"

"I'm not altogether sure. Cousin Silas left close on a quarter of a million, but the death duties are colossal."

"I expect there will be enough left for your simple needs," said Sir Adrian.

Jim grinned. "More than enough, I should think. But my needs aren't going to be quite so simple in the future. I'm engaged to be married."

Sir Adrian looked mildly surprised. "Dear me, are you? I don't think you mentioned that in your letter, did you?"

"No, I didn't think it went well, cheek by jowl with the announcement of Clement's death."

"Ah, artistic discrimination! Have I the pleasure of knowing the lady?"

"Rather, sir! It's Patricia Allison, Aunt Emily's companion."

Sir Adrian frowned slightly. "I don't think I've met her."

"Yes, you have, Adrian, the last time you were here."

"If you say so, no doubt it is so. I find, as I grow older, that people make very little impression on me. Is this what your mother would consider a suitable alliance?"

"Very much so, I assure you."

"I feel sure you know your own business best," said Sir Adrian. "By the way, didn't I send Timothy here?"

"You did, and he's very much here."

"Yes, I thought I did. I couldn't recall, when I got back to town, what arrangements I had made, but it occurred to me on the train that I must have sent him here. To turn to more important matters, have you come across old Mr Kane's stamp collection?"

"No, had he got one?"

"My dear Jim!" Sir Adrian sounded genuinely shocked. "He had a unique collection. I have on more than one occasion offered to buy at least three of the specimens from Silas, who, I may say, had no feeling for them other than a purely Kane desire to hold fast to his possessions. I will buy them from you, if you like to sell."

"Good Lord, Adrian, you can have the whole collection, if you want it! It doesn't mean a thing to me."

"I shan't impose on your innocence as much as that," replied Sir Adrian with a faint smile.

The door opened at this moment to admit Timothy, who bounced in, saying: "I say, Jim, I've asked Mr Roberts—oh, hullo, Father! I didn't see you." He went up to shake his parent by the hand. "I quite thought you'd gone to Scotland. How did you get here?"

"My arrival seems to cause you and Jim a great deal of quite unmerited surprise," said Sir Adrian. "I had five days of unbroken sunshine and then came home."

"Oh, I see! I say, Jim, I've asked Mr Roberts in to tea. Is it all right? I met him outside the cinema, and he asked whether I thought you'd mind him coming up to see you some time. You don't, do you? I told him I knew you wouldn't."

"And, as you see, I took him at his word and ventured to come," said Oscar Roberts from the open doorway. "But you've only to say the word and I'll catch the next bus back to Portlaw."

"Of course not! Do come in!" said Jim. "Adrian, may I introduce Mr Roberts? My stepfather, Sir Adrian Harte, sir."

"Pleased to meet you, Sir Adrian. Your son and I have been getting along fine together—or rather we were till this durned sergeant from Scotland Yard came and cut me right out of the picture," he added with a twinkle.

"Oh, I say, sir, that's not fair!" protested Timothy. "It was only that I wanted to see how a detective really works."

Oscar Roberts dropped a hand on his shoulder and pressed it. "Sure you did, sonny. I was only kidding. Well, I fancy you don't want a stranger butting in on your family party, Mr Kane. Maybe if I came along to-morrow . . ."

Sir Adrian said: "I seem to be in the way. I'm sure you would like some private conversation with my stepson, Mr Roberts. I was just about to go up to my room. You may come with me, Timothy."

He bore Timothy off with him. Oscar Roberts took the chair his host pushed forward and said: "I've not come to persuade you into falling in with my proposition."

Jim laughed. "Thank God for that!"

"Yes, I thought you'd perhaps be receiving a visit from one or other of your partners." He accepted a cigar from the box Jim held out to him and sought in his pocket for his cutter. As he lit the cigar he said, peering at Jim through the smoke: "Say, I'd like us to be frank, Kane."

"By all means."

Roberts leaned forward to lay his dead match in the ash tray on the table. "That certainly makes it easier to say what I want to. I wouldn't like you to get me wrong over this little business deal I'm trying to put through. If I can get them, I want Kane and Mansell's nets for my firm to handle down under. But I'm not out to start a general holocaust all to get the best when the next best will suit pretty near as well."

"I beg your pardon?" Jim stiffened a little.

The cool, calculating eyes did not waver. "Guess we'll leave it at that, Kane. There's been some mighty queer happenings in this house, and I'm bound to admit they seem to hang together a piece with my coming onto the scene. Maybe that's just a coincidence; maybe it's not. But I'd like to have you know that I'm not pressing your partners for an answer. I've a notion they'll try and put the screw on you. Well, I'm not turning it. I certainly shall be glad to get the matter settled one way or the other, but I appreciate your position, and I wouldn't be the one to push you into a deal you don't properly understand and might regret. That's no way to do business. I like to have you think it over and get some impartial advice. You won't keep me waiting any longer than is reasonable. I'll treat myself to a little vacation."

"It's extraordinarily decent of you," said Jim. "I do want time to find my feet; but isn't it asking rather a lot of you to keep you kicking your heels while I try to get abreast of this infernal net business?"

"If I see a chance of putting the deal through, I'll be content to kick my heels for a space." He regarded the tip of his cigar inscrutably. "It's not uninteresting— kicking my heels in Portlaw."

"You're interested in my cousin's murder?" said Jim bluntly.

"Well"—Roberts glanced at him with a slight look of amusement—"I feel I might be responsible in a roundabout way. You'll admit it's a fairly cute little problem the police are up against."

"A filthy case. They've called in Scotland Yard now."

"Yes, I'd the pleasure of receiving a call from Superintendent Hannasyde this morning."

"I believe he's pretty good. Rather a nice chap, I thought."

"Sure. I reckon he's the competent type they breed up at Scotland Yard. He's smart enough to get right onto Silas Kane's death. The trouble is, he's got mighty little to go on. Somebody certainly handled that business well. You have to hand it to them."

"You've always thought my cousin Silas was murdered, haven't you?" Jim asked curiously.

"I wouldn't say that. I thought maybe his death would bear some more investigating than it got."

"Yes, it looks like that now; but at the time I don't think any of us suspected there might have been foul play. It's going to be investigated now all right."

"That's so; but when you get a kind of family affair like this, it always seems to me the police have to work under a big handicap. This superintendent from London's no fool, but he doesn't know the folks he's dealing with. He can find out a lot through asking questions, but he can't get to know them the way a man moving amongst them like I am can. They're just naturally on their guard with him."

"You ought to have been a detective," said Jim, laughing.

Oscar Roberts smiled but said nothing.

"Do you mind telling me," said Jim; "have you got hold of something the police haven't?"

There was a slight pause. "Why, no, I wouldn't say that," replied Roberts in his measured way. "I'm not holding out on the police. Maybe I've got a hunch. I don't want you to feel sore at me chiselling in on what isn't, strictly speaking, any of my business. You've got to remember I was one of the first to see your cousin after he'd been shot. What's more, it sticks a bit in my head that I was to get Mr Clement Kane's answer to my proposition that day. It looked a cinch he was going to turn me down flat. Well, he didn't get a chance to do it. Someone bumped him off first. Guess that gives me an excuse for taking an interest in the case, Kane."

"Oh, I've no objection!" Jim said. "Good luck to you!"

"Thanks." Roberts uncrossed his long legs and prepared to get up. "There's just one other thing I'd like to say." He rose and hesitated for a moment. "Don't misunderstand me, Kane: I'm going on a hunch only. But I'm bound to say that, if I stood in your shoes, I'd watch out for trouble."

Jim got up, a spark of anger in his eyes. "I think your hunch is fantastic, sir; but by God, if the Mansells think they can frighten me into falling in with their damned schemes they've got another guess coming to them!"

Oscar Roberts chuckled. "That's the spirit. But all the same, I wouldn't sit around by open windows all by yourself, Kane. An easy target's kind of tempting."

Jim's chin jutted mulishly. "If I thought there was a word of truth in it, damn it, I'd turn the whole Australian project down now!"

"Now, that's not what I want at all!" said Roberts. "I appreciate the way you feel, but I certainly didn't come here to put you right against my proposition."

Jim gave a reluctant laugh. "I'll try and keep an impartial mind. And thanks for the warning! Come out and join the tea party now."

Roberts demurred a little but allowed himself to be overpersuaded. Tea had been taken out on to the terrace some minutes before, and quite a large party was already gathered there. Emily, hearing of Sir Adrian's arrival, had come down in her best black silk dress, an honour not accorded by her to many, and was sitting with him beside her, listening to his cultured, rather languid voice with a less forbidding air than usual. Sir Adrian to every Kane but Jim was the unknown quantity. Kane instinct bade Emily despise him for a fool who had never done a stroke of work in his life; Kane sense told her that, though he might be vague and impractical, he was no fool. His conversation was strange to her but gave her pleasure; his point of view nearly always clashed with her own, but though she might pour scorn on it, secretly she respected his judgment.

Rosemary and Betty Pemble were next to each

other. Betty, having spent an hour alternately sympathizing with Rosemary for having been left only Clement's private fortune and agreeing with her that it wasn't as though Jim had ever done anything to deserve the inheritance of the Kane estate, and that there was a hard streak in Patricia Allison, due undoubtedly to her spinsterhood, had leaped into the front rank of Rosemary's close friends. With the reappearance of her children upon the scene, however, Betty's attention had become necessarily diverted from Rosemary. She had settled them at a small table at a discreet distance from the rest of the party and was engaged, when Jim Kane and Oscar Roberts came out on to the terrace, in hushing them whenever their voices rose to obtrusive heights, which was often, and in remonstrating with them on the size of the portions they saw fit to cram into their mouths. Occasionally she explained apologetically to Rosemary that they weren't usually a bit like this. Timothy had ensconced himself beside Patricia at the tea table. Whenever the children offended his sense of propriety he glared at his plate and muttered: *"Gosh!"* in accents of repulsion.

Emily greeted Oscar Roberts without much cordiality. She was not in the habit of attempting to overcome her prejudices and saw no reason to make an exception in this case. Roberts' way of drawing his heels together and bowing as he took her hand she condemned as foreign. She knew no more disparaging adjective. She gave him a curt "How-de-do?" and immediately turned again to Sir Adrian and requested him to tell her what his wife was doing, gallivanting about Africa at her age.

"I really don't know," replied Sir Adrian.

"Then you ought to know!" said Emily tartly.

He smiled but merely said that he never presumed to question Norma's activities.

This was the kind of remark which Emily found baffling. In her opinion men ought to question their wives' activities. She would have said as much to most people but had just enough respect for Sir Adrian to refrain. She said instead: "She'll get eaten by cannibals one of these days."

"Oh, I don't think so!" replied Sir Adrian with easy optimism. "She's very capable, you know. An amazing woman! I find myself quite unable to keep pace with her extraordinary vitality." His glance wandered to Timothy's face, and from his to Jim's. "I fancy neither of her sons has inherited her forceful character."

"A good thing too!" said Emily. "What do you mean to do with that boy of yours?"

Sir Adrian looked rather alarmed. "Do with him?" he repeated.

"Yes," said Emily, impatiently. "What are you going to put him into?"

"Oh—ah! Well, it is rather too soon to think about that. He seems to me singularly ill suited to any profession which I can at the moment call to mind."

Emily gave one of her croaks of laughter and said after a moment: "I suppose you know the police suspect Jim?"

"I imagine they would be very likely to do so," he replied, gently polishing his eyeglass.

"A lot of nonsense! I've no patience with it."

Sir Adrian got up to take his cup to Miss Allison and, as Oscar Roberts began to talk to Emily, remained standing by the tea table, sipping his tea and exchanging a few commonplaces with Patricia. He presently drifted away to a vacant chair beside Betty Pemble's, who at once engaged him in conversation. Her children, having finished their tea, had gone off in search of their new friend the gardener, so that Betty was able to give her undivided attention to Sir Adrian. She thought him a most distinguished-looking man and was only too glad to be given the opportunity of telling him how much she felt for the family, and how she wished there was something she could do to help. Sir Adrian replied courteously but in a rather bored voice, and when Betty said that she expected he felt as though Jim were his own son, he said: "Dear me, no!

Not in the least," with a good deal of mild surprise. He might have added that he had little or no parental feeling for Timothy, either; but happily for Betty's opinion of him, he was not in the habit of talking about himself, and so did not. He had, however, said enough to make Betty confide later to her husband that, charming though he was, she could not help feeling that there was something rather sinister about Sir Adrian.

Miss Allison did not find him sinister, but he seemed to her unapproachable. It was quite impossible to discover whether one were making a good or a bad impression upon him, for his manner was the same towards everyone. She could fancy that one saw him through a mist, which he had carefully wrapped round himself, and behind which he dwelt, blissfully aloof. He seemed to take more interest in the whereabouts of old John Kane's stamp collection than in Clement's murder, and when Jim, in the privacy of his own bedroom, recounted his interview with Roberts to him, he said with a faint look of distaste: "Rather lurid, don't you think?"

"Yes, I do," replied Jim "Lurid and absurd. But you can't get away from the fact that, whether because they disliked the Australian scheme or for some other reason, Cousin Silas and Clement are both dead."

"Are you feeling nervous, Jim?"

"No, not exactly nervous. I'm not sitting about by open windows much."

"Well, I see no harm in that, if you feel there might be danger in it," said Sir Adrian. "But I find that my mind is quite unable to accept the possibility of a third murder taking place while the police are investigating the first and the second."

"Highly improbable," agreed Jim. His eyes narrowed at the corners in a rueful smile. "If you're apparently the third victim, it's surprising how much improbability you can swallow."

"Yes, I have no doubt it obscures your judgment," said Sir Adrian.

Jim laughed. "If ever I get badly rattled, I shall come and hold your hand, Adrian. You're the most tranquillizing person I know. With you about the place, even the first two murders seem a bit farfetched. If you stay long enough, we shall begin to doubt whether they ever really happened. I'm sure you never had any murders in your family, did you?"

"No, we have always contrived to keep out of the penny press," replied Sir Adrian, looking through his stud box for a pair of cuff links.

Jim shook his head. "You must loathe being mixed up with a vulgar lot like us," he said solemnly.

"Don't be absurd, my dear boy."

Jim strolled towards the door. "I'll go and change. Oh, Adrian, can you bear it? I've gone into Trade—at least, it looks as though I probably shall."

"I can bear it; but I doubt whether your mother will like it. She will think it very unenterprising of you."

"Oh, Mother will want me to finance an expedition to the North Pole, I expect," grinned Jim.

"You are quite wrong. Unless my memory is at fault, your mother wishes to make Central China her next objective," said Sir Adrian, busy with his tie.

Later that evening Miss Allison, finding herself alone with him for a few moments, broached the same subject to him. "Mr Roberts told me he had warned Jim to take no risks," she said. "Do you think it possible that the Mansells could—could really contemplate murder just to get their own way over this business deal?"

"No, I do not," replied Sir Adrian. "It is, of course, a temptation to believe an ill-conditioned young man like the younger Mansell to be capable of almost any crime, but one should guard against allowing mere prejudice to colour one's judgment."

"I have told myself that," said Miss Allison. "I expect I'm being stupidly anxious; but you see, it means rather a lot to me. When you care for a person your reason gets rather swamped."

"I hope you are not implying that I am the callous stepfather of legend?" said Sir Adrian, looking quizzically down at her.

She smiled. "Of course not. But he's not like your own son, or—or your fiancé, is he?"

"Certainly not in the least like my fiancé. And, I am happy to say, not much like my own son either. Though I have no doubt that Timothy will improve as he grows older."

"You are an unnatural parent, Sir Adrian."

"I am afraid I must be."

"And you don't think that any danger threatens Jim?"

"Extremely unlikely, I should imagine. From what I have heard of it—but I am lamentably ignorant on such matters—it does not seem to me that the proposed expansion of the business in Australia is of sufficient moment to provide a motive for three murders. There is, however, another possibility that occurs to me."

"Yes? Please tell me what it is!"

"No, I don't think I will do that," he replied. "It is a mere supposition which a very little investigation may easily disprove. I will have a talk with the superintendent from Scotland Yard tomorrow. That reminds me: I must request the butler to ring up the police station the first thing in the morning."

"If you'll give me the message I'll pass it on to Pritchard, Sir Adrian. That's part of my job, you know."

"That would be very kind of you. If you would tell the butler to inform the station sergeant that I should be obliged if Superintendent—I do not know his name, but perhaps you can supply that—would call at Cliff House some time during the course of the day, I should be most grateful."

She could not help laughing. "I will, of course; but when I think how terrified most of us are of these grim policemen, it seems positively asking for trouble calmly to summon them here!"

"Oh no, I hardly think so!" he replied gently.

"Well, anyway, it's a superb gesture," she said. "The rest of us, if we wanted to see the superintendent, would probably crawl humbly down to the police station and beg an audience."

He looked rather surprised. Miss Allison confided later to Jim Kane that intercourse with his stepfather made her feel that Clement's murder and her own fears were social solecisms.

"Oh, he thinks they are!" said Jim. "The whole thing is in very bad taste."

"Are you fond of him, Jim?"

"Very."

"Does he like you?"

"I think so. Why?"

"I only wondered. He seems such a withdrawn person. Still, it was nice of him to come down. What do you suppose he wants to see the superintendent for?"

"I haven't a notion. However, I'm all for it. He definitely adds tone to the proceedings. Obviously no member of his entourage would be vulgar enough to commit a murder."

"If the superintendent has a grain of sense, it won't be necessary for him to see your stepfather to realize that you couldn't possibly have done it," said Miss Allison stoutly.

Whatever the superintendent felt about it, Sergeant Hemingway quite agreed with her. "You've got to take psychology into account, Chief," he said. "To my way of thinking, a nice young fellow like James Kane doesn't waltz about murdering his relations."

"I agree; but there's also the question of motive to be taken into account. He had more than anyone else."

"Too much," said the sergeant briskly. "He's what I might call dripping with motive. I've a strong idea, myself, that what we want to look for is something a bit more recherché. This isn't one of your clumsy, hit-you-in-the-eye murders. It's got class. Who's this Sir Adrian What's-his-name that wants to see you?"

"Your young friend's father, I imagine."

"What, Terrible Timothy? You don't say! Well, if

he's half the turn his son is, you ought to have a lively morning of it, Super."

Superintendent Hannasyde, however, was unable to detect much resemblance between Timothy and his father. He went up to Cliff House shortly after eleven o'clock and encountered Timothy in the porch. He bade him a pleasant good morning but received a gloomy, though civil response. "You don't look very cheerful," he remarked. "I hope you haven't mislaid a clue?"

Timothy acknowledged this poor jest with a perfunctory smile and replied with cold dignity that no one could be expected to look cheerful with people simply being rottenly selfish the whole time.

"No, it certainly must be very difficult for you," agreed Hannasyde.

"It isn't that I care two hoots, because actually I don't particularly want to go out in any rotten motorboat," said Timothy bitterly. "Only, considering I asked first, I think it's pretty mean of Jim to take Patricia, that's all."

Superintendent Hannasyde, who had a mind trained to grapple with elusive problems, was able fairly accurately to guess the cause of Mr Harte's discontent. He replied suitably; but said that in his opinion jaunts upon the sea for one engaged in solving a mystery would be a waste of time. "Is your stepbrother out now, then?" he inquired.

"Yes, and I should jolly well laugh if Patricia was seasick!" said Mr Harte. "I shouldn't be a bit surprised if she was, either."

Pritchard came to the door in answer to the superintendent's ring at this moment, so Hannasyde parted from Mr Harte, docketing in his brain the fact that Mr James Kane, possible murderer, was apparently feeling carefree enough to disport himself in a motorboat with his fiancée.

Sir Adrian Harte received the superintendent in the library. He screwed his monocle into his eye, favoured Hannasyde with one of his calm, aloof glances, and said, "Ah, good morning, Superintendent! Sit down, won't you?"

Hannasyde took a chair. "Good morning, sir. You are Mr James Kane's stepfather, I understand? You wanted to see me?"

"I did, yes." Sir Adrian sat down, hitching his beautifully pressed trousers carefully at the knee. "There is an aspect to this extremely unpleasant affair which I should like to discuss with you. I did not know if you are aware of it, but a gentleman of the name of Roberts has seen fit to warn my stepson that he may shortly figure in this case as the third victim."

"No, I didn't know that, sir," Hannasyde replied, not taking his eyes from Sir Adrian's face.

"So I had supposed. What Mr Roberts' reason is for uttering this somewhat dramatic warning I am unable to tell you. But it seems to me highly undesirable that any unnecessary mystery should attach to the case."

"Highly undesirable," corroborated Hannasyde with emphasis. "Did Mr Roberts tell Mr Kane whom he suspected of wanting to murder him?"

"I gather that he threw out a hint—ah, a sufficiently broad hint, Superintendent!—that the Mansells would not allow my stepson to stand in the way of their schemes."

Hannasyde's brows drew together. "I take it you refer to the Australian scheme, sir? Did Mr Roberts utter this warning by way of threat?"

"Far from it. According to my stepson, he seemed genuinely disturbed to think that he might have been the unwitting cause of the two other deaths."

Hannasyde said slowly: "Yes, he said as much to me. I think it a trifle farfetched, sir."

"I agree with you. But a point occurred to me which might perhaps be investigated with advantage. I am not familiar with the exact terms of Matthew Kane's will, but no doubt you have gone into it." He paused, took his monocle out of his eye, polished it, and replaced it. "In the event of my stepson's death, Superintendent, who inherits his share of the business?"

Hannasyde nodded, as though he had expected this question. "Mrs Leighton would inherit it, sir."

"You are sure of that? It would not, by any chance, failing a male heir, go to the other two partners?"

"No, certainly not."

Sir Adrian frowned a little. "Ah! Yet if the Mansells wished to acquire complete control over the business, I imagine a lady would not be as hard for them to handle as my stepson might be. She might even agree to being bought out. My stepson tells me that he informed Paul Mansell that he had no desire to be bought out."

"Oh! Mansell actually suggested that, did he? That's interesting. Does Mr Kane attach much weight to Mr Roberts' warning?"

"Oh, not undue weight, I think. He has a certain value for my opinion," said Sir Adrian placidly.

"What is your opinion, sir, if I may ask?"

"I think it most improbable that anyone should have the courage to attempt a murder under your nose, Superintendent."

"It would take some nerve," admitted Hannasyde. "Still, I'm glad you have told me all this, sir."

"It is always well to be on the safe side," said Sir Adrian, getting up.

Hannasyde looked at him under his brows. "Do you want me to give your stepson police protection, sir?"

"That I leave entirely to you, Superintendent. I hardly think it should be necessary."

Hannasyde rose. "Well, I can promise you that the matter will have my very careful consideration, sir. Is that all you wished to say to me?"

"Yes, I think so, thank you," replied Sir Adrian, walking over to the door.

Hannasyde went out before him into the hall and bent to pick up his hat from the chair on which he had laid it. As he did so, he was startled by the sound of an eldritch shriek proceeding from the direction of the front drive. He jerked himself upright; but Sir Adrian, wholly unperturbed, merely raised his eyebrows and murmured: "My son, I fancy."

Mr Harte's voice, raised to a pitch of delirious excitement, floated clearly to Hannasyde's ears. *"Mum!"* screamed Mr Harte.

Sir Adrian stood perfectly still for a moment. Hannasyde thought he seemed to stiffen. Then he said tranquilly: "And apparently my wife also."

CHAPTER NINE

Sir Adrian walked forward to the door, which stood open, and stepped unhurriedly out into the porch. From a taxi piled with luggage, which seemed to consist mostly of battered tin trunks and canvas holdalls, a weather-beaten-looking lady of medium height and stocky build had alighted and was fervently embracing young Mr Harte. Her hat, a battered felt, was set rakishly over a crop of thick grey hair; she wore a coat and skirt of light tweed which needed pressing, heavy brogue shoes, and a handkerchief-scarf knotted round her neck.

"This is most unexpected, my dear," remarked Sir Adrian, advancing towards her.

Lady Harte released Timothy and greeted her husband in a brisk, cheerful voice. "Hullo, Adrian! My dear man, you're thinner than ever!" She kissed him vigorously and turned immediately to direct the activities of the taxi driver and a young footman. For several minutes her attention was fully occupied, and the air seemed to resound with her incisive commands. "Keep the large trunk the right way up, and be careful how you handle the knapsack. I shan't want the hold-all: you'd better store it somewhere for me. No, wait a moment! I think I packed the python's skin in it. Leave it in the hall: I'll unpack it there. Had the luck to stumble on a full-sized python my first day out on safari, Adrian. Beautiful skin, and not much damaged. First shot I fired with the new Grand and Lang too. S.S.G. shot, of course. I'm thinking of having it stuffed to make a standard for a lamp. No, don't bring that packing case into the house: I shan't want it. One or two rather good heads, Adrian, including a sable. I meant to send them to be mounted when I was in town, but I've had so much to think of I forgot. Where's Jim?"

"I think he has gone out in his speedboat," replied Sir Adrian. "What has brought you back so unexpectedly, Norma?"

"I'll tell you all about that in a minute," responded his wife. "I must see this stuff disposed of first. I see I seem to have brought my canvas bath with me. That was a mistake, of course. I meant to have left it in town. It had better be put in the garage, or somewhere. Yes, and the canteen: I shan't want that. I've been in such a rush ever since I landed that I've had no time to sort things out yet. However, it doesn't matter: there's plenty of room here to store everything."

"Mummy, when did you get back?" demanded Timothy. "Do you know Cousin Silas and Cousin Clement have been murdered? Do you know I was actually here when it all happened, Mum? Oh, Mum, do listen!"

"I am listening, my pet. Don't pick that topee case up by the handle: it's broken. Yes, Timothy, I know: thrilling for you, darling! You shall tell me all about it presently."

By this time the footman had been reinforced by the arrival of Pritchard. Lady Harte, announcing that she could safely leave everything to him, thrust a hand through her husband's arm and marched him into the house, saying: "Well, it's nice to see you again, Adrian. Of course, I haven't looked at a paper for weeks; but I got all the news in town. They have been going it down here! Poor old Clement!" She became aware of Hannasyde's silent presence and demanded an instant introduction. Upon hearing that he was a member of the C.I.D. she shook him vigorously by the hand, said she was glad to see him, and promised herself a chat with him as soon as she had settled down.

Hannasyde responded to this by saying that he would very much appreciate an interview with her, whereupon she replied: "If you want to interview me, there's no time like the present. I never believe in putting off until tomorrow what can be done today. In fact, you'll find me very businesslike. First, I must take my hat off and have a wash; then . . . ."

Hannasyde tried to tell her that he had no wish to intrude upon her so unreasonably soon after her reunion with her family, but she interrupted him, saying with great decision: "Nonsense, my good man! There's no silly sentimentality about me. Sit down and make yourself at home! I shan't keep you waiting long. I want to get to the bottom of this business."

Hannasyde, who felt that an explanation of her sudden and unheralded return to England was called for, thanked her and retired, at Sir Adrian's suggestion, to the library.

In about twenty minutes time both Lady Harte and Sir Adrian joined him, Lady Harte having discarded the battered felt and the handkerchief-scarf and dragged a comb through her short, crisp grey locks. Sir Adrian said: "Is there any objection to my presence, Superintendent?"

"None at all, sir. Lady Harte will, I am sure, understand that, taking into consideration her relationship with the present owner of this property, it is my duty to ask her one or two questions."

"Perfectly!" said Norma, striding up to the table and selecting a cigarette from a box on it. "Don't beat about the bush with me! I'm not afraid of plain speaking! You won't offend me. Got a light, Adrian?"

Sir Adrian struck a match for her. She lit her cigarette, threw up her head slightly to inhale a deep breath of smoke, and took up a stance by the table, her stoutly shod feet well apart, and her hands thrust into the pockets of her tailor-made jacket. Her grey eyes, sharp between lids slightly puckered as though from being constantly in the glare of a tropical sun, met Hannasyde's without flinching. "Now, Superintendent: what is it?"

"I should like to know, please, when you landed in England," said Hannasyde.

"Nothing easier. August ninth. I came by plane. I don't think I shall go anywhere by sea again, by the way, Adrian," she added over her shoulder.

"On August ninth?" repeated Hannasyde. "The day before Mr Clement Kane's death, in fact?"

She nodded. He glanced towards Sir Adrian and saw that he was looking at his wife with a kind of patient expectancy not unmixed with amusement.

"My dear Norma," said Sir Adrian, "I feel sure you had some excellent reason for returning so hurriedly, but do tell us what it was!"

"Really, Adrian, you're hopeless!" she said roundly. "You must have seen the news of George Dickson's illness in the papers! Now, don't look vague, my dear soul! You know perfectly well we've been expecting it for months."

"George Dickson?" said Sir Adrian. "I don't think I know——"

"Member for East Madingley!" said Norma impatiently.

"Oh!"

"Yes, he's applying for the Chiltern Hundreds. I got the news—hideously overdue, of course—by runner. I was on safari at the time. I broke camp, and marched back to Kyongo Bwarra, got the lorry there, and had a pretty stiff trip of it to the airport."

"Good God!" said Sir Adrian in accents of deep foreboding.

His wife, paying no heed to this ejaculation, began to stalk up and down the room, occasionally smoking her cigarette, but more often waving it in the air to illustrate her points. "I may have a fight, but I don't mind that. I'm used to overcoming difficulties. Roughing it in the wilds teaches one that, at least. Besides, the Socialist candidate's a bad speaker. Makes a poor impression on the platform. I'm confident I shall get in. I've been up there already, of course; seen our agent, the local committee——"

"My wife," explained Sir Adrian to the superintendent, "intends standing for Parliament."

"Certainly I do!" said Norma. "I feel it's my duty, and thank God I've never been one to shirk that!"

"Quite, Lady Harte. Do I understand that upon landing in England, you went north immediately to East Madingley?"

"Immediately? No, certainly not. I had a great deal of business to attend to in town, and several people to see. I left for my constituency the following evening. In fact, I've been in the devil's own rush ever since I got the cable in the Congo."

"I'm sure you have," said Sir Adrian. "That would account for your not having warned me of your arrival."

"Rubbish, Adrian! Don't be so forgetful. You must have had my cable." He shook his head, smiling. "Well, that's most extraordinary," she said. "I'm pretty sure I sent you one. I know I sent cables to Jevons and Sir Archibald. However, it's possible that in the hurry I may have forgotten. It doesn't really matter. I knew you'd be in Scotland, anyway."

"May I ask where you went when you landed in England, Lady Harte?"

"Ask me anything you like!" said Norma with a lavish gesture. "I went all over the place, seeing first this person and then that. First, of course, I had to hand my guns in and attend to all that nonsense; then I saw Sir Archibald for a few minutes, rushed off to buy a pair of gloves——"

"Did you spend the night at home, Lady Harte?"

"No, I only went home to dump my luggage. Most of the servants are on holiday. There's only the butler and his wife there, and I can't stand furniture muffled in holland covers. I just collected my car from the garage, and went down to Putney, and parked myself with an old servant of mine who lets rooms."

This seemed to Hannasyde an odd procedure. Lady Harte noticed his look of incredulity and gave a laugh. "My dear man, you needn't look so surprised! Why shouldn't I spend the night with my own son's old nanny? I get better attention with her than at any hotel, let me tell you!"

"I quite understand," said Hannasyde. "A devoted old servant would——"

"Devoted! She's practically one of the family. She took my eldest boy from the month, and my younger one too!"

"I see," said Hannasyde. "And you stayed with her until you went to East Madingley?"

"Of course I did!"

"All the following day, in fact?"

Lady Harte looked exasperated. "Yes! If you mean, was I in her house all day, certainly not! You don't seem to realize that I had a lot to do when I got back. I was in London, shopping, all the morning, dashed back to Putney after lunch to repack my suitcase, dashed up to King's Cross, and just caught the 7.15 train north."

"Were you aware of Mr Silas Kane's death, Lady Harte?"

"Yes, Nanny told me all about that. I can't say I was surprised. He'd had a weak heart for years."

"You did not make any attempt to get into touch either with your son or with anyone here?"

She gave her head a decided shake. "No time. There was nothing I could do, and it was extremely important I should present myself in my constituency without any further loss of time. I always keep my personal affairs and my public life strictly apart. It's by far the best plan."

"When did you learn of Mr Clement Kane's murder, Lady Harte?"

"Actually, I never heard anything about it till I got back to town last night. Usually I make a point of studying *The Times* from cover to cover, but my mind was occupied with more pressing business. Nanny told me about it as soon as I arrived at her place, of course, so I collected my baggage from Pont Street first thing this morning and managed to catch the ten o'clock train down to Portlaw." She threw the stub of her cigarette out of the window and added kindly: "If there's anything more you want to know, don't hesitate to ask me!"

"Thank you, Lady Harte. You will understand, I expect, that it is of importance to this case that I should know exactly where you went on August tenth."

"Was that the day Clement Kane was murdered?" inquired Norma. "Oh well, naturally you must know what my movements were! Now let me see!" She paused in her striding about the room and took another cigarette out of the box on the table. Once more her husband held a light for her, once more she inhaled the first breath with that characteristic little toss of the head. "Very difficult," she pronounced at last. "You know what it's like when one gets back from the wilds—or perhaps you don't. I spent the day shopping. New toothbrush, and hair lotion, and that sort of thing. I expect I could make out a list if I gave my mind to it, but I'm not sure I can remember the shops I went to. Some chemist or other in the Brompton Road, but God knows which one. I went to Harrod's, too, and various other places."

"The shops are really quite immaterial, Lady Harte. If you could tell me where you lunched it would be helpful."

"Oh, at some teashop or other! I rather think it was at a Lyons' Corner House—or, no, wait!—it might have been Stewart's. Somewhere in Piccadilly."

"Whichever restaurant it was, it was a crowded one?"

"They all are," said Norma. "If it weren't so out of

the way, I should have gone to my club; but it's in Cavendish Square. Waste of time!"

"And in the afternoon?" inquired Hannasyde.

"I hadn't done all the shopping I had to, so I went back to Putney—it was Saturday, you know. Early closing day in London." She gave a sudden laugh. "Good Lord, of course you can't prove any of this, no more can I! You're thinking that old Nanny would lie like a shot. So she would, bless her! Well, I've done most things—experience is the most important thing in life—but I've never yet been suspected of murder. Now, don't misunderstand me! I don't mind a bit; in fact, it'll provide me with a grand piece of copy for the book I'm writing."

Hannasyde could not help smiling, but he said: "There is another question I should like you to answer, Lady Harte. Were you conversant with the terms of Matthew Kane's will?"

"Do you mean, did I know that my boy stood next to his cousin Clement in succession? My dear good man, of course I did!"

"Did you ever mention the matter to your son?"

"No, certainly not."

"You seem very sure of that?"

"Well, I am sure. I never thought there was the least likelihood of him coming into the property. I'm not at all certain I wanted him to. I don't believe in young men rolling in wealth. I believe in them having to make their own way and fight for what they want. I've always done it. I only wish my boys had half my push. When I make up my mind to do a thing, I can't rest till it's done."

A singularly pugnacious expression came into her face as she delivered herself of this announcement, but just then Jim Kane walked quickly into the room and the expression vanished at once. "Jim, my dearest!" Norma cried and held out her arms to him.

Mr James Kane caught her in a bear's hug. He was laughing as he kissed her. "Mother, where did you spring from? Why weren't we warned? Or were we, and did Adrian forget all about it?"

"Well, I certainly was under the impression that I sent one of you a cable," said Norma. "Not that it matters much. Darling, what a dreadful coat! It's fraying at the cuffs. You really can't go about like that!"

"Why not?" he retorted. "Look at the wicked example you set me!"

"Oh, it doesn't matter about me!" she said. "Besides, I'm perfectly respectable. Now, you must sit down and not interrupt, Jim. I'm being interviewed by the police. Darling!" The last word was murmured in an idolatrous voice quite at variance with Lady Harte's usually incisive accents. Hannasyde watched one thin brown hand go swiftly up to pat Jim's cheek, saw the sharp eyes misty, and turned to find Sir Adrian meditatively polishing his monocle.

Sir Adrian met his look with a faint smile. "Yes, Superintendent?" he said gently.

"Nothing, sir. I have asked Lady Harte all I wish to just now. I'm sure she would like to be alone with her family."

Norma said: "Very decent of you, but my motto is business first. Of course, if you've really done with me——"

"I have," Hannasyde said.

Sir Adrian escorted him out of the room, closing the door on his wife and stepson. In the hall he said: "Have you a piece of paper and a pencil, Superintendent? If you have, I will give you that address you want."

Hannasyde produced both articles. "Thank you. I was going to ask you for that. As a matter of form, I must check up on Lady Harte's story."

Sir Adrian wrote a name and an address down in a leisurely fashion. "Incredible, isn't it?" he said.

"I wouldn't say that."

"That shows insight, Superintendent. My wife is one of the most truthful people I have the pleasure of knowing. Here is Nanny Bryant's address for you."

"Thank you." Hannasyde folded the paper, slipped it in his notebook, and picked up his hat.

He was in time to catch the omnibus that passed the lodge gates and was soon in Portlaw, in conference with Sergeant Hemingway and Inspector Carlton.

The sergeant heard the news of Lady Harte's arrival with the look of a terrier scenting a rat, but the inspector shook his head. "She's a caution, she is," he said. "Well, I ask you! Fancy a lady of her age, and with a family and all, careening about on the backs of camels the way I'm told she does!"

"It isn't my taste," agreed the sergeant. "In fact, there's only one thing worse than a camel ride, in my opinion, and that's an elephant ride. But the point is, she's not careening about on a camel. She's here. This is interesting, Chief. Brings in a new motive. Mother love! What did you make of her?"

"Energetic, determined woman, with a one-track mind and plenty of courage."

"She'd need to have, hobnobbing with a lot of gorillas," remarked the inspector. "Generally you're safe to rule the women out when it's a case of shooting, but I dare say her ladyship wouldn't think twice about pulling a trigger. I'm bound to admit the tale she put up was a thin one, and it don't seem natural she wouldn't let her people know she was coming home, but you've only got to talk to the servants up at Cliff House to know she's a regular cough drop."

"I certainly noticed that, although her husband and her elder son were surprised to see her, they didn't seem to be surprised that she hadn't let them know," agreed Hannasyde. "At the same time, I think the fact that she landed in England on the day before Clement Kane's murder, coupled with her subsequent behaviour, requires investigation. I've no doubt we shall find that her story, as far as she has told it, is quite true. She came home in a hurry to fight a by-election; whether she already knew of Silas Kane's death is, I think, uncertain. If she knew of it, it seems just within the bounds of possibility that she might have conceived the idea of shooting Clement and thus winning a fortune for her own son. That would account for her decision to stay with the old nurse—who, she herself admits, would certainly lie on her behalf—or James Kane's. There's a great deal I haven't fathomed in Lady Harte, but one thing she couldn't help showing me, and that was her feeling for her elder son. I should say he's the very apple of her eye. She greeted Sir Adrian and Timothy with affection, but her whole face changed when James Kane walked into the room."

The sergeant nodded wisely. "I've seen 'em like that often. What's more, I'd as soon handle a nest of wild cats."

Hannasyde smiled but said: "Oh, she seems quite reasonable. Did it strike you that Oscar Roberts was keeping anything back, Hemingway?"

"No," replied the sergeant, looking interested. "Got something on him?"

"Oh no, not that! But apparently he's seen fit to warn James Kane that he may be the next victim."

"Paul Mansell!" said the sergeant instantly. "Now I come to think of it, he did drop a hint we'd do well to keep an eye on Pretty Paul. Said he was anxious to cooperate with us too. Funny what a lot of people you meet who fancy themselves as detectives."

"Well, I don't know," said Inspector Carlton. "He didn't strike me as being a know-all, not Mr Roberts. Come to think of it, he may see a bit more than what we do, not being official."

"That's always possible," agreed Hannasyde. "I'll have a talk with him."

His talk with Oscar Roberts, however, was not productive of very much. Roberts admitted that he had let drop a word of warning in Jim's ear, but when Hannasyde asked him what grounds he had for thinking a warning necessary, he hesitated for a moment and then looked frankly at Hannasyde and said with the shadow of a smile: "I'd like you to get this, Superintendent: it's not my intention to hold out on you. If I were to stumble on something that might help you, believe me, I'd be right along at the police station with it."

"Very kind of you," said Hannasyde. "It would certainly be your duty. Am I to understand that you had no grounds for warning Mr Kane that his life might be in danger?"

"Call it a hunch. And maybe I'm wrong at that."

"Oh, a hunch!" Hannasyde said, an inflexion of contempt in his voice.

Roberts' smile broadened. "I kind of figured you'd feel that way about it, Superintendent, which is why I kept my mouth shut. I don't know what you think of the case, but to my mind, when two men who don't see eye to eye with their partners die within a fortnight of each other, it's time to sit up and look around."

Hannasyde said dryly: "I think I ought to warn you, Mr Roberts, that that kind of innuendo, unsupported by evidence, is actionable."

"Sure," agreed Roberts amiably. "Go right along and tell Mr Paul Mansell I said it, if you wish, Superintendent. Maybe he'll bring an action against me. And maybe he won't."

This enigmatic remark rather annoyed Hannasyde, who told his sergeant later, with unaccustomed acerbity, that he hoped Timothy Harte and Oscar Roberts between them would succeed in clearing up the case for him.

"I don't know about Terrible Timothy," replied Hemingway; "but it's my belief Roberts is a downy bird. Give him his due, he was onto old man Silas having been pushed off the cliff from the start."

"So he says. We've no proof that Silas Kane was murdered."

"That's true," conceded the sergeant. "Of course, if Lady Harte shot Clement, it looks as though the old man wasn't murdered. If you were to ask my opinion, I should say that this case is my idea of a mess. However, I'll see what I can get out of Master Jim's faithful nanny."

"James Kane was out joy-riding in that speedboat of his today," said Hannasyde inconsequently.

"Well, it may be his idea of pleasure. It wouldn't be mine," said the sergeant. "What with camels and speedboats, they seem to me an unnatural lot. There's some sort of a motorboat race billed to take place in Portlaw this month. Young Timothy tells me his brother's entered for it, so I dare say he'll be cavorting about in that boat of his a good bit."

"Either he has an easy conscience or a cast-iron nerve," said Hannasyde. "I'm not sure which."

"Bit of both," said the sergeant. "Gets it from his mother, I expect. Most mothers 'ud try and stop him monkeying around with racing boats and cars, and I don't know what besides; but according to what young Timothy tells me, there's nothing her ladyship likes better than watching her sons get up to dangerous tricks."

He was only partly right, for Lady Harte, hearing of the forthcoming race from Timothy, said that she was glad Jim was going to have some amusement after the stress of the past few days, but she wished he were a stronger swimmer.

Timothy, though offended with Jim for not having taken him out in the boat, never let anyone but himself criticise the paragon, so he said perfunctorily: "Oh, he can swim all right, Mother!"

"All right!" said Lady Harte with great energy. "I want my sons to do everything *well!* Always remember, Timothy, that mediocrity is *fatal!* Whatever you do, you must make up your mind to excell at. Look at me!"

Jim came into the room at that moment and, hearing only the last part of this invigorating speech, promptly asked: "What for, Ma?"

"Success!" answered Lady Harte. "I've always succeeded because I make it my business to do everything thoroughly. I hate half-measures. It's about your speedboat. You ought to be able to swim."

"But I can swim!"

"Not nearly well enough," said his mother sternly. "There's a tide race here too. Not that I wish to keep you tied to my apron strings, for I don't. Did you want me for anything in particular, darling? I shall be down as soon as I've sorted this collection."

"Yes," said Jim firmly. He cast an eye over the chaos reigning in the room and added: "You'd better let one of the skivvies put all this junk away."

"Look here, are you going to take me with you when you try the Seamew out properly, or aren't you?" demanded Timothy belligerently.

"I'm not. I'll take you some other time."

"Well, I call it absolutely rotten of you! I bet I can handle her as well as you can, what's more!"

"Clear out now! I want to have a chat with Mother. You've had your innings."

"I don't see why, just because you——"

Mr James Kane interrupted this speech by advancing purposefully upon his young relative. Mr Harte retreated in good order, promising vengeance.

Jim shut the door upon him. "Getting altogether too uppish. Can you bear a shock, Mother?"

Lady Harte looked up from the task of stowing clothes away haphazard in a large chest of drawers and stared at him with foreboding in her eyes. "You're engaged to be married!"

He laughed, his brows lifting in surprise. "How did you know? Quite right."

"Of course I'm right! What else could it be? Who is it?"

"It's Patricia Allison."

For a moment she seemed puzzled; then her brow cleared. "Do you mean Aunt Emily's secretary, or whatever she calls herself?"

"Yes."

"Oh, that's not so bad!" said Lady Harte, relieved. "I was afraid you were going to say it was that tow-headed little fool Adrian and I disliked so much. Patricia Allison! From what I remember, there's no silly nonsense about her. I always like these girls who *do* something, even if it's only looking after Aunt Emily. What I can't stand is a parasite. I hope she won't encourage you to live a life of idleness now you've come into all this money."

"I think I'm going to take an intelligent interest in netting."

Lady Harte said despairingly: "How I could ever have given birth to a son with so little ambition passes my comprehension! When I think what you might do——"

"But, darling, I hate travel!" objected Jim. "Can I bring Patricia in to see you?"

"Very well; but you know I don't get on with modern girls," said Lady Harte gloomily.

However, when Patricia presently came into the room, looking very cool and charming in a severe linen coat and skirt, her future mother-in-law said approvingly: "That's what I call a sensible kit. I hate frills and furbelows. Jim tells me you are going to be married. I should think you'll suit one another very well. It's always been my dread that he might marry something out of a tobacconist's shop, so you can imagine what a relief it is to me to know he's had the sense to choose a really nice girl. Not that I'm a snob, but there are limits, and young men are such fools."

"I know," said Patricia. "It's nice of you to take it like that. I was afraid you might feel that he could have done a lot better for himself."

Lady Harte seemed to find this amusing. She gave her jolly laugh and said that she had no use for pampered young women who had nothing to do except lacquer their fingernails and drink too many cocktails. While Patricia sorted and put away her scattered belongings she walked up and down the room, energetically planning a useful future for her elder son and laying her commands upon Patricia not to allow him to fritter away his time either in money grubbing or more frivolous pursuits.

By lunchtime she was on the best of terms with Patricia and had even favoured her with a brief sketch of her own (parliamentary) plans. She evinced not the smallest interest in the shocking events that had taken place at Cliff House during the preceding fortnight, and Patricia, feeling that Jim's mother was hardly the person in whom to confide fears for his safety which might, after all, be groundless, made no attempt to talk to her on the subject.

At the luncheon table Lady Harte dominated the company. She ate casually of any dish that happened to be placed in front of her and described in trenchant yet picturesque terms the adventure she had lately been through. Emily, who liked hearing about foreign lands, listened to her with a good grace, only interrupting her occasionally to say either that she had never heard of such a thing, or that she had no patience with such outlandish ways.

On Norma's proposed excursion into the realm of politics she spoke with vigour and decision, condemning it from the outset as ridiculous nonsense and announcing that she didn't know what the world was coming to. Norma then delivered a stern lecture on her responsibilities as a citizen, and the lunch party came to an end without anyone having mentioned murders, clues or policemen—a change which Miss Allison at least felt to be an advantage.

CHAPTER TEN

THE NEWS of Lady Harte's spectacular arrival at Cliff House reached the offices of Kane and Mansell within two hours of her taxi's return to Portlaw. The taxi driver described it, with humorous embellishments, to a man selling newspapers, who passed it on in due course to a junior clerk, who retailed it to his senior, who thought proper to mention it to Joe Mansell. Joe, surprised, told his son over the lunch table. Paul Mansell, stirring his coffee, said reflectively: "Oh!· . . . That's funny. Dam' funny."

Joe cast a quick look at him and then averted his eyes. "She's a very unaccountable woman, Norma Harte—very. Of course, she may have heard of Silas' death."

"Wonder if she had anything to do with Clement's death?" said Paul. "Violent sort of female, what?"

Joe stirred restlessly in his chair. "Really, my boy, really!"

"Well, I don't know," pursued Paul, watching his parent's discomfort with rather a mocking expression in his eyes. "Seems to me she might well be the guilty party. Rather a good shot, isn't she?"

Joe set his coffee cup down. "Now, look here, Paul!" he said in an angry undertone; "I'll tell you something! You make a great mistake to talk like that —a very great mistake! There's nothing looks worse than trying to cast the blame onto someone else!"

"Someone else?" repeated Paul lifting his brows.

"Well, you know what I mean! The less you say, the better. This is a very nasty business. I—upon my soul, it's taken years off my life! I've never been through such a fortnight, never!"

Paul leaned back in his chair, smiling and keeping his eyes, under their drooping lids, fixed maliciously on his father's face. "I do believe you think I killed Clement!" he said softly.

"You know very well I think nothing of the sort! I wish you wouldn't talk in that silly way. It's folly, rank folly! Of course, I know you wouldn't dream—good God, the very idea is preposterous! There's no need to discuss it. All I mean is that most unfortunately you've no alibi—that is, you can't prove an alibi—for the time of poor Clement's death. The police are bound to be suspicious of you. Well, they are suspicious: no use blinking facts."

"I'm not afraid. It's you who seem to have got cold feet. The police can't prove a thing against me. You needn't worry, Dad."

"I am worrying!" Joe said with suppressed violence. "You don't seem to realize what a ghastly business this is. Silas and Clement both gone within a fortnight."

Paul shrugged nonchalantly, took out his thin gold cigarette case, and opened it. "Speaking for myself, I don't look on their deaths as much loss," he drawled.

For a moment Joe did not answer. Then he said in a low voice: "Sometimes, Paul, you seem to me to be utterly callous! How you can sit there and say such a thing of two men you've known from the day you were born——"

"Oh Lord, don't pull out the pathetic stop, Dad!" Paul interrupted. "You know dam' well you agree with me."

"I deny that—I utterly deny that! I had the greatest regard for them. Silas was my oldest friend. Don't you dare say such a thing again! It's—it's an impertinence! A gross untruth!"

"Oh, all right!" replied Paul. "Sorry I spoke!" He tapped a cigarette on his case and put it between his lips. "I suppose you're only too glad to have young Jim Kane all ready to step into Clement's shoes."

"I've nothing against Jim, nothing at all!" Joe said. "He's a very nice boy; but of course as for his knowing anything about the business—well, that's absurd, and he'll be the first to realize it. If he likes to learn it, I shall be only too glad to help him and teach him the ins and outs of it. I don't anticipate that he'll be anything more than a sleeping partner, actually, but——"

"Oh, don't you!" Paul struck in. "You wait till you see his highness! It won't be long before there'll be nothing he won't know about the business."

"I know Jim Kane, thanks. I've no doubt you handled him badly. Got his back up. I never wanted you to tackle him. I was against it from the start. I'll have a talk with him myself when I think fit."

"And I'll bet you'll find I'm right," said Paul. "He's going to be a dam' nuisance to us. He's showing his teeth already, and, if I know these Kanes, that's nothing to what he'll be like once he's found his feet. It'll be Silas over again. Pig-headed, stick-in-the-mud——"

"That'll do, my boy, that'll do! You're talking very indiscreetly. There's nothing wrong with Jim. I dare say he wouldn't listen to you, but he'll listen to me, you'll see."

"I hope I shall," said Paul, getting up. "Meanwhile, how much longer do you expect Roberts to hang about?"

"Roberts quite understands how we're placed. He's being most reasonable, really most accommodating!"

"It strikes me he's being a dam' sight too accommodating," said Paul. "I'd like to know just what he's playing at, telling Jim Kane not to let himself be rushed into the deal!"

Joe looked at him narrowly. "What's this? How do you know that? Who told you?"

"Roberts himself. Came lounging into my office this morning and had the nerve to tell me, in front of Jenkins and Miss Clarke, that I was making a great mistake to press Kane, and that he'd like me to know he'd told him not to let himself be hustled. Darned cheek, I call it."

"He said that, did he?" Joe stared up at his son frowningly. "Roberts thinks Silas was murdered, Paul."

"He thinks too much. What's it got to do with him, anyway? Anyone would think he was investigating the crime instead of that beefy superintendent."

Joe said, moistening his lips, "I suppose he's interested. He was first on the scene, wasn't he?" He hesitated, and moved a fork on the table, and studied it. "I wonder whether he saw anything—anything that might give him an inkling——"

"Of course not!"

"How do you know?" Joe said, glancing up momentarily.

"Good Lord, if he'd seen anything, he'd have told the police! What would be the point of keeping it back?"

"I don't know. He's a queer chap. Never can make him out, quite."

"Well, I wish he'd stop poking his long nose into what doesn't concern him!" said Paul sharply. "I'm all for doing a deal with his firm, but I'm about fed up with having him cropping up at every turn! I suppose you mean he thinks I killed Clement. He can think what he likes, but I can tell you this much! It'll take a cleverer man than Friend Roberts to bring Clement's death home to me!"

"Gently, gently!" Joe said, looking round apprehensively. "Don't forget you're in a public restaurant, my boy!"

"I don't forget it, and I don't care who hears what I say!" retorted Paul.

Joe rose and picked up his hat. "You've let this appalling affair get on your nerves. Much wiser to say as little as possible. Are you coming straight back to the office?"

"No, I'm going down to the harbour to see Fenwick about that last consignment," snapped Paul.

"Oh yes! Quite right, my boy: a breath of fresh air will do you good. Blow away the cobwebs, eh?"

Paul deigned no reply to this but walked out of the restaurant to where he had parked his car and, getting into it, drove off in the direction of the old town.

He found his quarry in conversation with a couple of old salts at the end of the stone jetty. Some fishing smacks, with sails furled, lay at anchor in the harbour, with kittiwakes and herring gulls wheeling and circling above them; and a quantity of lobster pots decorated the jetty. A small tramp steamer and some rowing- and motor-boats, dipping and rising with the slight swell, were the only other craft visible.

Paul Mansell, concluding his business with Mr Thomas Fenwick, lingered for a few moments, watching a kittiwake swoop down to the water and rise again. A drawling voice spoke at his elbow. "A fine day, Mansell."

Paul turned, a spasm of annoyance contracting his features. "Oh—good afternoon! I didn't see you."

"I often take a stroll down this way," said Oscar Roberts, leaning his elbows on the low stone wall before them and gazing out across the wide bay. "Kind of peaceful. Say, you don't have much shipping here, do you?"

"No, very little nowadays. You won't find much use for those things," replied Paul, indicating with a faintly contemptuous smile the field glasses which hung round Roberts' neck.

"You never know," said Roberts. "I get a kick out of watching the gulls. Wonderful things, aren't they? Ever watched them through glasses?"

"No, I can't say I have. Not much in my line." He paused and added with an attempt at cordiality: "About that deal, Roberts; I've just been having a talk with my father. He is confident he can handle Kane."

Roberts had raised his field glasses and focussed them on the opposite headland, some two miles across the bay. "If you'll pardon me, I wouldn't advise you to handle Mr James Kane too much. I've a notion it won't pay."

Paul's face darkened. "What do you mean by that?" he demanded.

Roberts still kept his glasses trained on the opposite headland. "Oh, just one of my hunches!" he said amiably. "I'd leave that young man alone, if I were you." His glasses raked the white cliff gleaming on the other side of the bay. "Seems extraordinary what you can pick out with these things, doesn't it? I can see the whole line of the cliff path over yonder, and the very spot where old Mr Kane went over the edge." He lowered the glasses and turned to Paul. "Like to take a look?"

"No!" Paul said angrily.

Oscar Roberts regarded him with a faint smile. "Say, is anything wrong? You sound kind of put out."

Paul met his look and held it. "Not in the least. What should be wrong?"

He took the glasses which Robert was still holding out to him and focussed them on the headland. "Yes, a very fine pair," he said in his normal voice. "I see Kane's speedboat's tied up to the landing stage under the cliff. Do you know if he's entering for the race next week?"

"So I believe," answered Roberts. "Why?"

"Oh, no reason! Seems a bit callous, considering everything. Hullo, someone's going out in the boat!"

"That'll be Kane himself, trying her out, I fancy. We'll have a look at his form."

"I'm afraid I've got something better to do than waste my time watching Kane handle a speedboat," replied Paul, giving back the glasses.

Roberts took the glasses and looked through them. He said suddenly: "That's not Kane! That's the boy!"

Paul Mansell was preparing to walk away, but he stopped. "Timothy? I say, isn't that a bit dangerous?"

"I'll say it is! The durned little fool!"

Paul said uneasily: "You know the current's very strong here. I don't believe that kid's got any right to take Kane's boat out. Do you think we ought to do something? I mean——"

"Sure I think we ought!" Roberts said briskly. "Can you drive one of these things?" He pointed at a small motorboat tied up alongside the jetty.

"Well, no, I can't say I ever have, but I dare say——"

"Hold these glasses, then. Guess I can manage," Roberts said, and, thrusting the glasses into Paul's hands, ran towards the boat, and lowered himself into it. After a quick inspection he lifted his head and shouted: "By the Lord's mercy she's full up!" and cast off.

Paul saw him thread his way between the fishing-smacks to the mouth of the harbour and went back to watch the speedboat's progress.

Timothy was heading across the bay towards the harbour, steadily gaining speed. Through the glasses Paul could see the froth of foam about the Seamew's lifting bows and just the top of Timothy's head as he crouched over the wheel. The roar of the engine sounded across the water; Paul guessed Timothy to have opened the throttle to the full and bit his lip. Nearer at hand Roberts' borrowed motorboat chugged to meet the Seamew.

Mr Fenwick came along the jetty and said: "What's up, Mr Mansell? Who's that gone off with Bob Aiken's boat?"

"It's that blasted kid from Cliff House, monkeying about with Mr Jim Kane's Seamew!" Paul replied. "He'll capsize her for a certainty!"

Mr Fenwick smiled indulgently. "What, Mr Timothy? He's all right, Mr Mansell. He won't do no harm. He's more like a fish than a boy, he is."

"He's got no right to be in that boat. Anything might happen!"

"Oh, you don't need to worry your head over him, Mr Mansell! The way I always look at it is this: boys ——" He stopped short, staring across the bay. "Hullo, what's up with her?"

The Seamew, which had been skimming across the water on a straight course for Portlaw, seemed to be losing speed. Paul rested his elbows on the wall to keep the glasses steady and said in a voice sharpened with apprehension: "She's keeling over . . . her bows are right out of the——Good God, she's gone down!"

"Lord-love-a-duck, what's he done to her?" exclaimed Mr Fenwick. "Can you see him, Mr Mansell? Is he all right?"

"I can't make out. There isn't a sign—yes, there he is! He's all right, if he can hold out till Roberts reaches him."

"He'll do that easy enough," said Mr Fenwick, shading his eyes under one horny hand. "It beats me how he come to lose her like that. Wasn't turning, was he?"

"I couldn't see. She just seemed to disappear. He's making no headway against the current. What the devil possessed the little fool to do it?"

"Ah, now you're asking!" said Mr Fenwick, his

calm gaze upon the motorboat forging steadily through the water. "That's a boy all over. Proper varmints they are. How's he doing?"

"He's still there. He's seen Roberts, I think. . . . Yes, it's all right: Roberts has reached him. Gosh!" He lowered the glasses and wiped his forehead. "Bloody little fool!" he said angrily. "I hope he gets it hot!"

Out in the middle of the bay Oscar Roberts, having hauled an exhausted boy into the motorboat, was saying very much the same thing. Timothy lay on the floor of the boat gasping for breath and spitting salt water. Roberts said: "Guess there's a mighty big kick in the pants coming to you, son," and opened the throttle again, steering, not for Portlaw, but for the landing stage on the farther side of the bay, under Cliff House.

Mr Harte was quite unable to speak for a minute or two, but as soon as he was able to catch his breath he jerked out: "She simply sank! I didn't do a thing!"

Roberts smiled a little and said: "Don't waste that one on me. You keep it for that stepbrother of yours."

"But I didn't!" Timothy asseverated, sitting up. "She was going perfectly!"

"Maybe you struck a rock, then."

"I did not!" Timothy said indignantly. "Good Lord, I should know if I'd hit anything!"

"You should," agreed Roberts somewhat dryly. "But a boat doesn't sink for no reason, sonny, does it?"

"Of course not; but I swear it wasn't anything I did! Oh, I say, I forgot! Thanks awfully for pulling me out. There's a most frightful current. I couldn't make any headway against it." He added gruffly: "As a matter of fact, I expect I'd have been drowned if you hadn't come along. Thanks awfully, sir!"

"That all right. It's just lucky I happened to be around. How are you feeling?"

"Oh, I'm O.K.! But I don't understand about the Seamew. Honestly, I do know how to handle her! Well, you *saw* I could, didn't you?"

Roberts laughed. "I can't exactly say that, son. It didn't look too good to me, which is why I'm here now. Maybe you'd best be half drowned for a while: your stepbrother's on the landing stage."

Timothy glanced towards the shore. "Well, I don't care. There was something wrong with the boat: one minute she was all right, and the next—I don't know: I think the bottom was ripped off her. She—she just filled with water. But I swear she never hit anything!"

"The fact of the matter is," said Roberts, putting the engine astern as they drew near to the landing stage, "speedboats weren't meant to be handled by schoolboys."

They came gently up to the landing stage, where an extremely wrathful young man awaited them. "What the hell? . . ." exploded Mr James Kane.

His saturated relative clambered out of the boat and said unhappily: "I'm *frightfully* sorry, Jim; but, honestly, it wasn't my fault!"

"Where's the Seamew?" demanded Jim.

"Well, she—she sort of sank," said Mr Harte more unhappily than ever. "But——"

Jim interrupted him without ceremony. He spoke with admirable fluency for two blistering minutes. Mr Harte wilted perceptibly and gave several watery sniffs. Roberts, having tied up the boat, stepped out of it and suggested mildly that Timothy had better go and change his wet clothes. Jim, though expressing a savage hope that Timothy would contract pneumonia and die of it, agreed and told him to get out before he was kicked out. Timothy fled.

Jim turned to Roberts. He still looked very angry, but the alarming note left his voice. "What happened, sir?"

"That's more than I can tell you," replied Roberts. "I was on the end of the jetty yonder, with young Mansell, when we saw the kid get into the Seamew and cast off. Watched him through my field glasses, which, now I come to think of it, I told Mansell to hold for me. It didn't seem to me he was handling the boat any too well, so to be on the safe side I set out to meet him. What he did to the Seamew I can't make out, but she went down within about thirty seconds of my first seeing her lose speed. It looked to me as though he must have hit something and torn the bottom out of her."

Jim said, frowning: "Damned little ass! He ought to know the bay well enough by now! He must have been steering an idiotic course if he hit the rocks!"

"Maybe he had his hands too full to think much about his course," said Roberts, smiling a little. "He's not precisely in the habit of taking speedboats out, is he?"

"No, certainly not. He did it to get back on me for not taking him this morning. I'll teach him!"

"Guess he's had a bit of a fright already, Kane. There's an almighty strong current out there."

Jim gave a reluctant grin. "It would take more than that to put the wind up Timothy, sir. By the way, thanks very much for going to the rescue. You must come up and meet my mother. She arrived quite unexpectedly this morning."

"Is that so? I'd like to meet her very much; but I think I ought to take the boat back. Maybe the owner will be looking for it."

"Mansell's sure to explain. Come on up to the house and have a drink," said Jim, leading the way to the path that zigzagged up the cliff face. He glanced back, grimacing. "You can imagine my feelings when I heard the Seamew start up! I was on the terrace at the time. I guessed it was that devilish brat, of course. The worst of it is, my mother will probably be rather bucked about it, so Timothy will get the idea he's done something fairly clever."

Lady Harte, still wearing the crumpled tweed coat and skirt, met them as they came across the lawn at the top of the cliff. She shook Oscar Roberts warmly by the hand and said that it was very decent of him to have pulled Timothy out of the water. "Not but what he's a good swimmer for his age," she added. "However, he tells me the current was a bit too much for him, so I'm very grateful to you. Darling, I'm so sorry about the Seamew, but you can buy another, can't you?"

"Yes, but for God's sake don't let Timothy think he's a hero, Mother! He deserves to be flayed."

"No, I can't agree with you there, Jim," she said decidedly. "Of course he'd no business to take your boat out—I grant that—but you must admit it showed an adventurous spirit." She turned to Roberts. "I hate milksops, don't you?"

He agreed smilingly, but Jim groaned. "I knew it!" he said. "You're rather pleased Mother!"

"Well, I admit I didn't think he had as much enterprise. However, he's very upset at having lost your boat, so don't be unkind to him, darling. After all, it might just as well have happened to you. Timothy says there was something wrong with the boat."

"There was nothing wrong with her whatsoever!" said Jim. "What that loathsome whelp of yours did was to run her over the Pin rocks."

They had by this time reached the terrace. Rosemary was seated there, becomingly dressed in floating black draperies. While Jim went into the house to fetch a cooling drink for his stepbrother's preserver, she informed Lady Harte and Oscar Roberts that she had had a premonition that something dreadful was going to happen, and added, somewhat unwisely, that, fond as she was of Timothy, she could not help seeing that he was getting very out of hand. This led, not unnaturally, to a spirited defence of her son by Norma, and Jim, returning with beer and glasses, found both ladies engaged in a highly acrimonious argument. Though considerably annoyed with Timothy, he felt impelled to defend him against Rosemary's attack, with the result that Rosemary, looking offended, withdrew into the house, saying that no one seemed to have the least consideration for her.

"That young woman," said Lady Harte, accepting a glass of beer from her son, "badly wants an Object in life."

"She's got one. You wait till you see him," said Jim involuntarily. Recollecting the presence of a stranger, he added hastily: "Beer or a gimlet, Roberts?"

"I'll have beer, thanks. But don't mind me," replied Roberts, twinkling. "I've seen him too."

Jim laughed. "Awfully Nordic, isn't he? He's bunked to town, I understand. My own feeling is that he's too Nordic to be a murderer. Hullo, Adrian! Have some beer?"

Sir Adrian, who had come out on to the terrace from the drawing room, declined this offer but desired his stepson to tell him what had been happening. He appeared to be quite unmoved at the thought of the danger Timothy had been in, merely remarking that he hoped Jim did not expect him to enact the role of avenging parent.

Timothy presently joined the party on the terrace, chastened but anxious to justify himself. Failing, however, to induce Oscar Roberts to support his statement that he had been steering a course well outside the line of Pin rocks, or to win from his stepbrother any sign of belief in his story or forgiveness for his crime, he went away to nurse his sorrows in solitude.

He bore himself with unaccustomed lowliness throughout the rest of the day and retired early to bed. He bade Jim good night in a painstakingly offhand voice, received in reply the curtest of valedictions, and flushed to the ears. This quite melted Miss Allison's heart, and she presently slipped out of the drawing room and went upstairs to tap on his door. After a slight pause she was told gruffly to come in and entered to find Timothy reading in bed. He lowered his book and said in a goaded voice: "What is it?"

Miss Allison went to sit on the edge of the bed. "I know you're sick to death of the whole subject," she said; "but do you mind telling me just what happened?"

"You wouldn't believe me if I did," he replied bitterly.

"Well, you might give me a chance, anyway."

"I don't care whether anyone believes me or not!" said Timothy.

Miss Allison removed the book from his grasp. "Come off the roof! You know as well as Jim does where the rocks are. If you say you were beyond them, I believe you."

"Well, I was."

"Cross your heart, Timothy?"

"Yes, I swear I was. Besides, if I'd hit anything, I'd have felt it."

"And absolutely between ourselves, you didn't muck something up in the engine?"

"Course not. She wouldn't have sunk if I had."

Miss Allison twined her fingers together and said: "Timothy, what do you think was wrong?"

Something in her voice made him look at her sharply. "I don't know."

"Just exactly what happened?"

"Well, nothing at first. She was running perfectly. I opened her up awfully gradually too. As a matter of fact, I didn't mean to take her at full speed at all, but she was going so well, and it was such a grand day for it, that I simply couldn't help letting her out. I was steering an absolutely straight course, and the engine was running as sweetly as anything, when suddenly I felt her check a bit, and then I saw the water rising up in the boat, and she heeled right over. It happened so quickly I don't really know what did happen, except that I was chucked clean out of the boat. I can tell you, it was a pretty ghastly feeling."

"It must have been awful!" Miss Allison said, her face quite pale.

"Well, it was, because for one thing it took me completely by surprise, and for another the current got me. Gosh, I was glad to see that motorboat chugging along!"

"If Mr Roberts hadn't been there you'd have been drowned."

"I expect I should, really."

Her fingers gripped together in her lap. "It might have been Jim."

"Yes, I know; that's what I keep on telling him, but he doesn't believe a word I say. He thinks I capsized the rotten boat or ran her on the rocks. But he *knows* I can handle her, because he's often let me when I've been out with him. I'm frightfully sorry I took her out and—and lost her, but it's no use going on saying it. He simply doesn't listen. He said . . ." Timothy's voice shook suddenly. He found himself quite unable to repeat what Jim had said, and instead announced that he was tired and wished to be left alone.

Miss Allison got up. "Don't go to sleep yet. I'm going to fetch Jim."

Mr Harte sat up with a jerk. "You jolly well aren't! I don't want to see him!"

"I don't care a damn what you want. I mean to get to the bottom of this."

"I'll lock my door! It doesn't matter a hoot to me what Jim says or thinks, and if you make him come here, I won't ever speak to you again as long as I live!" declared Mr Harte, anguished.

"Don't be an idiot! Can't you see that this may be important?" said Patricia fiercely. "If you didn't run her on the rocks, *why did she sink?*"

Timothy stared at her. "Do you mean, she was tampered with?" he demanded. "But—but—why?"

"To get rid of Jim," said Patricia, but in a low voice, as though she were afraid of her own words.

"Gosh!" ejaculated Timothy, round eyed.

She left the room and went downstairs to find Jim. He was just coming out of the drawing room as she reached the hall, and said: "Oh, there you are! I was coming to look for you. Do you feel like going out?"

"No, not a bit. I want you to come up to Timothy's room, if you don't mind."

"But I do mind. I haven't the least desire to see

Timothy, and I have got a most burning desire to have you to myself for a bit."

"Don't be vindictive, Jim. It's mean."

"I'm not. I haven't done a thing to him."

"Yes, you are. You know perfectly well he thinks the world of you. I think he's rather upset by what you said to him. So do make it up with him. Besides, I want you to listen to his story carefully, because I think he's speaking the truth. Do come, Jim!"

"All right, but why have I got to listen to his story all over again?" he asked, allowing himself to be led upstairs.

"Never mind. I'll tell you why when you're heard it. You haven't really listened to him yet, you know."

Timothy was still sitting up in bed when they reached his room. His manner towards his stepbrother would not have led the uninitiated to suspect that he desired a reconciliation. He said: "You needn't think I wanted her to fetch you, because I didn't. I've told you I was sorry about half a million times already, and if you don't want to listen, you jolly well needn't!"

"If you give me any lip I'll wring your neck," said Jim. "You meddlesome, cocksure little beast."

Mr Harte's countenance lightened at this form of address. "Oh, Jim, honestly I'm most frightfully sorry about it!" he said thickly.

"All right, put a sock in it. Pat says I've got to listen to your utterly unconvincing narrative," replied Jim, sitting down on the side of the bed.

"Well, I wish you would," said Timothy; "because when Mr. Roberts says I ran on the rocks, he simply doesn't know what he's talking about! I didn't."

"What did you do, then?"

"Tell him exactly what you told me, Timothy!" commanded Miss Allison. "And do listen with an open mind, Jim! It's important."

"I can't for the life of me see why, but carry on!" said Jim.

Timothy drew his knees up, and hugged them, and repeated the story he had told Miss Allison. Jim heard him out in silence but at the end said: "Look here, my child, you may think you didn't hit anything, but a boat doesn't go down in thirty seconds for no reason. You must obviously have ripped one of the bottom strakes clean off her. I don't say you crashed bang into a rock, but, according to you, you were going all out. At that speed it would be enough if you merely grazed a rock."

"Jim, if I'd done that, wouldn't I have felt it?"

"I should have thought so. Never having piled her up myself I can't say for certain."

"Give me a piece of paper and a pencil!" ordered Timothy. "I'll draw you a diagram."

"What on earth does it matter? The thing's done now. Forget it!"

"No, let him show you!" said Patricia.

Jim sighed, and produced a pencil from his pocket, and handed it over. Timothy directed Miss Allison to give him the notebook that lay on his dressing table, licked the pencil, and began to sketch. "Well, that's the bay, roughly. *Here* is Portlaw, and *here* is the landing stage below our cliff. Now the Pin rocks run like *this*, don't they?"

"More or less," agreed Jim, watching the pencil's progress.

"Right!" Well, *this* is the course I steered. If anything, I was drawing away from the rocks. It must have been just about here that the Seamew went down. Anyway, I'll swear it wasn't within a quarter of a mile of the rocks. Now what about it?"

Jim shook his head. "It's beyond me. Without wishing to be offensive, I should imagine that, while that was the course you meant to steer, you actually were much nearer the shore."

"Oh gosh!" said Timothy, disgusted. "You must think I'm a pretty average ass!"

"I do," replied Jim promptly.

"When you let me handle the Seamew before, did I do all right or not?"

"You did. But I was with you."

"Look here!" interposed Patricia; "will you for the

sake of argument assume that Timothy's right, and he wasn't near the rocks?"

"Certainly ma'am! So what?"

"He couldn't have sunk the boat like that through doing something wrong with the engine, could he?"

"No."

"Could one of the bottom boards—or whatever you call them—have been loose from the start?"

"No."

"Are you sure?"

"Of course I'm sure. Didn't we have her out this morning?"

"Well, are you sure you didn't graze her on something?"

"God give me strength!" gasped Jim. "Talk about adding insult to injury! Are you two beauties trying to make out *I* sank the boat?"

"No, but are you sure?"

"I am!" said Jim emphatically.

"Then if Timothy didn't run her on the rocks, and there was nothing wrong with her this morning, *why did she sink?*" demanded Patricia.

"She didn't. What I mean is, she wouldn't have if——" He stopped and glanced quickly from Patricia's face to Timothy's. "Good Lord you don't think someone tampered with her, do you?" he exclaimed.

"Yes," replied Patricia. "I do."

CHAPTER ELEVEN

FOR A MOMENT Jim stared at Patricia, then he put his arm round her and drew her close to him. "Of all the lurid ideas! Darling. I'm sorry to have to say it, but you're definitely batty."

"No, she isn't," said Timothy. "Everyone knows you've entered for the race next week, and I should think a whole lot of people knew you were going to try the Seamew out tomorrow."

"Do try and pull yourself together," begged Jim. "I was out in her this morning! Who on earth could have had a chance to monkey about with her between the time I came in and the time you went out?"

"Anybody!" replied Timothy promptly. "It was a safe bet you wouldn't go out again today. You brought her in just after Mum arrived, which must have been just after eleven, and I didn't go down to the landing stage till three o'clock. There was loads of time."

"But, my good lad, nobody would dare tamper with my boat in broad daylight!"

Patricia sat down beside him on the edge of the bed. "I don't see why not. Nobody ever comes along this side of the bay. There's no sand to attract the Portlaw gang. Besides, you know what those mud flats are like between us and Portlaw if you walk round the bay at low tide. Supposing someone did something or other to the Seamew between one o'clock and two o'clock? None of us would have been on the shore, because we were having lunch. I call it a pretty good time."

"Well, I don't," said Jim. "If I were going to put someone else's boat out of action, I should choose a nice dark night for the job."

"No, you wouldn't, because you couldn't see to do it," said Timothy instantly. "You'd have to have a lantern, and that might attract attention. Golly, I bet Pat's right, and someone is trying to do you in!"

"You needn't sound so darned pleased about it, viper!"

"I'm not, but I do think it's jolly exciting."

Jim grinned his appreciation of this point of view but said: "I suppose I should be unpopular if I suggested that the bottom might have been ripped off the Seamew by a floating spar or something of that nature?"

Patricia gave a little shiver. "I've got a feeling . . ." she began, and then stopped and laughed.

Jim looked at her with deep foreboding. "Are you also—whatever else you may be—honest with yourself, darling?"

"Shut up!" said Patricia. "This isn't a joke."

"My error," murmured Jim.

"Jim, Mr Roberts warned you only yesterday you might be the next victim."

Timothy, who had relaxed upon his pillows, bounced up at this, his blue eyes sparkling with pleasurable anticipation. "*Did* he? I *say*, do you think there's a Hidden Killer in the house!"

"Timothy!" gasped Miss Allison, instinctively clasping Mr Kane's arm.

"Well, if you come to think about it, this is just the sort of house where you might have a Hidden Killer lurking, 'cept that it isn't really old enough, and I shouldn't think there's a secret passage or anything. But it's got two wings, and three staircases, and lots of attics leading out of one another and——"

"Stop!" commanded Miss Allison, pale with fright. "I know it's nonsense; but if you go on like that I shan't be able to sleep a wink all night."

"Calm yourself, my love," said Mr Kane. "If the Hidden Killer tried to do me in by tampering with the Seamew, there doesn't seem to be much point in him lurking in the house."

"No, of course not," said Patricia. "Let's get back to the point. You're the only one of us who knows anything about boats, Jim. Would it be possible for anyone to do something to the speedboat that wouldn't show at first—I mean, if you simply knocked a hole in it it would fill with water at once, and the Seamew didn't."

"I suppose you could plug your hole," replied Jim.

"How?"

Jim reached out a hand for the pencil and Timothy's notebook. "Well, imagine this is one of your bottom strakes. If you cut a wedge-shaped hole, and plugged it so that the broad end of your plug stuck out a bit, presumably it would stay put until you got some way on the boat. It would work loose, and of course as soon as you were going full speed it would be bound to come out, and the force of the water would be enough to rip the strake right off."

"I see. Do you think that's what was done?"

"No," said Jim cheerfully.

"Why not?" demanded Mr Harte.

"Probably because I haven't got that kind of mind. Moreover, to do that job you'd have to have the boat out of the water, come armed with a bit and a brace, a pad saw, and a bit of putty to fill up the gaps—it's too darned silly!"

"When was low tide today?" asked Patricia. "Lunchtime, wasn't it?"

"Twelve forty-five," said Jim.

"That means that the Seamew must have been lying on the slipway then, doesn't it?"

"Yes," he agreed reluctantly.

"Jim, don't you see how it all fits in? You tied her up just after eleven, she was high and dry an hour later, and floating again by the time Timothy got to her. It was all thought out, and the time calculated!"

"Rot!" said Jim.

"It isn't rot! It's jolly sensible!" retorted Mr Harte. "Only, who's the Killer? I rather thought Mr Dermott was the person who did Cousin Clement in, but I don't see why he wants to do you in too."

"Nor anyone else. I do wish you'd get this silly idea out of your heads."

"Jim, I shouldn't have thought anything of it if it weren't for what Mr Roberts said to you. But in face of that——"

"My dear girl, Roberts was talking through his hat. In any case, he saw the whole thing happen, and if there were anything in your theory, he'd presumably be the first to suspect there'd been some dirty work done on the Seamew. But he didn't even suggest it."

"It looks to me," said Mr Harte, pursuing his own line of thought, "as though it must be one of the Mansells. The only other person I can think of who might want to get rid of you is the next heir—Cousin Maud, I mean."

"Who is living in Sydney," said Jim. "Try again."

"Perhaps she isn't!" said Timothy, loath to abandon this original idea. "Perhaps she's been here all the time, in disguise!"

"Very likely, I should think. Now explain how she managed to post a letter to Aunt Emily from Australia when she was in England at the time, and we shall be all set."

"Say, wise guy!" said Mr Harte, suddenly becoming trans-atlantic. "You ever heard of a Blind?"

"Often," replied Jim. "I've even been on one."

"Not that kind, you ass! The other! Get a load of this, now. What if she wrote the letter before she came to England and left it with someone to post on a certain date?"

Jim sighed. "Now I'll tell one!"

"No, but——"

" 'The Idiot Boy,' by William Wordsworth!" said Jim. "I suppose she knew by instinct that Cousin Silas always went for a walk after dinner, and which night there'd be a fog, and a few other little details like that? Had the whole thing mapped out to the minute two months before she did the deed. You make me tired!"

"I hadn't thought of that," admitted Mr Harte.

"Well, while you are thinking of it you might also ask yourself whether cutting holes in speedboats is really a womanly trick," said Jim, getting up.

Timothy relinquished his theory, though reluctantly. "Oh, all right! It was only an idea. Actually, I shouldn't be a bit surprised if it turned out to be someone we've never even suspected. Pritchard, or someone like that. I say, I wonder if Cousin Silas possessed some frightfully valuable thing which someone else wants? You needn't look like that! I know I've heard of it happening. Something you don't know about. A priceless manuscript or—or—good Lord, if that's it, there probably *is* a Hidden Killer in the house!"

"I don't quite see why killing Jim should help him to get hold of the Stolen Treasure," objected Miss Allison.

"I expect there's some frightfully complicated reason," said Mr Harte wisely.

"Well, we'll leave you to think it out," said Jim. "Come on, Pat!"

"You go down. I'll join you in a minute," she replied. "I'm just going along to my room."

She did not go to her room immediately, however. As soon as Jim had gone downstairs she returned to Mr Harte and said: "Timothy, I wish you'd tell Superintendent Hannasyde what happened today. I know Jim thinks it's all nonsense; but I can't rid myself of the feeling that he is in danger."

"All right, I will," promised Timothy. "Not," he added gloomily, "that they'll believe a word I say, because I know jolly well they won't. No one ever does."

Telling him to comfort himself with the reflection that she at least had believed his story, Miss Allison withdrew, leaving him to occupy himself until sleep overtook him in evolving a highly elaborate theory to account for the presence in their midst of an Unknown Killer. She went along the passage towards the west wing, where, next to Mrs Kane's, her room was situated. For the first time she thought the passage very inadequately lit, and when she encountered Ogle not two steps from Timothy's door, she gave an uncontrollable start of sheer nerves.

Ogle, though Miss Allison had not questioned her presence in the passage, immediately began to justify it, so that Miss Allison, knowing her to be extremely inquisitive, guessed that she had been listening outside Timothy's room. She could hardly blame her, for it was one of Emily Kane's least agreeable traits to cull all the information she could from Ogle's expert spying upon the rest of the household. Not unnaturally there had been a good deal of incentive during the past fortnight for Ogle to listen at doors. Miss Allison, accustomed to this unamiable habit, merely smiled and said: "All right, Ogle, don't apologize!"

The maid's sallow cheeks flushed; she said somewhat naïvely: "The less the police come nosing round here the better it will be, miss. What's done can't be undone. You will pardon me, but if Master Timothy sank Mr James' boat, it was only what anyone would have expected, and there's no call to drag the police into it."

Miss Allison raised her brows. "Why not?" she asked.

"They're not wanted here," Ogle said sullenly. "They won't find out anything, any more than they did over Mr Clement. They only worrit the mistress."

"The case of Mr Clement isn't finished," said Miss Allison "I told you before, the inquest was merely adjourned."

"They won't find out anything," Ogle repeated. "No more they're not wanted to. The impudence of them asking the mistress questions! Well, they didn't get anything out of me, that's one thing."

Miss Allison did not think this worthy of being replied to. She passed on to her bedroom and presently rejoined the party in the drawing room.

As usual, she took Emily up to bed at ten o'clock, but when she had delivered her into Ogle's care, she went downstairs again and permitted Mr James Kane to take her for a moonlight stroll through the gardens.

The night was fine and very warm, but a rustle heard in a cluster of flowering shrubs quite destroyed Miss Allison's pleasure in being alone with her betrothed. She was reasonable enough to admit that the noise had probably been caused by a cat or a night bird, but it put her in mind of the dangers threatening Jim, and she very soon made an excuse to go back into the house.

Norma and Rosemary were the sole occupants of the drawing room, Sir Adrian having drifted away to the library. When Jim and Patricia came in through the french windows Norma was seated bolt upright at a card table, energetically playing a complicated Patience and telling Rosemary at the same time how much happier she would be if she found an Object in life.

Rosemary was quite in agreement with this but explained that her Russian blood made it impossible for her to remain constant to any one Object for longer than a few months at a stretch.

"My dear girl, don't talk nonsense to me!" said Norma bracingly. "You're lazy, that's all that's wrong with you. Why don't you take up social work?"

"I don't think my health would stand it," replied Rosemary. "I'm one of those unfortunate people whose nerves simply go to pieces as soon as they're bored."

"Thank God I don't know what it is to have nerves!" said Norma.

"Yes, you're lucky. I don't suppose you even feel the *atmosphere* in this awful house," said Rosemary shuddering.

"All imagination!" declared Norma, briskly shuffling the cards.

"Of course, I knew you would say that. All the same, there is a dreadful atmosphere here. I expect you have to be rather sensitive to it."

Lady Hart raised her eyes from the cards. "I do not in the least mind being thought insensitive, Rosemary; but as I fancy you meant that remark as a slur on my character, I can only say that it was extremely rude of you," she said severely.

This rejoinder was so unexpected that Rosemary, colouring hotly, was for the moment bereft of speech. Lady Harte, laying her cards out with a firm hand, took advantage of her silence to add: "The sensitiveness you vaunt so incessantly, my good girl, does not seem to take other people's feelings into account. If you talked less about yourself and thought more of others, you would not only be a happier woman but a great deal pleasanter to live with into the bargain."

"Of course, I know I'm very selfish," replied Rosemary with the utmost calm. "You mustn't think I don't know myself through and through, because I do. I'm selfish and terribly temperamental and fickle."

"You are not only selfish," said Lady Harte; "you are indolent, shallow, parasitic and remarkably stupid."

Rosemary got up, roused at last to anger. She said in a trembling voice: "How *very* funny! Really, I can hardly help laughing!"

"Laugh away," advised Lady Harte, her attention on Miss Milligan.

"When you have seen your husband shot before your very eyes," said Rosemary, a trifle inaccurately, "perhaps you will have some comprehension of what it means to suffer."

Lady Harte raised her eyes and looked steadily up at the outraged beauty. "My husband, as I think you are aware, died of his wounds twenty years ago. I saw him die. If you think you can tell me anything about suffering, I shall be interested to hear it."

There was an uncomfortable silence. "Sometimes I feel as though I should go out of my *mind!*" announced Rosemary. "No one has the least understanding of my character. Good night!"

"Good night," said Lady Harte.

The door shut with a decided bang behind Rosemary. Jim moved forward from the window, where he and Patricia had remained rooted during this remarkable duologue. "Really, Mother!" he expostulated.

"A little plain speaking is what is wanted in this house!" said Norma roundly. "The idea of that young baggage telling me I don't know what it is to suffer! She! . . . Why, she's revelling in being a widow! Do you think I can't see what's under my nose? Atmosphere! Bah!"

Patricia smiled but said: "I don't much like identifying myself with Rosemary, but I'm conscious of that atmosphere, too, you know."

"A dose of salts will probably do away with it," replied Norma crudely.

This prosaic suggestion did much to restore Miss Allison to her usual placidity, but when she presently went up to bed her mind crept back to the conversation in Timothy's room. The pleasing theory that an Unknown Killer lurked in their midst did not seriously trouble her, but she would have been happier could she but have been assured that Jim would lock his bedroom door before going to bed. But nothing was more unlikely than that he would take this simple precaution against being murdered.

Further reflection compelled Miss Allison to admit to herself that it would not be a very easy matter for anyone to murder Jim in his bed without running the risk of instant detection. In the warmth and bright light of the bathroom she decided that her fears were foolish; on the way back to her room along the shadowy passage she was not quite so sure; and lying in bed with the moonlight filtering into the room through the gaps between the curtains, and a tendril of Virginia creeper tapping against the window, she began to consider the possibility of Timothy's being right after all. In her mind she ran over the male staff of Cliff House and fell asleep at last with a conglomeration of fantastic thoughts jostling one another in her head.

It did not seem to her that she had been asleep for more than a few minutes when she was awakened suddenly by the echoes of a scream. She started up, half in doubt, and switched on the light. The hands of her bedside clock stood at a quarter-past one, she noticed. Just as she was about to lie down again, believing the scream to have occurred only in her unquiet dreams, it was repeated. Miss Allison recognized Mr Harte's voice, raised to a wild note of panic, and sprang out of bed, snatching up her dressing gown. As she flung open her door she heard Timothy shriek: "Jim! Jim!"

She raced down the passage to his room and found to her surprise that it was illumined only by the moonlight. Switching on the light, she discovered Mr Harte cowering at the end of his bed, sweat on his brow, his eyes dilated and glaring at her.

"There's a man, there's a man!" gasped Mr Harte in a grip of a rigor. "Jim, Jim, there's a man!"

Miss Allison, her own nerves not quite normal, gave a choked exclamation and faltered: "Where? Who?"

Mr Harte paid no attention to her but panted. "It's the *Killer!* I saw his eyes g-glittering! He's there! I saw him. Jim!"

Miss Allison spun round to look in the direction of his terrified gaze. She saw nothing to alarm him, and at that moment Jim walked into the room, looking sleepy and dishevelled. "What on earth's the matter?" he demanded.

"I saw him, I saw him!" bubbled Mr Harte. "There's a man in the room!"

"Oh!" said Jim, running an experienced eye over his relative. "Wake up, you ass!"

He flashed his torch in Timothy's face, and Timothy came to himself with a gasp and a shudder and clutched his arm. "Oh, Jim!" he said sobbingly. "Oh, Jim! A m-man in a m-mask! Oh gosh! I swear there was s-someone in the room!"

"Rubbish! You've had a nightmare, that's all," said Jim, giving him a little shake.

"Yes, I kn-know, but—*who's that?*"

The rising note of terror made Miss Allison look round involuntarily, but all that met her eyes was the spectacle of Sir Adrian Harte, swathed in a brocade dressing gown and with not a hair out of place, entering the room.

Jim moved so that Timothy could see the door. "Only your father. Pull yourself together!"

Mr Harte relaxed his taut muscles but still retained his grip on Jim's arm. "G-gosh, I thought it was the K-Killer!"

"You thought it was what?" inquired Sir Adrian, slightly taken aback.

"It's all right, sir; the little idiot started a wildcat

theory that there was a Hidden Killer in the house and gave himself a nightmare. Pat, you cuckoo, you're just about as bad! The kid was only dreaming!"

"Yes, of course," said Miss Allison, who was feeling a little shaken. "Silly of me. I ought to have known. Only his eyes were wide open, and I suppose I was half asleep myself, and it didn't occur to me." She became aware all at once of the appearance she must present, with her head in a shingle-cap, and a kimono caught round her like an untidy shawl, and said distressfully, "Oh dear, I must look like nothing on earth!"

However, Lady Harte walked into the room just then, and in face of the appearance she presented, with her grey hair on end and a tropical mackintosh worn over a pair of faded pyjamas, Miss Allison could not feel her own deshabille to be in any way remarkable.

"Hullo, Timothy. Had one of your bad dreams?" inquired Lady Harte.

"Oh, Mummy, I thought there was a man with a mask in the room! It was ghastly!"

"Have a drink of water," recommended his mother, stalking over to the washstand and pouring out a glass for him.

Timothy took the glass and gulped down some water.

"I suppose there isn't anyone prowling about?" said Lady Harte. "I noticed that the hall light was on as I came past the head of the stairs. You'd better go and have a look round, Jim. If I'd a gun I'd go myself; but thanks to the wretched laws of this country, mine are still in custody."

"Don't trouble," said Sir Adrian. "The light is on because I switched it on. I was downstairs looking for something to read when Timothy created all this commotion. If the excitement is now over, I propose to continue my search. Do you think a volume of sermons would be a soporific?"

"Excellent, I should say. Bring one up for your offspring, Adrian," replied Jim.

"What Timothy wants is not a book but a Dose," said Norma.

"Oh, *Mother!*" protested Mr Harte.

"Bad luck!" sympathized Jim. "Not but what it serves you right for putting the wind up Patricia."

He and Miss Allison left him in his mother's expert hands and went back to their rooms. There were no further alarms during the remainder of the night, and Mr Harte appeared at breakfast later in excellent spirits and full of strenuous plans for the day. Rosemary, who, in spite of being (she told them) a very light sleeper, had slept peacefully through the disturbance, explained this seemingly unaccountable phenomenon by describing her slumbers as a coma of utter nervous exhaustion and said that from then onwards she had been very restless, oppressed by the atmosphere of doom that hung over the house.

"That's quite enough!" interposed Lady Harte, helping herself to marmalade with a liberal hand. "We don't want any more nightmares."

Mr Harte, inclined, in the comfortable daylight, to look upon his exploit as a very good joke, said that he hadn't had such a cracking nightmare since the occasion when Jim took him to see *The Ringer*. "It's because I'm interested in Crime," he said. "Old Nanny says things prey on my mind."

"When Jim took you to *The Ringer*," said his prosaic parent, "it wasn't Crime preying on your mind that gave you a nightmare, but lobster preying on your stomach. I remember very well when I asked Jim what he'd let you have for dinner he recited a list of all the most indigestible dishes anyone could imagine, beginning with lobster and ending with mushrooms on toast. So don't talk nonsense!"

This shattering reminiscence not unnaturally took the wind out of Mr Harte's sails, and after a growl of: "Mother!" he relapsed into silence, and as soon as he had finished breakfast withdrew from the dining room and went in search of more congenial company.

An encounter with Superintendent Hannasyde later

in the morning was almost equally dispiriting. The superintendent listened to his account of the foundering of the Seamew with an air of gravity wholly belied by a twinkle at the back of his kindly grey eyes. This did not escape Mr Harte, and when the superintendent said solemnly that it was too bad no one believed his story, he retorted with asperity: "No, and no one believed me when I said Cousin Silas had been murdered, but I'll bet he was! And what's more, you think he was!"

"Leaving your cousin Silas out of it," said Hannasyde, "what do you want me to do about the Seamew? Salvage her?"

"No, because Jim says if she was tampered with, the strake with the hole in it would have been torn clean off. But I do think you might keep an eye on Jim. Patricia—Miss Allison, you know—believes he's in danger just as much as I do, and so does Mr Roberts."

"Oh, I'll keep an eye on him all right," promised Hannasyde.

Timothy cast him a smouldering look of dislike and went off to find his friend the sergeant.

The sergeant soothed his injured feelings by listening to him with a proper display of interest and credulity and asked him what his theory was. Greatly heartened, Timothy took him into his confidence and propounded his theory of the Hidden Killer.

"I wouldn't wonder but what you're right," said the sergeant, shaking his head. "The Hand of Death, that's what it is. I've read about such things."

"Have you ever come across cases like that?" Timothy asked eagerly.

"Well, I haven't actually worked on one," admitted the sergeant. "Of course, they generally keep that kind of case for the Big Five."

"Say, it 'ud be a big feather in your cap if this did turn out to be a Hidden Killer, and you unmasked him, wouldn't it?"

"That's what I was thinking," said the sergeant.

"But the Chief wouldn't like it if I was to drop my routine work and go hunting for Killers on my own."

"I expect there's a lot of jealousy at Scotland Yard," said Timothy darkly.

"You'd be surprised," replied Hemingway. "Awful, it is."

"Well, don't you think people ought to be watched? Couldn't you keep your eye on Pritchard, for instance? It often is the butler, and, as far as I can see, no one's even suspected him yet."

A diabolical scheme presented itself to the sergeant. He said: "That's right; but you see, we're handicapped, being policemen. What we really want is an assistant. Now, if you were to watch Pritchard, and all the rest of them, you might discover something."

"Well, I will," said Mr Harte, his eye brightening. "Then if he does anything queer, I'll come and report to you."

"That's the ticket," said the sergeant. "You stick to him!" Later, recounting the episode to his superior, he said: "And if we don't have that butler turning homicidal it'll be a wonder."

"I call it a dirty trick," said Hannasyde.

"It is," agreed the sergeant cheerfully. "But the way I look at it is this. If it has to be me or the butler, it had better be him. What did you make of the Wreck of the Hesperus, Chief?"

"Nothing very much. It sounds most improbable. As far as I could gather, Oscar Roberts, who was the original scaremonger, made nothing of it, either."

"No, he's blotted his copybook properly, he has," grinned the sergeant. "Terrible Timothy's got it in for him all right. You didn't get anything more on Paul Mansell, I suppose?"

Hannasyde shook his head. "No. He certainly went to Brotherton Manor to play tennis, precisely as he says. He arrived at a quarter to four, the day Clement Kane was murdered, having been invited for half-past three. It all fits in quite clearly with the possibility of his having shot Clement Kane, but it doesn't make it any more than a possibility. According to his story, he lunched with a Mrs Trent that Saturday and went on from her house to Brotherton Manor afterwards. She corroborates his story down to the last detail."

The sergeant, who knew his chief well, cocked an intelligent eye and said: "Oh, she does, does she? Pretty Paul make it worth her while to do so?"

"It wouldn't surprise me to learn that he had, but I've nothing to go on. She's a flashy blonde widow. Quite cool and collected. I couldn't catch her out."

"Ah, one of the hard-boiled Hannahs," said the sergeant, nodding. "There's just a bit of talk about her and Master Paul. Does she happen to remember what time he left her on Saturday to go to this tennis party?"

"Oh, she says he left her at five-and-twenty minutes past three. From her house in Portlaw to Brotherton Manor is just over twelve miles, by the coast road running past Cliff House. It's a good road, and not crowded. I should think he could have made the distance in twenty minutes, if he stepped on it a bit, which he says he did."

"Any servants to corroborate Mrs Trent's valuable testimony?" inquired the sergeant.

"No. One general servant, who went off for her half-day immediately after lunch."

"Slight smell of dead rat about this story," said the sergeant; "looks to me like a put-up job. Any bright young fellow on point duty happen to remember seeing Paul's car leave the town?"

"Not a hope," replied Hannasyde. "She lives in Gerrard Avenue, and the only big crossing he had to negotiate before getting clear of the town is governed by traffic lights."

The sergeant said disgustedly: "That's what they call Progress, that is. It beats me what the world's coming to."

Hannasyde smiled a little but said, "Someone may have seen the car. Carlton is going into that."

"Not they," said the sergeant bitterly. "Or if anyone did, they won't be able to say for certain whether it was at a quarter-past three or a quarter to four. I've had some!"

"Well, it is just possible that if he's lying, and he did shoot Clement Kane, someone may have seen his car pulled up outside Cliff House. He didn't drive in the main gate, and I should think it unlikely that he drove in the tradesmen's gate. It's true there's no lodge there, but he'd hardly dare park his car inside the grounds. If he murdered Clement, I think he must have left his car in the road, entered the grounds by way of the tradesmen's gate, and reached the house under cover of the rhododendron thicket. Quite simple."

"Super," said the sergeant; "how many cars have you seen parked along the cliff road with their owners having a nice picnic inside?"

"Oh, I know, I know!" replied Hannasyde. "Any number. But Mansell's car must be well known in this district and might well have caught the attention of anyone familiar with it. It's a long shot, but sometimes our long shots come off, Skipper."

"Come unstuck, more like," said the sergeant, still in a mood of gloom. "A proper mess, that's what this case is. We don't know where it started, and if Terrible Timothy's right, we don't know where it's going to end. You don't know where to take hold of it, that's what I complain of. It's more like my missus's skein of knitting wool, after one of the kittens has had it, than a decent murder case. I mean, you get hold of one end and start following it up, and all it leads to is a damned knot worked so tight you can't do a thing with it. Then you grab hold of the other end, and start on that, and what you find is that it's a bit the kitten chewed through that just comes away in your hand, with the rest of the wool in as bad a muddle as ever. Well, I ask you, Super! Just look at it! First there's the old man. Perhaps he was murdered and perhaps he wasn't. And if he was murdered the same man did in Clement, unless it was another party altogether making hay while the sun shone. It makes my head go round. It doesn't make sense."

"Not as told by you," agreed Hannasyde. "It is a teaser, I admit. There are so many possibilities, and the worst of it is, we weren't in at the start."

"If it was the start," interposed the sergeant.

"If it was the start, as you say. I don't think we shall ever know for certain what happened to Silas Kane, though we may get at it by inference. The local police accepted Clement's story of his own movements that night, and he, on the face of it, was the likeliest suspect. But the fact of his having been murdered doesn't make it look as though he killed Silas."

"Unless the whole thing's a snowball," said the sergeant, "with each new heir doing in the last. I wouldn't put it beyond them."

"A trifle unlikely," said Hannasyde. "Try and get the case straight in your mind, Skipper. We have to consider it in several lights. First, we'll assume that both men were murdered, and by the same person, and presumably for the same motive. That rules out Dermott, Mr Kane, Ogle, Lady Harte and Rosemary Kane. Lady Harte wasn't in England at the time of Silas Kane's death, and neither she nor Rosemary could have pushed a man over the cliff edge. They haven't the necessary strength. So we're left with James Kane and both the Mansells. Any one of the three could have committed both murders. James Kane has no alibi for the time of Silas Kane's death; Joe Mansell's depends entirely on his wife's testimony; Paul's once more on the ubiquitous Mrs Trent, with whom he spent that evening."

"Yes, but there's a snag in all this, Super," objected the sergeant.

"There are several, because so far we're only working on assumption. We've got to look at the case from a second angle. Let us suppose that both men were murdered, but by different people and for different motives."

The sergeant moaned: "I can't get round to that."

"Most unlikely," assented Hannasyde. "But it could have happened. I'm by no means satisfied that Clement could not have motored his wife home on the night of Silas' death and himself driven back to Cliff House without her knowledge. They didn't occupy the same bedroom, remember. Clement wanted Silas' money badly, not for himself, but for his wife, with whom he seems to have been utterly infatuated. Assuming for the moment that he killed his cousin, just glance over the subsequent events. Upon his coming into the Kane fortune, Rosemary Kane, who, if gossip is to be believed at all, was on the verge of leaving him for Trevor Dermott, immediately gave Dermott the air. Well, you've seen Dermott. He's exactly the type of unbalanced man who sees red on very little provocation and behaves violently."

The sergeant stroked his chin. "It fits," he admitted. "The trouble is, all the theories fit. You can even have that one without making the old man's death out to have been murder."

"Oh, that's looking at the case from the third angle," said Hannasyde. "I haven't finished with the second yet. Having considered the combination of Clement Kane and Dermott, let's glance at the other combination. Clement remains fixed as Silas' murderer—"

"What about the Mansells?"

"Certainly not. The Mansells and James Kane must belong to the first angle—that both men were killed by the same person for the same motive. Retaining Clement, then, let's put Dermott aside. We are left with Mr Kane, Ogle, and Lady Harte as suspects for the second murder. None of them very likely, but all of them possible. Now we'll take a look at it from the third angle, that Silas Kane met his death by accident."

"That's the worst of the lot," said the Sergeant. "It gives us the whole boiling to suspect."

"No, not quite. I think we must rule the Mansells

out. If they didn't murder Silas for standing in their way over a business deal, it isn't very likely that they murdered Clement for doing so."

"Well, I suppose that's something," said the Sergeant. "All the same, it doesn't alter the stage much, does it? We've still got Jim Kane and his mother, Mrs Kane and her maid, Rosemary Kane and her fancy boy, and, for all we know, Terrible Timothy. I make that seven."

"I refuse to consider Timothy," retorted Hannasyde. "Six."

"Don't know so much. What with these gangster films, and him being pretty well nuts on Crime, I wouldn't say it wasn't him. Still, I'll call it six."

"There may be a seventh," said Hannasyde. "But that depends on whether someone really is trying to make away with James Kane or not."

The sergeant blinked. "But that brings it round to the Mansells again, doesn't it, Chief?"

"Not quite conclusively. There's the cousin alleged to be living in Australia," said Hannasyde. "To be on the safe side, I've cabled to the police at Sydney for any information they can give us."

CHAPTER TWELVE

DISCUSSION, incessantly promoted by Mr Harte, on the probable cause of the Seamew's end was put a stop to by his mother, who forbade him to mention the matter again in her hearing. She herself, disbelieving his story, had no particular objection to his exercising his imagination in speculating upon the possibility of his stepbrother's life having been threatened, but Emily Kane, overhearing one of his more lurid flights, demanded to be told the whole and was so much disturbed by it that Patricia had considerable difficulty in soothing her alarms and coaxing her back to tolerably good humour.

Agitation in Emily invariably made her short tempered. She would have scorned to betray a feminine weakness or to ask for reassurance. She reassured herself by denouncing the bare idea of Jim's life being in danger as stuff and nonsense and saying she had never heard anything to equal it, found fault with everyone who came near her, and supposed that Timothy got his silly notions from his mother.

Norma took this in good part, laughing in genuine amusement and saying: "Quite wrong, Aunt Emily; he got these particular notions from his friend Roberts. I think they're ridiculous."

Emily's mouth worked. She glared at Lady Harte and said: "That man! What's it got to do with him? Encroaching ways! I've no patience with him!"

Jim came into the room in time to hear this familiar phrase and said promptly: "Somebody been annoying you, Aunt? You look horribly fierce."

From no one but Jim would Emily have tolerated such a teasing form of address, but since he could do no wrong in her eyes she merely nodded at him and replied: "If you take my advice, you'll send him about his business!"

"Who?" inquired Jim, beginning to fill his pipe.

"That Roberts. Your cousin wouldn't have anything to do with his flibbertigibbet scheme. I don't know what he wants here, treating the house as though it belonged to him!"

Jim let this somewhat unfair accusation pass unchallenged. "I imagine he's trying to unravel the mystery of Clement's death. Sometimes I think he's on to something the police haven't discovered, but he doesn't give away much."

Emily's twisted hands gripped the handle of her

ebony stick more tightly. "Impudence! Poking his nose into our affairs! I'd like to give him a piece of my mind!"

"You probably will," said Jim, smiling down at her over the lighted match he was holding above the bowl of his pipe.

"Serve him right!" said Emily. "If people would mind their own business it would be a better thing for everyone."

"Well, I don't know," replied Jim. "If Roberts can clear up the mystery, I'm all for it. I think we've had about enough of it, and the police don't seem to be doing much, do they?"

"They're doing more than they're wanted to!" said Emily angrily. "Getting us into the papers and digging up what's best left alone! I don't know what your great-uncle would say if he were alive to see it."

"It's got to be dug up, Aunt, whether we like it or not."

She made no reply to this, but folded her lips, and sat with her remote stare fixed on the space before her. Lady Harte said: "I don't think the publicity matters at all. One gets used to that sort of thing. I've had so much of it I never think twice about it."

"I dare say," said Emily disagreeably. She transferred her gaze to Jim's face. "What's this pack of nonsense I hear about your being in danger?"

"Just that," he answered. "A pack of nonsense."

"One of that Roberts' tales. What next, I wonder! The sooner we see the back of him the better. Putting ideas into Timothy's head!"

"To do him justice, I don't think he mentioned the matter to Timothy at all. He warned me. And though I personally think it's rot, you must admit it was a kindly act on his part."

Emily gave a short laugh. "Trying to get round you to fall in with his scheme, I've no doubt. Don't you go making any rash promises!"

He smiled and shook his head. Emily glared suspicion. "Have those Mansells been at you again?" she demanded.

"No. I met Joe Mansell in Portlaw today, and he said he wanted to talk things over with me. I've arranged to call and see him at the office tomorrow morning. I expect he'll bring the question up then."

"What are you going to say?"

"Nothing. I've been talking to Adrian about it——"

"I should like to know what he thinks he knows about it!" interjected Emily scornfully.

"Oh, Adrian's no fool!" said Lady Harte.

"As a matter of fact, he doesn't think he knows anything about it," said Jim. "His advice is that I should go up and lay the proposition before Everard and Dawson—which I propose to do as soon as things have straightened themselves out a bit here."

Emily was unable to find fault with this, so she relapsed into silence.

"Does Patricia know you're going to see Joe tomorrow?" asked Lady Harte.

"No. I haven't said anything to her about it."

"Then don't. She'll only start imagining things."

"I'm not going to. You two—and Adrian, of course —are the only people I've told. Not that I think the most jumpy person, which Pat isn't, could possibly expect any harm to overtake me. Even if the Mansells were out for my blood, they'd hardly try to bump me off in their own offices. However, Pat's a trifle worked up over the whole show, so there's no point in saying anything about it to her."

Lady Harte looked at him consideringly. "The whole idea's absurd. All the same, there's no harm in being prepared. Do you carry a gun?"

He laughed. "No, my dear, I don't."

"I should, if I were you. Whenever I change my camp I make it a rule to set up a line of bottles and have a little revolver practice in full sight of the village. I've never had a bit of trouble. Never even been robbed."

"You're a turn in yourself, Mother," said Jim appreciatively. "But this isn't Darkest Africa, and I doubt whether anyone would be impressed by my marksmanship."

"Nonsense, you're not a bad shot! Don't depreciate yourself so much!" said his mother severely.

However, when he set out for Portlaw the following morning, Mr James Kane was unarmed and unaccompanied. For this last he had to thank his stepfather, who rescued him from the toils of Mr Harte.

Jim found Sir Adrian in the garage, inexpertly replenishing his cigarette lighter from a large tin of petrol. Like most men more accustomed to working with their heads than with their hands, he had contrived to make a major operation of a small task. He wore an expression of profound distaste and, when his stepson walked into the garage, said that it was a pity he had not arrived sooner.

"What a Godforsaken mess!" remarked Jim. "Why don't you get the thing filled at a tobacconist's?"

"Can I?" said Sir Adrian vaguely. "I have never owned one of these infernal things before. Your mother gave it to me. I wish that she would try to curb her generous impulses." He wiped his hands on an oily rag and looked at the result with patient resignation. "Are you going to see Joseph Mansell now? Your mother has been talking arrant nonsense to me about the advisability of your carrying a gun. I hope you are not infected by the general atmosphere of melodrama reigning in this absurd house."

"Not noticeably," replied Jim, putting away the tin of petrol and stepping up to his car. "Did Pat go with Aunt Emily?"

"No, she took the omnibus into Portlaw. Your mother went with Mrs Kane."

Jim smiled. "I like to think of Mother driving sedately out for an airing in a large and respectable Daimler. Do you want anything in the town, sir?"

"No, nothing, thank you. Ah, Jim!"

Jim had stepped into his car, but he turned his head inquiringly towards his stepfather.

Sir Adrian polished his monocle and said blandly: "Don't commit yourself in any way, Jim."

"Not going to," said Jim.

"You may find it a trifle awkward, dealing with a man old enough to be your father. You can with perfect propriety point out to Mansell that you have as yet no certain knowledge of your financial position. And, Jim!"

"Sir?"

"If you see that ill-conditioned son of Mansell, do not let your very natural desire to—er—push his face in run away with you."

Jim laughed. "You know, you really ought to come with me, Adrian."

"I should be quite out of place, believe me, my dear boy. Well, Timothy, what is it?"

His son, who had entered the garage, said: "Nothing. Oh, I say, Jim, are you going out? Can I come too?"

"Certainly not," replied Sir Adrian. "Jim is going into Portlaw on business."

"Well, I could wait for him, couldn't I?"

"No. Strange as it may seem to you, you are not wanted," said Sir Adrian.

"He can come if he likes, sir," said Jim, starting his engine. "I don't mind."

"You will do much better without him. No, Timothy."

"But, Father, why can't I . . ."

Sir Adrian's aloof gaze came to bear on his son's face. "No, Timothy," he repeated in a patient voice.

Mr Harte sighed and refrained from further speech. Jim backed the Bentley out of the garage and said with a twinkle: "How do you get your results, sir? Is it the power of the human eye?"

Sir Adrian smiled faintly. "Just force of personality," he replied.

His son, guessing correctly that this interchange referred to himself, gave an injured sniff and walked off in a dudgeon.

Jim covered the five miles by the coast road round the bay into Portlaw at his usual swift speed and threaded his way through the streets of the town to the offices of Kane and Mansell, situated in one of the busiest roads. A policeman, taking exception to his evident desire to leave his car parked in the main street, directed him firmly down a side street to the yard at the back of the building. Here Jim found Paul Mansell's sports roadster standing under the shelter of a lean-to roof. He ran the Bentley up alongside it, and got out, and entered the building through the back door. Being quite unfamiliar with the place, he plunged into a labyrinth of packing and ledger rooms and created a sensation amongst the female staff. These damsels, recognizing the new head of the firm, and most favourably impressed by his appearance, found his arrival in the back premises extremely funny, or— as they themselves later described it—a perfect scream. There was much staring, a good deal of giggling, and any number of Oh—Mr Kanes! before one, less impressionable than her sisters, volunteered to escort him to Mr Mansell's office. Mr James Kane was not a shy man, but under the battery of admiring, curious or amused eyes he perceptibly changed colour and was thankful to find himself presently in a less populous part of the building.

Joe Mansell was alone and greeted his young visitor with almost effusive kindliness, patting him on the shoulder, settling him in the easiest chair the room held, and thrusting a box of cigars towards him. From his opening gambit of: "Well, Jim, I expect you're feeling all at sea, eh, my boy?" Jim realized that his stepfather had been right in prophesying an awkward interview.

In actual fact it was not as difficult as he had anticipated. Paul Mansell put in no appearance, and for the first half-hour Joe Mansell confined his discourse to an exposition of the firm's aims and standing. Jim attended to him closely, asked several intelligent questions, and was warmly complimented upon his grasp of the business.

"Well, then there's this Australian proposition we're interested in," said Joe. "I'd better give you some idea of what it all means."

Jim said politely that he would be very grateful to have the matter explained to him, and sat in interested silence while Joe talked. Joe, becoming more bluff and fatherly every minute, soon inspired him with some of his dead cousin's contempt for his mental capacity. He found himself growing steadily more hostile to a scheme put forward so speciously and presently interposed to put forward a tentative suggestion of his own that the firm should be turned into a public company. Even as he said it, he knew that he had not the smallest intention of allowing Joe Mansell to get control. It would seem like a betrayal of Clement and Silas, and John, and old Matthew Kane, the founder of the house. He was conscious for the first time in his life of family pride stirring in him. These Mansells aren't going to control my business! he thought. Damn it all, I'm a Kane!

Joe, watching him, saw the hardening of his mouth and jaw, and a steely light in his eyes unpleasantly reminiscent of his cousin Silas. Quelling his own exasperation, he became even more paternal and told Jim he could well appreciate his point of view but thought that Jim must just trust him to guide his footsteps aright.

Before Jim could think of a polite way of saying that he had no intention of being guided by a Mansell an interruption occurred. A knock fell on the door, and immediately following it Oscar Roberts walked into the room.

Jim, who had expected to see Paul Mansell, and had turned his head with a gathering frown on his brow, got up with a look of relief.

Joe's expression said plainly that he had not expected this visit and did not appreciate it. He greeted

Roberts with a bare assumption of cordiality and said pointedly that he was having a private chat with the firm's new head.

"So they told me," replied Roberts, his coldly calculating gaze resting for a moment on Joe's heavy countenance. "Guess what you're talking about is as much my show as anyone's, isn't it?" He shook hands with Jim. "Say, Kane, if you want anyone to explain my firm's proposition to you, I'm the man you're looking for."

"Naturally, naturally!" Joe said. "You—er—you have come at a most opportune moment, Roberts. We *were* discussing your proposition."

"I thought maybe you were," said Roberts ironically. He glanced round the room with a look of surprise. "I don't see Mr Paul Mansell. Is he out?"

Joe reddened a little. "My son has a lot of work on hand. His presence is really not necessary."

"Well, I certainly thought I should find him here," said Roberts, lowering his long limbs into a chair. "What do you want me to tell you, Kane?"

"Really, I don't think you need tell me anything," replied Jim. He laid his hand on a typescript lying on the desk. "It's all here, isn't it? With your permission, Mr Mansell, I'll take it home with me and study it at my leisure."

"Of course! Certainly! But time presses, you know, Jim. Can't keep our good friend here hanging about indefinitely."

"It's O.K. by me," said Roberts. "I'd like to have Kane go into it by himself and come to an unbiased decision. If he feels he'd rather not take it on, why, I shall quite understand and go elsewhere."

Joe Mansell looked dissatisfied but gave a reluctant agreement. After a few minutes of somewhat idle talk the interview came to an end. Joe shook hands with Jim, prophesying that he would soon acquire a grasp of the business, and Jim and Roberts went out together.

Jim said, with a slight touch of annoyance: "Are you by any chance constituting yourself as a bodyguard to me, sir?"

"I won't say just that," replied Roberts carefully. "Though you sure are walking right into the lion's den when you visit that office."

"Really, sir, don't you think you're being a trifle absurd? Did you expect to find a corpse, or what?"

Roberts laughed. "No, no, it's not as bad as that. Maybe I thought it would do no harm to let the Mansells know I'm wise to your visit. You want to watch your step, Kane."

"I don't wish to seem ungrateful, but, to tell you the truth, I've had about enough drama. Joe Mansell's been a friend of the family for half a century, and——"

"That's fine," said Roberts imperturbably. "What's the drama you speak of?"

"My stepfather calls it melodrama. I could wish you had not repeated your dark warning to my fiancée, you know."

"Is that so? Well, I certainly am sorry if I've upset Miss Allison. I didn't mean to do that."

"The trouble is, she's got things a bit out of focus since the accident to my boat," said Jim.

Roberts looked at him. "The accident to your boat?" he repeated.

Jim gave a rueful laugh. "Oh, Timothy started a hare over that, you know, and he and Patricia have been chasing it ever since. He even told Superintendent Hannasyde about it. The genial theory is that the boat was tampered with, with the idea that I should go down with her. Nothing will get it out of their heads."

"No?" said Roberts.

Jim stopped dead in his tracks. "Look here, sir, you're not going to tell me you believe such a damned silly story?"

"Well," said Roberts, "I wouldn't go so far as to say I actually believe it, but if I were you, I wouldn't dismiss it too carelessly. I'm sorry Miss Allison got hold of the notion: I hoped she wouldn't. Guess that was a trick that can't be pulled twice, so there was no sense in alarming the ladies unnecessarily."

"Good God, sir, did it occur to you, then?"

"Sure it occurred to me," replied Roberts calmly. "But when there's no way of proving a thing, there's no sense in talking about it. What did the superintendent make of it?"

"I don't think he made anything of it. It's obvious Timothy must have hit something."

"Maybe if the superintendent occupied himself with what isn't so obvious he'd get along better," commented Roberts.

They had traversed the side street by this time and come to the entrance of Kane and Mansell's yard.

"Well, sir, I still think the whole thing's impossible," said Jim. "I've got my car parked here. Can I give you a lift anywhere?"

"That's very good of you; but I've only a step to go. You take that proposition of mine home with you and study it." He pointed to the typescript under Jim's arm. "Maybe you'll give me a ring some time, and I'll be glad to come along and discuss it with you."

"Very good of you, sir; I will," said Jim, shaking hands.

He extricated his car from the yard and drove up the side street to the main road. As he paused, awaiting his opportunity to cut across the traffic, he saw Miss Allison, waiting by a bus stop and laden with parcels. Half a minute later he drew up alongside her and said: "Taxi, miss?"

"Good Lord, where did you spring from?" said Patricia, thankfully climbing into the car. "I didn't know you were going to——" She stopped and looked accusingly at him. "You've been to the office!"

"I have."

"Jim, you idiot, do you mean to tell me you deliberately kept it dark from me? Why on earth?"

"Well, seeing as how you go into a sort of flat spin

every time anyone mentions the accursed name of Mansell, I thought it might be kinder to say nothing."

"I call that absolutely insulting!" declared Miss Allison. "As though I should be afraid of your going to your own offices! If there's one place where you're bound to be safe, it's there. Look here, I do wish you wouldn't drive at a hundred miles an hour!"

"This, my girl, is a limit area, and I'm driving within the limit," said Mr Kane.

"I'm sure you were doing at least forty. Anyway, do go slowly! I want to talk to you."

"My sweet, I'll drive you in third all the way home. There shall be nothing to alarm you."

"I'm not exactly *alarmed,*" said Miss Allison, "because I know you're an expert; but you must admit that the way you streak along the coast road is enough to put the wind up anyone."

Mr Kane promised humbly to mend his ways and indeed proceeded to drive Miss Allison home at a decorous speed. In fact, so decorous did it become that he broke off in the middle of a sentence to say: "Darling Jim, is there a hearse ahead?"

"There is no pleasing some people," said Mr Kane, accelerating slightly and swinging round a big bend in the road. "First she slangs me for speeding, then——" He stopped. The car was not responding to his hands on the wheel. He felt the front wheels floating, threw the car swiftly out of gear, and jammed on his brakes.

Miss Allison, looking inquiringly up at him, saw his face set and rather white, became aware of the car pursuing a most erratic course, gasped: "Look out! You'll have her in the ditch!" and the next instant found herself flung half out of the car into a quickthorn hedge, with her betrothed on top of her. Mr Kane extricated himself swiftly and hauled Miss Allison up. "Sorry, darling!" he said rather breathlessly. "Hurt?"

"No, not particularly," said Miss Allison with admirable calm. "What happened?"

"The steering went," he replied. "By God's grace we

were going slow. If we'd been travelling at any speed we would have been a couple of goners by this time. You've scratched your cheek, darling."

"I have also bruised my shoulder," said Miss Allison, dabbing her cheek with a handkerchief. She looked at the car, lying drunkenly against the bank, with two wheels in the ditch. "What do you suppose made the steering go?" she asked, in a painstakingly casual voice.

"No idea. I shall be able to tell when we've salvaged her," replied Jim, dusting his trousers. "Now, my love, the next move is to get you home. I'm afraid it'll have to be the bus after all."

"It'll be along in a minute or two. What are you going to do?"

"Walk back to Lamb's Garage and get hold of a breakdown gang to tow her in."

She nodded. "All right. Rescue my parcels, will you, Jim? I'll send the Daimler down for you as soon as Mrs Kane gets back with it."

"Tell Jackson to pick me up at Lamb's," he said. "And look here, Pat! Don't say too much about this at home."

"No, I won't. I'll just say we had a breakdown." She saw the omnibus approaching and hesitated. "I—wish I hadn't got to go home, Jim."

"It's all right," he said. "Nothing's going to happen to me."

She gave his hand a squeeze, bestowed a slightly tremulous smile upon him, and climbed into the omnibus.

Mr James Kane stood for a minute or two thoughtfully looking his car over. It was obviously impossible to discover much while she reposed drunkenly in the ditch, so after frowning at her in some perplexity he set off with his long easy stride down the road in the direction of the nearest garage.

Half an hour later the Bentley, hauled from the ditch and towed to the garage, stood jacked up in the middle of the workshop, and Jim, with the foreman and two mechanics, was inspecting the track rod, which hung loose on the right side, causing the left front wheel to float.

"You lorst the nut that holds the ball joint of the track rod, sir, that's what you done," explained the elder of the two mechanics, eager to impart information. "You look how it is on the right side, sir: that'll show you. You got this nut on the ball joint, and this split pin you see here to hold it in place. Now you can see what happens if you was to lose the split pin, and the nut come unscrewed-like."

The foreman interrupted him somewhat severely. "Mr Kane doesn't need you to tell him that." He looked at Jim. "Queer setout, sir. What beats me is how it ever happened."

"Yes," said Jim.

"Been smeared all over with muck too," said the foreman, peering at the screw thread on the track rod.

"I noticed that," said Jim.

The foreman shot him a quick, arrested look, and then turned to the elder mechanic, and sent him off upon some errand. The younger mechanic, a solemn Scot of few words, looked gravely at him and waited.

"Mr Kane, that didn't happen natural," said the foreman. "I know your car. That pin never came out on its own, nor that muck didn't get there without it was put. If you was to ask me, I should say there had been some dirty work done."

The young Scot delivered himself of an utterance. "Ay," he said weightily.

"Looks like it," said Jim. "Can you let me have a car? I want to go back to the spot where the nut must have come off and look for it."

"That's right, sir. I'll send Andy here with you."

It was Andy who, on the bend of the coast road where the Bentley had got out of control, found the nut, rolled to the side of the road, and delivered himself of a second utterance. "That'll be it," he said, holding it in a grimy palm. He paused to recruit his forces and added: "Lebber't ower wi' muck."

He did not speak again until they reached the garage. Then as Jim stopped the car he roused himself from deep reflection and said simply that he doubted somebody's plans had misgaed.

The foreman took the nut and said: "That's it all right. You didn't find any sign of the split pin, sir, I know."

Jim shook his head. "I didn't expect to. Look here, Mason, I'd rather you didn't talk too much about this."

"Mr Kane, sir, I'm ready to take my oath your car's been doctored. You ought to tell the police."

"I'm going to. They'll probably come and interrogate you."

"They're welcome. I'll tell them what I know, which is that your car was in beautiful running order when I had her for overhaul two days ago. She's a lovely piece of work." He laid an affectionate hand on one crumpled wing. "She's not one of these cheap tin kettles on wheels anything could happen to, and, what's more, you aren't the kind of driver who mishandles his car. Someone took the split pin out, and loosened that nut so it would work off. What do you say, Andy?"

"Ay," said Andy, slowly nodding his head.

Mrs Kane's chauffeur came into the workshop at this moment and touched his hat to Jim. "I've brought the car down, sir." He cast a curious, professional eye over the Bentley and looked inquiringly at Jim.

"Take a look at her," said Jim.

The chauffeur obeyed with alacrity. The foreman and Andy stood in silence, watching him.

"What do you make of it, Jackson?"

The chauffeur looked at the nut held out to him by Mason and then at Jim. "That's dirty work, sir, or I'm a Dutchman. That never happened on its own. My Lord, there's someone laying for you, sir! Master Timothy's right!"

"Looks like it," said Jim. "Run me in to the police station, will you? I'd better try and get hold of the superintendent."

As good luck would have it, Hannasyde was just coming away from the police station when the Daimler drew up and set Jim down. He stopped on the steps and said: "Good morning, Mr Kane. Do you want me, by any chance?"

"Yes, I do," replied Jim. "Can you spare me ten minutes?"

"Of course. Come inside."

Jim followed him into the police station and to a small bare office leading out of the charge room. Hannasyde shut the door and pushed forward a chair near the desk. "Sit down, Mr Kane. What can I do for you?"

"I don't know, but I hope you can do something," replied Jim with a rueful smile. "I've just had what might easily have been a fatal accident in my car."

"Indeed?" Hannasyde moved to the other side of the desk and sat down. "Go on, Mr Kane. Where did it happen, and how?"

"On the coast road, on my way home from Portlaw. I had Miss Allison beside me and mercifully wasn't driving at any speed. As I swung round the first big bend in the road I lost all control over the steering, felt my front wheels floating, and ended up in the ditch. Had I been driving at anything like my normal speed we should both of us have been killed. As it is, I was going slow, and we got off with a few bruises. Do you know anything about cars, Superintendent?"

"A certain amount. Not very much."

"Let me have that pencil then, will you? Thanks. Now, I had the car hauled out of the ditch and towed to Lamb's Garage. We discovered that the track rod —that's the rod that runs between the two front wheels, like this—was loose at one end." He sketched a rough diagram on the back of an envelope. "At each end of the track rod there's a ball joint which fits into it and is held by a nut, here. Do you see? Holding that nut is a split pin. When we inspected the car, the nut on the left end of the rod was missing. The pin also, of course. I went back along the road with one of the garage hands and found the nut. It had been smeared over with a lot of muck."

"Are you suggesting that it was done deliberately, Mr Kane?"

"No, I'm not suggesting," replied Jim. "I'm asserting. It *was* done deliberately: there can be no doubt about that. Someone removed the split pin securing the nut, and, I should say, unscrewed the nut down to the last few threads, messed it up thoroughly with a lot of oil and muck, and left it like that. The first big bend in the road, with the consequent pull on the wheels, did the rest of the trick. Had I not had Miss Allison with me it was a safe bet I should have been travelling somewhere between forty and fifty miles an hour, in which case I should have smashed myself and the car to glory."

Hannasyde raised his eyes from the diagram he had picked up and said: "Yes, I understand this all right. Do you suppose your car was tampered with at Cliff House, or elsewhere?"

"Elsewhere. I can't think that the nut, loosened as it must have been, would have held all the way to Portlaw and halfway back again."

"Did you leave your car anywhere in Portlaw?"

"Yes, I did," replied Jim. "I left it for about an hour in the yard at the back of Kane and Mansell's offices in Bridge Street."

CHAPTER THIRTEEN

HANNASYDE did not say anything for a moment or two but sat looking in his grave, considering way at the large young man before him. He had laid the diagram down again and was gently dropping the point of a pencil on the desk, running his fingers down the smooth sides and letting the pencil slip back again through them. "In the yard at the back of Kane and Mansell's offices," he repeated presently. "Nowhere else?"

Jim shook his head.

"I don't think I've seen the yard. Is it overlooked?"

"Yes, by the windows in the back of the house. But I ran the car under a lean-to shelter running down one side of the wall. I don't think anyone tinkering with the car under that roof would be seen from any of the upper windows, and the ground-floor ones are frosted."

"I'll go and take a look round," said Hannasyde. "Did you meet anyone in the yard?"

"No, not a soul."

"Were you expected at the office?"

"Yes, Mr Mansell asked me to call for the purpose of talking over the general situation."

"Does that mean the question of the Australian project?"

"Largely, yes."

"Forgive what may seem to be a somewhat intrusive question; but are you going to adopt that scheme?"

"I'm not sure. I'm not in love with it, and I'm not over-fond of being jockeyed into things."

"Does it seem to you that the Mansells are pressing you unduly?"

Jim thought it over. "Difficult to say. I suppose, since they're so keen on it, it's not surprising they should want to hustle me a bit. I found Joe Mansell a trifle too persuasive for my taste. I don't think there's much doubt he'd like either to get me out of the business or to make me into a sort of sleeping partner. You can't altogether blame him. It must be darned annoying for a man of his age and experience to have me foisted onto him as head of the firm."

"I take it you don't mean to become a sleeping partner?"

"No, I don't think so. It was originally a Kane show,

and somehow I don't fancy leaving it in the Mansells' hands."

"Have you said as much to them?"

"Well, hardly! I've made it pretty clear that I'm not going to be shelved."

"Have you given them any indication of what your views on the Australian scheme are?"

Jim reflected. "I haven't committed myself in any way. I did tell Paul Mansell that I knew neither my Cousin Silas nor Clement liked it. They've probably gathered that I'm not smitten with it."

"If the scheme were adopted, would you have to put up the necessary capital?"

"That seems to be the general idea. Sort of loan, to the tune of about twenty thousand pounds."

"I see. Was Mr Paul Mansell present at your interview this morning?"

"No, I didn't see him at all. I imagine he was in the building, as his car was parked in the yard, but he didn't show up."

"You had an interview with Paul Mansell at Cliff House not so many days ago, didn't you, as a result of which Mr Oscar Roberts also called upon you for the purpose of warning you that you might be in danger?"

"Yes."

"Did you set any store by that warning? Had you any reason to think that there might be a risk in visiting the offices of Kane and Mansell?"

"Far from it. I thought I couldn't be in a safer place, even supposing they were trying to bump me off. The idea of anyone doctoring my car didn't occur to me. I don't think it occurred to Roberts either. He seemed to think I was more likely to get knocked on the head, or something equally absurd."

Hannasyde frowned. "Did he tell you so?"

"No, but he walked in in the middle of my interview with Mr Mansell, quite obviously as a protective measure. I was rather fed up with him at the time, but, by Jove, I believe he was right!"

"Mr Kane, from your knowledge of the Mansells,

does it seem probable to you that they would murder two, if not three, people for the sake of putting through a business deal?"

"Not a bit," replied Jim promptly. "On the other hand, they undoubtedly think there's big money to be made out of the Australian deal, and you can't get away from the fact that an attempt—probably two attempts—have been made on my life. I admit it sounds pretty steep on the face of it, but you must remember that, if I'd gone down in the Seamew, or been smashed up in my car today, you'd have found it very hard to prove that I'd been murdered. As far as the Seamew's concerned, I doubt whether you'd find any evidence, even if you went to the expense of salvaging her. If a hole was really cut in her, the force of the water must have torn the bottom off her. And if I hadn't had Miss Allison with me this morning, I should have smashed my car up so good and proper that you'd have been hard put to it to find out what caused the crash."

"I quite appreciate that, Mr Kane. You are quite sure no one else could have access to your car?"

"No, of course I'm not. While it stood in the yard anyone could have walked in and tinkered with it. But who'd want to?"

"And at Cliff House?"

"Well, yes; but again, who'd want to?" Jim said impatiently. "Besides, the chauffeur was washing my great-aunt's car first thing this morning and didn't leave the garage until eleven. I had the car out late last night and locked the garage when I brought her in, so it can't have been done yesterday. I went down to the garage myself just after eleven this morning and found my stepfather there, so I should think that at the most the garage was empty for five minutes."

There was the slightest of pauses. "What was your stepfather doing in the garage, Mr Kane?"

"Filling his cigarette lighter. Look here, what the devil are you getting at?" demanded Jim, half starting from his chair.

"Merely checking up on everyone who was seen near your car," replied Hannasyde mildly.

"Well, please don't check up on my stepfather!" said Jim "The idea's quite absurd. I'm on the best of terms with him and always have been. You might as well suspect my young stepbrother."

"I don't think I suspect anyone, Mr Kane. On the other hand, you must see that I cannot exonerate any-one on your bare word. If I am to go into this attempt on your life, which I understand you wish me to do, you must allow me to make what inquiries I think nec-essary. You say Sir Adrian was filling his lighter, which strikes me immediately as being a somewhat un-usual thing to do. Lighters are generally filled at a to-bacconist's shop."

Jim smiled. "When you know my stepfather a little better, Superintendent, you won't see anything unusual in that. It's entirely typical of him."

Hannasyde inclined his head slightly, as though ac-cepting this statement. "And he was the only person you observed anywhere in the vicinity of the garage?"

"Yes—at least, no; my stepbrother blew in while I was there; but as he was very keen to go with me, I don't somehow think we need consider him as a pos-sible suspect."

Hannasyde paid no heed to this rather sarcastic speech. "He was keen to go with you? You didn't take him, did you?"

"No, my stepfather told him——" Jim broke off, his eyes going swiftly to Hannasyde's face. Then he burst out laughing. "Oh, this is too farcical!"

"What did your stepfather tell him, Mr Kane?"

"That I didn't want to be bothered by him. Which was perfectly true. Seriously, Superintendent, you must leave my stepfather out of this. Incidentally, I fail to see what his motive could possibly be."

"I take it you have never had any reason to suspect that he might be jealous of your mother's affection for you?"

"Not the slightest," said Jim emphatically.

"Very well," said Hannasyde. "I promise you I'll go into it carefully, Mr Kane. And, if possible, refrain from insulting Sir Adrian," he added, with the glimmer of a smile.

"Thanks," said Jim, rising and shaking hands. "I'll be getting along, then."

"Not got cold feet, Mr Kane?"

"Oh, not very! There seems to be a Providence watching over me, anyway."

Hannasyde agreed and saw him off the premises. After that he had a short conference with Inspector Carlton and went out to meet Sergeant Hemingway for lunch.

The sergeant, who had failed to elicit anything from Mr James Kane's old nanny but the most rigid corroboration of her mistress's story, was feeling disgruntled; but he cheered up when he heard what Hannasyde had to tell him, and pointed out that he had prophesied that no one could tell where the case was going to end. "That's one suspect less, at all events," he said briskly. "Looks like we can rule out the old lady, too, not to mention Lady Harte."

"You're going too fast for me," said Hannasyde. "I'm not ruling anyone out yet."

"What, not James Kane himself, Super?"

"I don't think so. I believe he's telling me the truth, but we can't leave out of account the possibility that he may have engineered this accident just to put us off the real scent."

"Him?" said the sergeant incredulously. "Don't you believe it, Super! He's not that sort!"

"Hemingway," said the superintendent, "you think that if a man plays first-class football and gets into the semifinal of the Amateur Golf Championship he can't be a murderer!"

The sergeant blushed but said defiantly: "Psychology!"

"Rubbish!" said Hannasyde. "However, Carlton's putting one of his young men on to keep an eye on James Kane, and I've promised to investigate the affair. I'm going to see the car and to question the garage hands immediately after lunch. I shall go on up to Cliff House. I want you to go around to Kane and Mansell's office, take a careful look at the building with respect to the yard, and see what you can get out of the personnel."

While the superintendent and Sergeant Hemingway were discussing the case over the lunch table, Mrs Kane's Daimler was bearing Jim home in state. He arrived to find that the rest of the party had started lunch and realized, as soon as he entered the dining room, that Miss Allison had not been able to allay his relatives' suspicions. As he took his seat at the end of the table, with an apology for being late, his mother said in her most businesslike and commanding voice: "Now, Jim! Without any beating about the bush, what happened this morning?"

"To the Bentley?" said Jim, shaking out his table napkin. "The steering went, and we ended up safely but ungracefully in the ditch."

"Don't try and throw dust in my eyes, Jim!" she said. "You needn't think my nerves won't stand the truth. I've faced too many dangers in my time——"

"Nerves!" interrupted Emily fiercely. "No one talked of nerves in my young days!"

"And a very good thing too!" said Lady Harte. "I don't know what they are. Never did."

"You don't know how fortunate you are," said Rosemary with a pitying smile.

"On the contrary, I do know. Jim, I insist upon being answered!"

"Well, Mother, a nut holding one of the ball joints had worked loose, and it fell off."

"That," said Sir Adrian, helping himself to salad, "of course explains everything. Enlighten our ignorance, my dear boy."

"I don't want to hear anything about nuts and ball joints," announced Emily. "If someone's been tampering with your car, say so!"

Jim looked up to find Miss Allison's gaze inquiringly on his face.

"Was it tampered with, Jim?" she asked.

"Traitress!"

"I did try to make out it was an accident, but no one believed me. If it wasn't an accident we'd all rather know."

"Of course it wasn't an accident!" declared Timothy scornfully. "And now perhaps you'll believe I did *not* run the Seamew on the rocks!"

"I think," said Sir Adrian in his tranquil way, "that since speculation is so rife, you had better tell us just what did happen, Jim."

"Well, sir, it seems fairly obvious the car was tampered with."

"That is very disturbing," said Sir Adrian. "If you have not already done so, you should inform the police."

"I have. That's what made me late for lunch. The superintendent's going to look into it."

"I should think so indeed!" snapped Emily. "I don't know what the world's coming to!"

"Of course, what I am waiting for," said Rosemary, "is for somebody to try and bring it round to Trevor. Or possibly even me."

No one but Emily paid any attention to this remark, and as she merely said that the least said about that Dermott the better, Rosemary was discouraged from pursuing the subject.

"I have yet to learn that I am an alarmist," said Lady Harte; "but it is quite obvious that we must take immediate steps. This is beyond a joke. Whom do the police suspect?"

"Adrian," replied Jim with a cheerful grin.

Even Emily laughed at this. Norma said: "Adrian? Good God, the police must be out of their senses! Adrian doesn't know one end of a car from the other!"

"It grieves me to think I made so ill an impression on the superintendent," said Sir Adrian, delicately dropping tarragon over his salad. "What, if any, is my motive, Jim?"

"Oh, stepfather complex, sir! Gnawing jealousy."

"Ah yes, of course!" agreed Sir Adrian. "But surely it is a little odd of me to have borne with you all these years and to choose the moment when you are about to leave my roof for ever to murder you?"

"Actually," said Rosemary, who had been listening with deep interest, "people suffering from inhibitions often behave quite irrationally."

Emily looked at her with acute dislike. "If you've nothing to say more worth listening to than that, you'd better hold your tongue," she said crushingly.

"Well, it's very funny, no doubt; but I'm not going to have such nonsensical things said of my husband!" announced Lady Harte. "It annoys me very much indeed, for no one could have been a better father to Jim than Adrian!"

"I utterly refuse to subscribe to that," said Jim. "He never came the father over me in all his life."

"Thank you, Jim," said Sir Adrian, touched.

"Something must be done!" said Norma in a martial voice. "If I had my revolver—well, anyway, this decides it! From now on you'll carry a gun, Jim."

"I haven't got a gun," replied Jim. "Besides, from the look of things, I'm to be done in by accident."

"The Killer's failed twice," said Timothy. "We've got to be prepared for absolutely anything now. I say, it's most frightfully exciting, isn't it, Jim?"

"Lovely," agreed Jim.

"The extraordinary thing is that I had an intuition from the start that it was the Mansells," said Rosemary. "I was laughed to scorn, of course, but when I get one of my premonitions——"

"I suppose there's no doubt it is one of the Mansells?" interrupted Norma, looking at her son.

Emily unexpectedly demurred at this. "Joe Mansell's a fool, and always was, but there's no harm in him that ever I saw, and I've known him for fifty years and more."

"Yes, but what about Paul?" asked Rosemary. "Do you know, I've always had a feeling about him? I can't describe it, but——"

Emily sniffed. "If you're telling me that Paul Mansell murdered my son and Clement, I don't believe a word of it. A whippersnapper like him!"

"If he didn't, Aunt, who did?" demanded Lady Harte.

"I'm sure I don't know. It seems to me people will do anything nowadays. I've no patience with it," replied Emily.

By the time the party rose from the luncheon table a great many methods of protecting Jim from his unknown enemy had been put forward and heartily condemned. The news that a plain-clothes man had arrived, and was apparently keeping the house under observation, afforded gratification to no one but Timothy, who at once dashed out to make his acquaintance. Emily, bristling, said that they had had enough of policemen prying about the place and upsetting the servants; Patricia agreed with Lady Harte that to send one man only to guard Jim's precious person was frivolous; and Rosemary complained that the sight of a detective "brought it all back to her." Jim, discovering that his bodyguard, a shy but very earnest young man, proposed to accompany him if he left the premises, not unnaturally decided to cancel an expedition to a ruined abbey which Miss Allison had expressed a desire to visit. When Patricia had seen Mrs Kane comfortably bestowed on the couch in her own sitting room for her customary siesta, she went downstairs again to join Jim in the garden, the edge of her pleasure in this programme being considerably dulled by Rosemary's saying thoughtfully that it must be rather horrid to reflect that behind any bush or tree a murderer might be lurking. When Mr Harte exercised a simple sense of humour by stalking his stepbrother down to the lake and suddenly commanding him in gruff accents and from behind a rhododendron to "stick 'em up!" Miss Allison came to the conclusion that two chairs on the terrace would be more agreeable to her shattered nerves than wandering about all too well-wooded grounds.

Mr Harte, roundly cursed by Jim, was quite una-bashed. "Made you jump, didn't I?" he said ghoul-ishly. "As a matter of fact, I'm guarding you."

"Thanks," said Jim. "Are you going to guard me the whole afternoon?"

"Well, while you're in the garden I shall. Sergeant Trotter—that's the new detective, you know—said I ought to."

"I'll have a word with Sergeant Trotter," said Jim grimly. "Come on, Pat, let's go and sit sedately on the terrace."

Mr Harte accompanied them back to the house, chatting with his usual insouciance. Halfway across the south lawn he stopped, his blue eyes gleaming with ex-citement. "Say, buddy!" he pronounced. "I got a swell idea! Only I must have some dough!" He planted him-self in front of Jim and raised an eager, beseeching countenance. "Have you got any money, Jim? Because if so, could I have some, please? There's something I frightfully want to go and buy in Portlaw, and if you gave me about ten bob—or perhaps a pound, if you can spare it—I could whizz in on my bike."

"Look here, is it something devilish?" asked Jim suspiciously.

"No, no, honestly it isn't! As a matter of fact, it's actually for you, and I *know* you'll be pleased!"

"Oh God!" said Jim, with deep misgiving.

Mr Harte danced with impatience. "Oh, Jim, don't be a cad!"

"Well, if you swear it isn't anything hellish, and if it really means that you'll remove yourself till teatime," began Jim, taking out his notecase.

"Oh, good of you!" exclaimed Mr Harte, waiting to hear no more. He pocketed a pound note with fervid thanks and was about to hurry away when a thought occurred to him, and he paused. "I say, can I keep the change?" he asked anxiously.

Jim nodded.

"Say, you're a swell guy!" declared Mr Harte in a burst of gratitude and vanished.

Jim and Patricia ensconced themselves on the terrace. They enjoyed peace for nearly an hour, at the end of which time a stately procession issued out of the house. Emily had cut her siesta short and elected to join the rest of the party. This entailed the summoning of the footman and the chauffeur to carry her downstairs; the butler to bear her favourite chair out on to the terrace; and Ogle to bring up the rear with her rug, her shawl, and her spectacles.

By the time Emily had been settled in her chair, a table placed at her elbow, her ebony cane propped up within her reach, and her sunshade fetched for her, the party had been further augmented by the arrival of Oscar Roberts. He was ushered on to the terrace by Pritchard and after bowing to Mrs Kane and Patricia went up to Jim and shook hands. "I met Timothy in the town," he said. "What he had to say made me feel I'd like to come right on up to see you. Are you still telling me I'm crazy?"

"I don't think I ever said that, did I?" replied Jim, pulling forward a chair. "Sit down, won't you? Cigarette?"

Roberts took one from the case held out to him and lit it. "Might I know just what happened to your car this morning, Kane? I can't say I made much of my friend Timothy's story. It sounded mighty lurid."

"Oh, it wasn't lurid at all!" replied Jim easily. "Just something put out of action in the steering. No damage done."

Roberts smiled. "Quit stalling, Kane!"

"Well, we're not saying too much about it, you know. A nut had worked loose and came off. We might have crashed badly, but we didn't."

"We?"

"Miss Allison was with me."

"Say, Miss Allison, you'd better stop riding around with this guy: it seems to be kind of dangerous!" Roberts said humorously. "If you take my advice, young man, you'll leave that car of yours in the garage till this case is cleared up."

"As she's a bit bent I shall probably have to," replied Jim. "Not that I think anyone would pull the same trick twice."

"What was the trick?"

"The nut holding one of the ball joints on the track rod was loosened. The split pin securing it was missing when we inspected the car."

Roberts interposed. "Sorry, Kane, but that doesn't mean a thing to me. What kind of a steering system is this?"

"Quite a usual one. Certain makes of car have it. I can soon show you." He produced a pencil and an envelope from his pocket and drew a rough diagram, elucidating it as he did so.

Roberts watched with knit brows, putting one or two questions as the drawing progressed. He took the envelope from Jim presently and studied it. "Guess you'd have to be familiar with the car to be able to pull this one," he remarked. "Now, this nut, you say, came off; if you knew the car, it wouldn't be a difficult job to pull that pin out and loosen the nut?"

"No. Dead easy, given a spanner and a pair of pliers."

"Could it have been done in a few minutes, do you suppose?"

"I should think so."

Roberts gave back the envelope. "Well, that certainly is interesting," he said. "Looks like you're up against something, Kane. Can't help blaming myself for this one. I ought to have thought of your car standing in that yard just crying out to be tampered with."

Emily, who had been listening to him with ill-concealed impatience, said crossly: "I don't know why, I'm sure. You're not a detective, are you?"

Roberts turned courteously towards her. "Mrs Kane, when a man sees murder rife under his very nose, he's apt to take notice of it."

"Scotland Yard has the matter in hand," said Emily in her stiffest voice.

Roberts smiled a little. "Sure they have. I expect when it comes to solving problems they're swell. Maybe they're not quite so clever at preventing crime."

At this moment Sir Adrian came out on to the terrace with Superintendent Hannasyde. Jim said at once: "My God, sir, has it come to this?"

"No, not yet," replied Sir Adrian calmly. "I am still a free man. The superintendent wishes to have a word with Mrs Kane."

Emily felt no particular animosity towards Superintendent Hannasyde, who had at their first meeting handled her with consummate tact; but her inevitable reaction towards anyone requiring anything of her was of hostility. She looked him up and down and said: "I don't know what he thinks I can tell him."

Patricia got up. "I expect you'd like to speak to Mrs Kane alone, Superintendent."

"Sit down!" said Emily sharply. "I've no secrets. If I knew anything I should have told it in the first place. Well, what do you want?"

Hannasyde took the chair Jim had thrust forward. "I take it that you have been informed of the accident to your great-nephew's car, Mrs Kane?"

"Yes, I have," said Emily; "and I'll thank you to see that nothing of the sort happens again! I don't know what the police think they're for."

"I'll do my best," promised Hannasyde. "I think you may be able to help me." He glanced fleetingly round the assembled company. "Do you wish me to speak frankly, or would you like to see me alone?"

"No, I shouldn't," replied Emily.

"Then I'm going to be very frank indeed," said Hannasyde. "I have seen the foreman of Lamb's Garage, and I have seen Mr Kane's car. I am satisfied that the accident did not occur naturally. It remains for me to discover who tampered with the car. Sir Adrian will, I hope, forgive me if I say that his presence in the garage this morning makes it necessary for me to consider the possibility of his being the guilty person."

"Stuff and nonsense!" interrupted Emily with a snort.

"A thought occurs to me," said Sir Adrian, disposing himself in a deck chair. "Had I a motive for murdering Clement Kane?"

Hannasyde's eyes twinkled appreciatively. "I have not yet discovered it, sir."

"Murder begets murder," said Jim. "You didn't murder Clement, Adrian. His murder just put the idea of murdering me into your head."

Sir Adrian wrinkled his brow. "I never take my ideas at second hand," he complained.

"Waiving you for the moment, sir," interposed Hannasyde, "I am apparently left with only two suspects."

"Joe Mansell wouldn't murder anyone, if that's what you mean," said Emily. "I don't know anything about his son, and I don't want to."

"We'll waive him too," said Hannasyde. "There is one other person who would benefit by Mr Kane's death, and that is his heir."

Emily stared at him. "Maud? Rubbish, she's in Australia!"

"Are you sure of that, Mrs Kane?"

"I had a letter from her, posted in Sydney. I don't know what more you want."

"May I see that letter?"

For a moment it seemed as though Emily would refuse; then she turned towards Miss Allison and commanded her to fetch it from the davenport in her sitting room.

Patricia got up and went into the house. Hannasyde said: "When did you last see your great-niece, Mrs Kane?"

"When she was a child," replied Emily. "I don't know when. I never took any stock in that Australian lot."

"Then it is safe to assume that you would not recognize her today?"

"I've no idea. She was a plain child. I remember they dressed her very unsuitably. Just like them! If they had a penny to bless themselves with it went on grand clothes and trips to England. They never got any encouragement from *me*."

"Do you know anything of the man she married, Mrs Kane?"

"Never saw him in my life. She used to write cadging letters to my son. Of course, we guessed *that* was at her husband's instigation. He was no good at all."

"You never even saw a photograph of him?"

"I never saw one, and if I had, I shouldn't have been interested. If you want to know anything about him, you'd better ask Mr Roberts. He comes from Australia."

Oscar Roberts had been listening with a slight frown in his cold, intelligent eyes. He said slowly: "I'm an Australian sure enough; but I don't know Sydney very well. What is the man's name, Mrs Kane?"

"Leighton," she replied. "That's what my great-niece signs herself, anyway."

"Leighton?" His frown grew. "The only Leighton I ever knew I met in a bar at Melbourne, and, as far as I know, he wasn't a married man."

From the recesses of her memory Emily unexpectedly brought a new fact to light. "That's nothing. He left her years ago. I remember her mother—she was an empty little ninny, always whining about something or other—wrote to my son about it. I don't know what she thought *he* could do about it. Of course, he did nothing at all. Maud was fool enough to take the man back again, but it didn't last. It wouldn't surprise me to hear of him posing as a bachelor in Melbourne, or wherever you say you met him. I've no doubt if he had sixpence in his pocket he wouldn't trouble his head over Maud."

"They are not divorced?" Hannasyde asked.

"If they are I never heard of it. Maud had no pride at all. Just like her mother."

Hannasyde turned to Oscar Roberts. "How well were you acquainted with the man you met in Melbourne?"

"Not so well. If he was the Leighton you want he certainly wasn't on the up-and-up when I knew him. He was picking up a living doing odd jobs for any firm that would use him. Chicken feed! The trouble with him was drink. Are you figuring he might be at the bottom of this racket, Superintendent?"

"He or his wife. Possibly both."

"That's ingenious," Roberts admitted. "That certainly is ingenious; but I can't get around to it fitting the hobo I knew."

"Would you know that man again if you saw him?"

"Sure I'd know him, unless he was wearing a wig, or something. Say, you've got me thinking, Superintendent. But there's a couple of snags I can see."

"Yes, Mr Roberts?"

"Well, the first is that, assuming the Leighton I knew is the Leighton you're after, I doubt whether he'd ever have got himself sobered up enough to tackle a job like this. Maybe we're not talking of the same man. Let it go. The second snag is the number of murders. It's too steep, Superintendent. The man who'd set out to commit no less than three murders so that his wife could inherit a fortune sure must be a mastermind! You can take it from me, all that amount of nerve don't fit my Leighton, and from what Mrs Kane's been telling us about the guy her great-niece married, it don't fit him either. Why, the man who could plan deviltry on a scale as grand as that must have brains enough to make a fortune for himself!"

"It doesn't always follow that a clever man chooses an honest way to make a fortune, Mr Roberts. I admit the improbability of his planning three murders, and I believe that if he is at the bottom of this case he didn't plan three. It is far more likely that, in common with

Mr Kane, he took it for granted that his wife stood next in succession to Mr Clement Kane."

Roberts regarded him with a faint smile. "You've got it fixed in your mind Mr Silas Kane and Mr Clement were murdered by the same man, haven't you, Superintendent? Does it ever strike you there's a queer difference in the methods employed?"

"In my profession, Mr Roberts, we guard against getting fixed ideas. I have as yet no proof that Mr Silas Kane was murdered."

"Guess he was murdered, all right; but whether you'll ever know by whom is another matter. I've a hunch that the man who pushed him off that cliff edge is dead himself now." He glanced at Jim. "A while back, Kane, you said something that was maybe sounder than you knew. You said: 'Murder begets murder.' I believe in this case it did."

"You take a great interest in this case, Mr Roberts?" said Hannasyde.

"Yes, Superintendent. It's a dandy little problem."

"Have you had much experience of crime?"

Roberts regarded him with his head slightly on one side. "Now, why do you ask me that?"

"You seem to look upon it almost from a professional standpoint."

"You're trying to flatter me, Superintendent. I've been—interested in crime for a good many years; but I don't aspire to your standards. But in my experience a murderer has only one trick in his repertoire. In this case you have one man killed so neatly you'll never prove it was murder; and another killed so blatantly there's no possibility it could have been anything but murder. Unless I'm mistaken, the two methods indicate two very different types of minds. One's subtle; one ain't."

"Aren't you rather leaving out of account the attempt upon Mr Kane's life? Doesn't it fall into the same category as Mr Silas Kane's murder?"

"Why, no, I think not, Superintendent. The accident to the Seamew and the accident to the car were tricks that could easily go wrong, and did go wrong. They look to me like a plain guy trying to be clever. Mr Silas Kane's murderer thought of a plan where there was no room for mistake. You have to hand it to him."

"If you don't mind, sir, I think we've had about enough of this conversation," interposed Jim. "It isn't very pleasant for my great-aunt."

Roberts turned at once with a swift apology on his lips, but Emily said fiercely: "I've supposed all along that my son was murdered. Not that the police would ever prove it. The Mansells! They didn't do it! Who stood to gain by his death?" She gave a short laugh and folded her hands closer in her lap. Patricia, coming out onto the terrace through the drawing-room window, thought that for a moment she looked almost terrible, a little stout old lady with a rigid back, and eyes like blue ice.

There was a constrained silence. "It can't be proved, Aunt, and—after all, Clement's dead," said Jim uncomfortably.

Her tight mouth relaxed slightly. "Yes. He's dead," she answered.

Hannasyde, watching her, said bluntly: "Do you seriously believe that he killed your son, Mrs Kane?"

Her stare abolished him; she replied in her curtest, most expressionless voice: "What I believe is my own concern. It won't help you. You'll never prove anything."

CHAPTER FOURTEEN

PATRICIA, who had been standing quite still just outside the drawing-room window, came forward, relieving a sudden tension. "I think this is the letter you want, Mrs Kane."

Emily glanced at it. "*I* don't want it. Give it to the superintendent."

Hannasyde took it with a word of thanks and carefully inspected the postmark on the envelope. He withdrew a folded letter and gave it back to Miss Allison. "If I may keep the envelope, Mrs Kane, that's all I want."

"Keep anything you like," said Emily. "I don't mind."

"Thank you." Hannasyde put the letter in his pocketbook and got up. "That's all, then, for the present."

Jim accompanied him through the house to the front door.

"Thanks for my bodyguard, Superintendent. Between him and my stepbrother I ought to be pretty safe."

"I hope so," Hannasyde answered.

"They're a bit of a nuisance," said Jim cheerfully; "but at least your nice Sergeant Trotter's presence does augur a certain measure of belief in my story."

"I'm sorry if I led you to think that I didn't believe your story."

"Very handsomely said, Superintendent. Do you, by any chance?"

"Believe you? Why not, Mr Kane?"

Jim laughed. "It only dawned on me, after I'd got back here, that you probably suspected me of staging the whole show just to put you off the scent. I can prove my innocence by requesting you to inquire of the personnel at my office whether my hands were dirty or not when I walked in the back entrance."

"I'm afraid that's no proof at all," replied Hannasyde with his slow smile. "You might have worn a pair of rubber gloves, mightn't you?"

"Damn! I never thought of that," said Jim. "I must remain a suspect. It's comforting to think that I'm in the best of company."

Hannasyde returned a light answer and took his leave, catching the next omnibus back to Portlaw.

He was met at the police station by Inspector Carlton, who hailed his arrival with satisfaction, announcing, not without pride, that he had news to report. "That alibi of Mr Paul Mansell's," he said. "Well, we've shook it, Superintendent. Your outside chance came off. I've got a young fellow here who's prepared to swear he saw Mr Mansell's Lagonda drawn up by the tradesmen's gate at Cliff House at 3.30 P.M. on the day Mr Clement was shot."

"That's interesting," said Hannasyde, hanging up his hat. "Reliable witness?"

"I'd say so. Garage hand. He's waiting in my office."

"Right, I'll see him at once."

The witness, a tall youth with a shock of resilient brown hair, was quite clear in his evidence. He told Hannasyde that, having Saturday afternoon leave from Jones's Garage in Portlaw, he had taken his young lady for a spin on his motor bike and had passed along the coast road by Cliff House at about half-past three, the time being fixed in his mind by the fact of the said young lady having kept him hanging about in Portlaw till it was a question whether they could reach Bransome, farther down the coast, in time for tea or not.

"Yes, I see," said Hannasyde. "You say you saw Mr Mansell's car outside Cliff House?"

"That's right, sir. A four-and-a-half-litre Lagonda it is."

"Did you notice its number?"

Mr. Bert Wilson scratched his head reflectively. "Well, I don't know as I actually noticed it, so to speak. I know the car, see? Come to that, I know the number of it, too, which is——"

"No, that isn't what I mean," interrupted Hannasyde. "There are many Lagondas on the road, after all. Are you quite sure that this one belonged to Mr Paul Mansell?"

Mr Wilson had no doubt of this. He offered to take

his dying oath it was Mr Mansell's car, adding: "I work at Jones's Garage, see? 'Smatter of fact, when I saw the car parked there, outside Cliff House, I passed the remark to my young lady, 'That's one of our cars, that is,' I said. Well, what I mean is, we had her in for oil and grease only two days before. We do all Mr Paul Mansell's work for him. Why, I know that Lagonda backwards, as you might say."

"Was anyone with the car when you passed it?"

"No sir. Parked with her rear wheels just off the road, she was, just by the tradesmen's entrance, as my young lady will bear me out."

Hannasyde favoured him with one of his long searching looks. "Do you know what happened at Cliff House on Saturday, August tenth?" he asked.

"What, Mr Clement Kane being done in like he was, sir? Yes sir, of course. Caused quite a bit of talk in the town it has. Well, what I mean is——"

"Why have you waited till now to come forward with this information?"

Mr Wilson shifted his weight from one foot to the other and looked embarrassed. "It's like this, you see, sir. I didn't make nothing of it, not at first. Kind of slipped my mind, if you know what I mean. Then I see the notice about anyone being able to give information, and I shows it to my young lady, and she says at once, 'Bert,' she says, 'do you know what?' 'No,' I says; 'what?' 'You ought to tell the police about Mr Paul Mansell's car,' she says, 'that's what.' 'Oh, all right, Doris,' I says—that being her name—not that I'm one to go poking into what don't concern me, because it's what I don't hold with and never did. So I tells Mr Jones, see? and he says as how I ought to come round to the police station right off, which I done."

"And now let's see Pretty Paul talk himself out of that one!" remarked Sergeant Hemingway, when he heard of this interlude.

"You're more prejudiced against Paul Mansell than I've ever known you to be against anyone," said Hannasyde.

"Not prejudiced," said the sergeant firmly. "I never let myself get prejudiced. All I say is that he's a nasty, slimy, double-faced tick who'd murder his own grandmother if he saw a bit of money to be got out of it."

"Very moderate," said Hannasyde, smiling.

"Well," said the sergeant, nettled, "it stands out a mile, doesn't it? Now, if you weren't my superior officer . . ."

Hannasyde sighed. "Never mind that bit: I've got it off by heart. What would you say if I weren't your superior officer?"

"I'd say," replied the sergeant promptly, "that you must be nuts to go round suspecting a decent young fellow like Jim Kane when you've got an out-and-out dirty swine like Paul Mansell fair stinking under your very nose. Of course," he added, "that's only what I'd say if you *weren't* my superior officer. As it is——"

"I do wish you'd try and get it out of your head that I suspect Jim Kane any more than I suspect any of the others. I don't. I suspect him a good deal less than I suspect some, but I try to be impartial. Have a shot at it yourself."

The sergeant cast him a reproachful glance but merely said: "Are you going to tackle Pretty Paul yourself, Chief?"

"Yes. Anything come through from the Yard for me?"

"Come to think of it, I believe something has," replied the sergeant and went to see.

He came back in a few minutes with a long envelope which he handed to the superintendent. While Hannasyde slit it open, spread open the several sheets contained in it, and read them quickly through, he stood watching him with an expression of birdlike interest. "Anything doing, Chief?" he ventured to ask presently.

"Not a great deal. The Sydney police know nothing of the Leighton I want. Mrs Leighton is there all right. Seems to have been living there for about a year. Melbourne cables nothing known of Edwin Leighton since

ne end of 1933, when he was discharged from prison
fter serving a short term for obtaining money under
alse pretences. Seems to have faded out."

"Well, anyway," said the sergeant, brightening, "if
e's been in prison, they'll have his fingerprints and
hotograph. Were they asked for?"

"Yes, if the police had them. Copies are being sent
y air mail."

"Any description?"

"Not very helpful. Age, forty-two; height, five foot
leven inches; hair, brown; eyes, grey."

"Fancy that!" said the sergeant ironically. "Wife
now anything of his whereabouts?"

"Apparently not." Hannasyde folded the sheets and
ipped them into his pocket. "Nothing much to be
one about that till we get the photograph. I'll go and
all on Paul Mansell."

He walked from the police station to the offices of
ane and Mansell and after sending in his card was
ery soon escorted to the room at the back of the
uilding on the first floor that was Paul's office. On his
ay up the stairs and down the broad corridor he took
wift note of his surroundings and did not miss the
oor on the landing, set wide to admit the fresh air,
hat gave on to the iron fire-escape leading down into
he yard.

Paul Mansell had his secretary with him when Han-
asyde was ushered into the room, and was apparently
usy with a heavy file. He did not look up immedi-
tely, but when Hannasyde walked forward to a chair
y the desk, he raised his eyes and said: "Ah, good af-
ernoon! Just a moment, if you please. Miss Jenkins,
ake this!"

He dictated a letter, which seemed to Hannasyde
ather unimportant, and then dismissed the girl and
aid: "Sorry to keep you waiting. What can I do for
ou?"

The overgenial note in his voice did not escape Han-
asyde. He replied calmly: "You can tell me, Mr

Mansell, what your car was doing outside Cliff House at 3.30 P.M. on August tenth."

Paul Mansell lost some of his colour. He countered with a swift question: "Who says my car was outside Cliff House that afternoon?"

"I have evidence that it was drawn up at the side of the road by the tradesmen's entrance, Mr Mansell. Do you care to explain this?"

Paul lit a cigarette and inhaled a breath of smoke before answering. "I should very much like to know where you got this tale from."

"I am sorry. I am not in a position to disclose the source of this piece of evidence," said Hannasyde, unmoved.

"Well, really, I——" Paul stopped, plainly undecided what to say. "I don't know that I feel inclined to answer this most extraordinary question, without knowing——" He met the superintendent's cold eyes and broke off again.

"Do you deny that your car was parked outside the grounds of Cliff House that afternoon, Mr Mansell?"

Paul looked at him for a moment under his lashes. "Deny it? No, I didn't say I denied it. But it has nothing to do with this case, I can assure you. As a matter of fact, the raison d'être is so simple——"

"I should be obliged to you if you would tell me what the raison d'être was," interrupted Hannasyde.

"Oh, certainly! I've no objection," said Paul. "As I told you before, I was due at a tennis party at Brotherton Manor that Saturday. I stayed talking to Mrs Trent longer than I meant to. I had to stop at Cliff House to pick up my racket, that's all."

"Why?"

"Why? Because I'd left it there, of course. If you don't believe me, you can go and ask my sister, Mrs Pemble, or her husband. They were both there."

"Both where?"

"At Cliff House, the day before Silas Kane's death. There was a small tennis party—well, hardly a party: just ourselves, and Patricia Allison. My people haven't

ot a tennis court, and Silas Kane let us use the ones
t his place whenever we wanted to. On that particular
ccasion it came on to rain just before tea, and we all
vent into the summerhouse—sort of glorified sun-par-
ur arrangement; I dare say you've seen it—hoping
hat it would clear up. Played silly games, you know.
Jp Jenkins, and Rummy, and that sort of thing, to
ass the time. The rain kept on, and we all went up to
he house for tea. I happened to leave my racket in the
ummerhouse: forgot about it, you know. The weather
idn't clear up, and in the end we—my sister, and
'emble and myself—drove home without returning to
he summerhouse. I remembered my racket when I got
ack to Portlaw, but I knew where I'd left it, and that
t would be perfectly safe and dry. I knew I'd put it in
ts press, too, which was all that mattered. Naturally I
lidn't go chasing back to Cliff House for it. Then all
his business of Silas Kane dying, and then Clement,
ame, and what with one thing and another I never
hought about the racket again till I had to play tennis
t Brotherton Manor on the tenth. Of course, I re-
nembered at once where the thing was, and I simply
icked it up on my way. That's all. Not really interest-
ng, is it?"

"Do you mean, Mr Mansell, that you just walked
hrough the grounds to the summerhouse without any-
ne's knowledge, abstracted your racket, and came
way again?"

"That's it. What do you suppose I'd do? Drive up to
he front door and send the butler to get the darned
hing?"

"I should suppose that a more usual form of proce-
ure would have been to have called first at the house
o ask permission to get your racket," replied Hanna-
yde.

Paul brushed that aside with one of his airy ges-
ures. "Quite unnecessary, I assure you. I know the
Kanes so well—I mean, I've always had the run of the
lace, pretty well. I don't say that, if I'd had twenty
ninutes to waste, I mightn't have done the polite as you

suggest, but the point is, I was late already. You must be fairly familiar with Cliff House by this time. Do you know where the tennis courts are situated? They're a day's march from the house—dam' silly place to have put them, I always thought—but that's beside the point. The point being that, if you nip in the tradesmen's entrance, and turn sharp to your left down the first path you come to, you reach the summerhouse in about half the time it takes you to start from the house. Anything more I can tell you?"

"Yes," said Hannasyde. "Why did you conceal this perfectly innocent errand?"

"Oh, come, Superintendent, I don't know that I *concealed* it!"

"Pardon me; but when I asked you for a precise account of your movements on the afternoon of August tenth, you not only made no mention of this episode but you must obviously have misstated the time of your leaving Mrs Trent's house after lunch. No matter how near to the side entrance of Cliff House the tennis courts may be, you could not, if you left Mrs Trent at 3.25, have stopped at Cliff House, collected your property, and still have contrived to arrive at Brotherton Manor at 3.45."

Paul smoked for a moment or two in uneasy silence. Then he said: "Well, if you must know, I got the wind up a bit. Silly of me, of course; but when I got the news of Clement's having been shot, and realized I must have been actually in the grounds when it happened, I saw that my perfectly ordinary behaviour might strike an outsider as being rather odd. Mind you, if I'd heard or seen anything I'd have come forward at once: that goes without saying. But I knew my being there had absolutely no bearing on the case, so I lay low about it. I don't say it was altogether wise of me, but——"

"It was the very reverse of wise, Mr Mansell. You must see for yourself that it places you in an extremely invidious position, to say the least of it. Can you bring anyone besides your sister forward to corroborate your statement that you left your racket in the summerhouse on the day of this tennis party?"

"Oh Lord, yes!" said Paul with an assumption of nonchalance. "Mrs Trent knew that I had to stop at Cliff House for my racket, because I told her so."

"You might ask yourself, with advantage, Mr Mansell, whether, in view of Mrs Trent's instant corroboration of a part of your original deposition which you now admit to have been false, her further testimony is likely to carry much weight with me," said Hannasyde unpleasantly.

"Well, I don't know whom you expect me to refer you to," said Paul. "Miss Allison might remember the incident; but it's quite possible she never knew anything about it. I didn't make a song and dance about having left the dam' racket in the summerhouse. She probably didn't notice that I didn't take it away with me. I dare say it sounds fishy to you, but I can't help that. And unless there's anything more you want to ask me——"

"There is," said Hannasyde. "Will you tell me, please, where you were between eleven o'clock and twelve this morning?"

"Look here, what on earth's it got to do with you where I was?" demanded Paul, his temper fraying a little.

"Have you any objection to telling me where you were, Mr Mansell?"

"I don't know that I've any objection, but——"

"Then let me advise you to answer my question."

Paul said with a flash of anger: "Damn it, I'm not bound to answer you!"

"Certainly not," said Hannasyde. "Am I to put it on record that you decline to answer me?"

"Good Lord, what a fuss to make—I don't mind answering you, but I dislike being interrogated without any apparent rhyme or reason!"

"Very well, Mr Mansell; then I will tell you that an

event has occurred which renders it necessary for me to check up on the movements during that hour of anyone connected with this case. Where were you?"

"I don't know. Here, I expect. Where should I be?"

"I must request you to be more precise, Mr Mansell. You are surely able to recall what your movements were this morning?"

"I don't sit and watch the clock! I've got something better to do. I did what I usually do—attended to my correspondence first, dictated some letters to my secretary . . ."

Hannasyde glanced round. "Does your secretary work in this room?"

"Of course not. She works in there," replied Paul, nodding towards a door communicating with an adjoining apartment.

"When did she leave this room this morning to type your letters?"

"Oh, round about ten-thirty! I don't know for certain."

"Did she return at any time between eleven and twelve?"

"No, I don't think so. In fact, I'm sure she didn't."

"What did you do?"

"Got on with my work, of course."

"In this room?"

"Mostly. I went down to the packing room once, and into the ledger department. That's all."

Hannasyde got up and walked over to the window. It overlooked the yard below, and beyond the cover of the lean-to shelter, built at right angles to the house, he could just see the tail of Paul Mansell's car protruding. The body of the car was hidden by the low roof above it.

Paul Mansell watched him with a shade of uneasiness in his face. "What's the matter? What are you getting at?" he asked.

Hannasyde turned his head. "I see that you look out on to the yard," he said. "Did you see Mr James Kane park his car there this morning?"

"No, I can't say I did. I don't hang out of the window to gape at every car I hear in the yard. Look here, what's this all about?"

Hannasyde came back to the desk. "Upon his way back to Cliff House, after his interview with your father, Mr Kane met with an accident," he said.

Paul Mansell half started to his feet. "Good God, you don't mean he's dead?"

"No," replied Hannasyde. "Mr Kane escaped injury. But investigation has disclosed the fact that the accident was caused by the loosening of one of the nuts holding the left ball joint of the track rod of his car in position."

Paul stared at him, his brows knit. "The inference being that I monkeyed about with his blasted car?"

"Not necessarily," said Hannasyde in his quiet way.

"I should dam' well hope not!" Paul said angrily. "What reason have I got to try and kill Jim Kane? Or his cousin Clement, for that matter! I think it's about the limit that you policemen should have the neck to suspect me! Do you suppose I'd be fool enough to murder a couple of men—oh, three, isn't it?—three men, just to put through a potty business deal?"

"There is no need for such heat, Mr Mansell."

"Well, I think there is! It's about time the air was cleared a bit. You needn't imagine I haven't realized what you've been getting at ever since you came down here! What's more, I know who put you up to it! It was that stagy fool Roberts, trying to do the giddy detective all over the shop!"

The door opened, and Joseph Mansell came into the room, looking worried and a little frightened. "What's all this? What's all this?" he said. "Paul, my boy, really! I could hear your voice in my office! No need to shout—no need to shout, you know! Good afternoon, Superintendent. Now, what is the trouble?"

"Oh, nothing!" Paul said, sinking back in his chair. "Superintendent Hannasyde is just accusing me of trying to murder Jim Kane, that's all!"

"Murder Jim? Good God, what's this, Superintendent?"

"Your son is labouring under a misapprehension, Mr Mansell. I have accused him of nothing. All I have asked him to do is to account for his movements this morning, while Mr Kane was in your office."

"Well, well, there's no harm in that: you have to do your duty. But what's this about Jim Kane?"

Hannasyde explained briefly. Joe looked very much shocked, said feebly that he felt sure there must be a mistake, and added that surely the superintendent could not seriously suspect his son of having had anything to do with the accident.

"That's where you're wrong," said Paul mockingly. "He thinks I killed Clement, and probably Silas too. Now I'm rounding off the job with Jim. And what I say is that such a cracked-brained idea would never have come into his head if that meddlesome know-all Roberts hadn't put it there!"

"Paul, my boy, Paul! Gently! I'm sure the superintendent doesn't think any such thing, or Roberts either. You're letting all this worry get on your nerves!"

"Well, and if I am, is it surprising?" retorted Paul. "I've had detectives nosing around till I'm sick of the sight of them, and, on top of that, I've had Roberts dogging my footsteps and coming as near to saying bang out that I murdered Clement as he dare!" He swung round in his chair to face Hannasyde and added venomously: "If you want to chase a wild goose, try him for a change! I've had enough of it! He had just as much motive as I had for killing Clement!"

"Paul!" said his father warningly. "Now, that's quite enough! There's no need to talk in that wild fashion. You know perfectly well that Roberts couldn't possibly have killed poor Clement, even if he had had a motive, which really, my boy, he hadn't. Must keep calm, you know! The superintendent's only doing his duty, after all."

Paul seemed to recollect himself. He flushed and muttered that he was sorry, but that the case was getting on his nerves a bit. Hannasyde, realizing that nothing further could be elicited from him, took his leave and left the room in company with Joe Mansell, who went with him to the head of the staircase, trying all the way to excuse his son's outburst.

From Kane and Mansell's offices Hannasyde proceeded to the Cedars, Joe Mansell's comfortable Victorian house situated in a wide avenue leading off the Esplanade. He found the household undergoing the doubtful pleasure of having-the-children-down-after-tea. This was a rite enjoyed only by Betty, but her deep-seated conviction that her mother, her husband, and any afternoon visitor who might have been unwise enough to call at the Cedars during her stay there were all filled with an overpowering desire to see the children made it impossible even for so forthright a lady as Agatha Mansell to protest against the daily invasion of her drawing room. It would have hurt Mrs Pemble's feelings too much. So the children, washed, brushed and dressed in their best clothes, burst into the drawing room regularly at five o'clock every day, loudly and insistently demanding sweetmeats and entertainment.

When Superintendent Hannasyde sent in his card, with a request for a few moments speech with Mrs Pemble, Jennifer and Peter, having been coaxed into shaking hands with two visitors and prompted to reply civilly to a number of the fatuous questions invariably addressed to the young by strangers, were engaged in the simple but enjoyable game of launching themselves bodily upon the sofa, mauling the cushions, scrambling off again, and repeating the performance. Their mother at first exclaimed in a shocked voice: "Oh, I can't come *now!*" but upon reflection consented to tear herself away from her offspring "just for a minute, sweethearts!"

This time limit, if adhered to, would have suited Hannasyde very well. He had not anticipated that his interview would occupy more than five minutes at the maximum, but he realized, within thirty seconds of

making Mrs Pemble's acquaintance, that she was no
one of those who could give a plain answer to a plai
question. It was indeed some time before he was give
an opportunity of asking his question. He had first t
gather as best he might from a confused rush of word
that Mrs Pemble had been playing with her children
that she always played with them after tea, and o
course at other times too; that she simply couldn'
imagine why he should wish to see her; that she knev
simply nothing about anything; that she could onl
spare him a minute; that she thought the whole affai
simply too frightful for words; that she was simpl
trying to put it out of her mind; and, finally, that sh
was terribly highly strung, though she made a point c
simply never talking about herself.

Superintendent Hannasyde, who had not had an
tea, felt a trifle dazed by these eager confidences bu
managed to break in on them and to put his question
Did Mrs Pemble recall what her brother had done witl
his tennis racket upon the last occasion when he ha
played tennis at Cliff House, the day before Sila
Kane's death?

By the time Betty had succeeded in recalling the oc
casion, which she did by the employment of such land
marks as the-day-Jennifer-had-a-bilious-attack, or the
day-Peter-fell-downstairs, her husband had com
into the room and was able to give Hannasyde ;
prompt answer. "Yes, rather!" he said. "He left it in th
summerhouse. I remember his saying so on the way
home."

This firmness had the effect of sobering Mrs Pemble
She said: "Oh yes, of course! I remember perfectly
We couldn't go back for it, because I'd promised th
children I'd be home in time to tuck them up in bed
hadn't I, Clive?"

"Thank you," said Hannasyde. "That is all I wantec
to know."

"If only there was anything else I *could* tell you I
should be simply delighted," said Betty earnestly. "I

mean, I think it's so appalling—it worries me frightfully, doesn't it, Clive?"

"Yes, rather!" said her dutiful helpmate.

Hannasyde thanked her, evaded an invitation to tell her what he had discovered, and departed. Mr and Mrs Pemble returned to the drawing room, and in the intervals of playing with her children Mrs Pemble discussed exhaustively the various causes which might account for the superintendent's strange question. When the children had been removed, under protest, by their nurse, she went away to invite Rosemary Kane, over the telephone, to motor to the Cedars after dinner for a nice, cosy talk.

Rosemary, undeterred by her oft-stated conviction that Joseph or Paul Mansell had murdered her husband, at once accepted this invitation, with the result that the rest of the party at Cliff House were able to spend an evening of comparative peace. Lady Harte showed Emily the snapshots she had taken in the Congo; Sir Adrian read a book; Jim and Patricia played billiards; and Timothy vanished on secret business of his own.

When Rosemary returned she found that Emily had already been carried up to bed, and that the others were on the point of following her. Asked whether she had spent a pleasant evening, she said that it had been a relief to get away from the atmosphere of Cliff House, but that she and Betty Pemble were on different planes.

Shortly before one o'clock Sir Adrian, whose habit it was to read far into the night, laid down his book and sat up in bed, listening intently. After a moment he got up, put on his exotic dressing gown, and went softly out on to the corridor, armed with a torch. The house seemed to be in darkness. He walked down the passage to his stepson's room and very quietly opened the door. He took one step into the room, and suddenly the silence of the room was rent by the shrill ringing of what seemed to be innumerable bells.

"Good God!" exclaimed Sir Adrian, annoyed.

Jim woke with a start and snapped on his bedside light. "What the blazes? . . . Hullo, Adrian! What's all the row about?"

"I haven't the slightest idea," replied Sir Adrian. "I came to tell you that I think someone is moving about downstairs, but I imagine whoever it may have been has by this time made good his escape. Will these bells never stop ringing?"

"Blast that infernal boy!" swore Jim, getting out of bed. "You bet this is his doing!"

The noise had by this time roused everyone in the house but Timothy. Lady Harte, Patricia, Rosemary, and a group of sleepy and scared servants all clustered on to the corridor, demanding to know what had happened, and from Emily's room came the sound of her voice calling to Miss Allison. While Patricia went to reassure the old lady, Jim located the cause of the disturbance, which proved to be an ingenious burglar alarm laid under the sheepskin mat before his bedroom door. It did not take him long to still the clamour, and in a few moments Rosemary was able to uncover her ears and to ask in an injured voice who was responsible for making such an unnecessary din.

"Timothy, of course," replied Jim. "And to think I gave him the money for it!"

"Really, I begin to think that boy may go a long way!" cried Lady Harte, her maternal pride aroused. "I call it extremely clever of him—much better than anything the police have done! What set it off?"

"I did," answered Sir Adrian. "I fancied I heard someone moving about under my room and came to wake Jim. It was not my purpose, however, to wake the entire household."

At this moment Ogle came up the front stairs, her hair in two plaits, a red-flannel dressing gown girt about her with a cord, and a steaming cup in her hand. "Who's making this outlandish noise?" she demanded angrily. "Frightening the mistress out of her senses, I'll be bound!"

"Have you been prowling about downstairs?" asked Lady Harte severely.

"No, my lady, I have not! Prowling, indeed! I've been making a cup of Ovaltine for the mistress. She can't sleep, and no wonder, is what I say! Such goings on!" She swept by the group on the passage and stalked into Emily's room.

"Thank you, Adrian!" said Jim in a broken voice. "I undoubtedly owe my life to you."

CHAPTER FIFTEEN

MR HARTE, learning at the breakfast table of the night's happenings, was torn between pride in the success of his invention and disgust at having slept through the disturbance. He thought it excessively funny that his father should have sprung the alarm, and when rebuked by his ungrateful stepbrother for having set such a booby trap outside his door, said indignantly that it was not a booby trap, and how on earth could he have guessed, anyway, that his father would go wandering about the house in the middle of the night? His mother staunchly supported him and agreed that the alarm should be set every night. Mr James Kane said that this was what drove a man from home and expressed a desire for the police to make haste and clear up the mystery.

"I must say, I think it's high time they did," said Lady Harte; "I begin to wonder whether they're doing anything at all. Most unsatisfactory!"

She might have been comforted had she known that Sergeant Hemingway was saying much the same thing.

"We get no forrader," he grumbled. "We've got no less than nine suspects for Clement Kane's death, and though this attempt on young Kane seems to whittle the number down a bit at first glance, when you go into it you find it's made the whole thing in a worse muddle than what it was before. Take Pretty Paul. You might have thought we'd got him in a cleft stick when we found out about him being on the premises when Clement was shot, but not a bit of it! He pulls out a highly unconvincing story of what he'd been doing, and those Pembles go and corroborate it. It's disheartening, Chief. Are we looking for one murderer or two murderers, that's what I'd like to know?"

"So should I," said Hannasyde.

"Well, to my way of thinking, there's just one person behind the whole show, and I've a strong notion it's Paul Mansell. Myself, I don't fancy Jim Kane. If he was clever enough to make away with two cousins without leaving a single clue behind him, I can't see what he wants with a couple of faked attempts on himself. We hadn't got a thing on him, which he must have known. What's more, if he loosened that nut on his car, he was taking a tidy risk. Suppose it had come off in the middle of the town, and he'd sailed into an omnibus, or something? Nice mess he'd have made of himself! Suppose there'd been another car coming towards him when the nut did come off? He fits the first two murders—I give you that; but he doesn't fit this latest denouement. If we're after someone who fits the two murders and the two attempts, all we've got is a couple of Mansells—and of the two I'd put my money on Paul—and this Leighton, whom we haven't seen. For the life of me, Super, I can't see why you're so shy of thinking it might be Pretty Paul."

"I don't like his motive," replied Hannasyde. "The stake isn't big enough."

"Well, I don't know," said the sergeant. "I've known a man to murder his own mother for the sake of a few hundred pounds insurance money."

"We're not dealing with a criminal of the poorer classes, nor have I known a man to murder three people for the sake of a few hundred pounds."

"Dare say he expects to make a few thousands."

"No doubt. But there's a difference between expectation and certainty. There's also another factor which you're leaving out of account. When Clement Kane was shot, James Kane, standing in the garden hall, saw nothing. Not so much as an agitation in the bushes. You may contend, if you like, that it would have been possible for the murderer to have shot Clement through the study window and to have dashed into the cover of the shrubbery in a very few seconds. But I've seen that garden hall. James Kane states that the door into the garden was open; if it had been shut he could still have seen out, because the upper panels are glazed. The sound of a shot so near at hand must have had the effect of making him look round immediately. An involuntary reaction. He says he did look round and stepped out at once through the open door. I've stood in that garden hall, Hemingway, and I've seen that it commands a view of the shrubbery. I can't understand how James Kane could have failed to observe any movement at all in the garden. If the murderer escaped, not into the shrubbery but by the path running along the side of the house to the front avenue, it is incredible that Kane should not have caught a glimpse of him when he looked out. He heard no footsteps on the gravel, either before or after the shot. One can argue that, as he had only just entered the garden hall when the shot was fired, he need not necessarily have heard anyone approaching the study. But surely he must have heard a hasty retreat? If we are to exonerate James Kane himself, we look like being faced with a far more fantastic possibility, which is that old Mrs Kane murdered Clement, and James Kane knows it."

"Revenge?" inquired the sergeant.

"That, and dislike of having him and his wife firmly established at Cliff House. She believes that Clement killed her son: that much seems to be certain. One of the doubts in my mind is whether she could have handled as heavy a gun as a 38."

"Yes, but if she did it, and Jim Kane knows it, what

about the attempts on him?" objected the sergeant. "Are you making Sir Adrian responsible for them?"

"It's a possibility. They may, on the other hand, have been faked by himself, partly to throw me off Mrs Kane's scent, partly to protect himself. Tortuous, I know, but the human brain is tortuous."

The sergeant sighed. "You're making it sound worse than ever, Chief. I'm blowed if I see where we are now."

"On the wrong track," replied Hannasyde promptly. "We've got to find the gun which shot Clement Kane."

"What you might call a tall order," remarked the sergeant. "If it was James Kane who did it, the odds are he took it out to sea in that boat of his and dropped it overboard. If it was Dermott, after all, we might find it at the bottom of the lake, but more likely he disposed of it miles from here. If it was young Mansell, there's no saying where he got rid of it. Of course, I had a look in the shrubbery, but there was no sign of the ground having been disturbed, and I can't say I expected any. It isn't in human nature to leave the weapon close to the scene of the crime, now, is it?"

"That's a ready-made argument which won't stand investigation," answered Hannasyde. "I agree that in nine cases out of ten you won't find the weapon near the scene of the crime, except of course in those instances where the murder has been faked to look like suicide. But the more I go into this case the more I feel convinced that we're up against a very astute mind. Moreover, unless the murderer was either Paul Mansell or Trevor Dermott, we have to remember that he had very little time in which to dispose of the gun before confronting Inspector Carlton. It's true Carlton didn't search anyone, but I hardly think the murderer would have been foolhardy enough to have run the risk of being found with the weapon on his person. Instinct would urge him to get rid of it immediately."

"Yes, that's good psychology, Super," conceded the sergeant. "What are we going to do? Drag the lake?"

"If all else fails. But neither James Kane nor Mrs

Kane could have disposed of the revolver as far from the house as that, let alone the certainty of their being seen by Dermott and Mrs Clement Kane, who were here. I think it must be concealed in, or near, the house."

"That bank of rhododendrons? Terrible Timothy searched there, and so I did myself."

"No, I thought of that; but I don't believe we shall find it there. If the murderer hid it there he must surely have buried it, for we were bound to search that bank. I don't see him doing that. It would have taken time, he might have been seen from the house, and at any moment one of the gardeners might have passed by. If he got rid of the gun on the premises he must have done it quickly. Now, isn't there a big rain tub standing not ten feet from the study window?"

The sergeant blinked at him. "There is, of course, but are you suggesting that anyone would have the almighty brass to drop the gun in there where it might be discovered any minute, Super? Why, he'd have to be crazy! The very fact of the tub being so handy would be enough to put him off!"

"Perhaps he banked on us thinking that," said Hannasyde with a slight smile.

The sergeant scratched his chin. "I'm bound to say it's about the last place I'd look for the gun. As a matter of fact, I've never banked much on finding it there at all."

"Nor I. Which is where I think we may have been wrong. We'll go and investigate that tub."

But when the sergeant was confronted with the big green rain tub standing so blatantly against the wall of the house, he shook his head and said: "He wouldn't have had the nerve."

"Whoever committed this crime had plenty of nerve," replied Hannasyde grimly. "See if you can find a long stick."

The sergeant said: "That's easy," and moved towards a round bed of roses beyond the edge of the shrubbery and calmly uprooted the stake that sup-

ported one of the standard trees. Hannasyde took it
from him, and, mounting the brick platform on which
the tub stood, lifted the wooden lid, and lowered the
stick into the dark water, probing and stirring. The sergeant watched him with interest but without hope.

"There is something lying on the bottom!" Hannasyde said. "I've just moved it." He withdrew the stake,
threw it aside, and stepped down from the ledge of
bricks. "Turn that spigot, Sergeant! I want the tub
emptied."

"That'll make us popular with the head gardener,"
murmured the sergeant, but he turned the spigot and
stood back while the water splashed down onto the
gravel path, forming first a pond and then a river.

It was not the head gardener who took exception to
the gathering flood, but Ogle, bouncing out upon the
two detectives from the garden hall. "You turn that
tap off this instant!" she commanded angrily. "The
idea of it, making all this mess! You've got no right to
come here ruining the flower beds and making the
place not fit to go near! What do you want with that
tub? Who gave you leave to touch it, I should like to
know?"

Hannasyde paid no attention, leaving the task of
getting rid of her to his subordinate, who accomplished
it in record time. She darted back into the house,
promising to tell Mr James what damage was being
done to his property, and in a few moments came back
with him at her heels. "There, sir!" she said. "Tell
them to stop it this instant! The mistress wouldn't
allow it, not for one moment! The impudence of it!"

"All right, Ogle! You trot along," said Jim. He
looked from the lake at his feet to the superintendent
and said, as Ogle withdrew reluctantly into the house:
"I say, must you? You're not exactly improving this bit
of garden. What's the great idea?"

"I shouldn't do it if I didn't think it necessary, Mr
Kane," said Hannasyde rather curtly. "It won't do any
serious damage to the garden, I assure you. The tub's
only half full."

"Thanks very much," said Jim, his jaw hardening a little. "And now perhaps you'll explain just what you're up to?"

"Certainly," said Hannasyde, looking at him under his brows. "I am pursuing an investigation. Have you any objection?"

"I have," said Jim. "I object most strongly to having any part of my property damaged without my permission being first obtained."

"I beg your pardon," said Hannasyde instantly. "Have I your permission to empty this tub?"

For a moment Jim's smiling eyes held no hint of a smile but, instead, a distinctly grim expression. Then his excellent temper reasserted itself and he gave a laugh and said: "Carry on!"

"Thank you," said Hannasyde, watching the dwindling flow of water from the spigot.

Jim lit a cigarette and stood half in, half out of the garden hall, leaning his big shoulders against the doorframe. "As an example of simple faith, this performance must be pretty well unrivalled," he remarked.

Hannasyde glanced up. "Yes? And why, Mr Kane?"

"Don't be silly," said Jim. "Do you suppose I haven't grasped what you're up to? You're quite obviously hunting for the fatal weapon. Of course it would be concealed in a rain tub bang on the scene of the crime."

"We shall see," said Hannasyde. "Give me a hand, will you, Sergeant?"

The sergeant, secretly in sympathy with Mr James Kane's evident scepticism, stepped into the flood and assisted his superior to lower the heavy tub off its platform onto the ground and to tilt it onto its side. A little muddy water trickled out of it, and, as they tilted it still farther, something was heard to slide inside it, grating on the wood.

"Right up!" Hannasyde said.

The sergeant got his hands under the bottom of the tub and gave it a hoist. A Colt 38 revolver clattered down the side of the tub and fell into the pool of water with a splash.

"Well, I'll be damned!" said Jim, staring.

"Sometimes, Mr Kane, the obvious place is the right place," said Hannasyde calmly and bent to pick up the gun.

It was at this somewhat inopportune moment that Mr Harte came wandering round the corner of the house, his whole bearing proclaiming the fact that he was bored and did not know what to do with himself. At sight of the two detectives the cloud left his brow, and he pranced up to them, full of zeal and curiosity. "Hullo, Sarge! What are you doing?" he demanded. "Golly, what a mess! I *say!* What have you found?"

The sergeant, who had been staring at the gun in Hannasyde's hand as one bemused, recollected himself with a start and said: "Look here, sonny, you trot off and tell yourself an anecdote! We're busy."

"You've found the gat!" cried Mr Harte. "Gosh! I say, what's that weird thing on the end of the barrel?"

Hannasyde raised his eyes from the revolver and glanced thoughtfully at Mr Harte's eager countenance. The sergeant was trying to edge him away, but Mr Harte had no intention of leaving. "All right, Hemingway," said Hannasyde quietly. "It doesn't matter."

The sergeant sent him a quick, puzzled look but stopped trying to get rid of Mr Harte.

Jim, frowning at the revolver, said: "I don't understand. Isn't that thing a silencer?"

"It is," replied Hannasyde.

"But then, that can't be the gun you're looking for," Jim objected. "It made the hell of a noise! They heard it in the hall."

"Very odd, isn't it?" said Hannasyde unemotionally. He slid the gun into his pocket and turned towards the house. His intent, questing gaze fell on the little brick platform built for the tub to stand on; he stepped up to it and bent, closely scrutinizing it. He picked something up very carefully. "Now I'm beginning to understand," he said.

The three others craned forward to see what lay in the palm of his hand. "That's a bit of burnt-out fuse!" im exclaimed.

"My Lord!" muttered the sergeant and went down on his knees by the platform. "Here's another bit, Chief. That seems to be the lot."

"About eighteen inches of it," said Hannasyde, measuring the fragments with his eye. "Say three minutes burning time." He glanced up at the pipe which fed the rain tub. "It must have slipped down behind the tub from . . ." He paused and raised a hand to one of the brackets clamping the pipe to the wall, feeling it carefully ". . . from this bracket," he concluded, bringing his hand away with another tiny fragment of the mottled fuse in it. "There should be a detonator." He looked down at Mr Harte and said with a faint smile: "If you want to be useful, see if you can find it."

"You bet your life!" said Mr Harte fervently and proceeded without any more ado to create havoc amongst the antirrhinums planted thickly in the bed along the wall of the house.

The sergeant, his eyes fixed on Hannasyde's face in an expression of shocked inquiry, opened his mouth to speak, encountered a steady look from Hannasyde, and thought better of it. He joined Timothy in the search for the detonator. It was Timothy who presently let out a squeak of triumph and held up between an earth-stained finger and thumb a brass object like a cartridge which had been pinched at the open end. "Look, is this it?"

"That's it," said Hannasyde, taking it from him.

Jim was still looking bewildered. "How did it work?" he asked.

"Quite simply," Hannasyde replied. "One end of the fuse was inserted at this end. Then the sides of the cap were very carefully pinched together so that they gripped the fuse. Do you see? It was then hung over that bracket, and the other end split and set light to. Standard fuse, which it is safe to assume this is, being white, burns at the rate of six inches a minute, and I

should judge that we've found just about eighteen
inches of it. What you and the others heard, Mr Kane
was not the shot that killed your cousin, but the detonator going off."

"Good God, then that accounts for my not seeing a
sign of anyone when I looked out!" Jim said. "My
cousin was shot some minutes earlier?" Hannasyde
nodded. "Yes, but I still don't quite get it. I gather that
it lets me out, but——"

"What do you suppose can have been the reason for
setting the fuse, Mr Kane?"

"Alibi!" gasped Mr Harte, executing a slight war
dance. "Whoopee!"

"Alibi," repeated Jim. "Yes, of course. Sorry to be
so dense. But——"

"Oh, Jim, you ass!" said Timothy. "You couldn't
have done it, because you didn't get yourself an alibi!
Golly, I do think this is fun!"

"I've grasped that," said Jim. "But what I don't
immediately perceive is, which of us *did* benefit by this
contraption. Neither of the Mansells established an
alibi, nor did Dermott, nor did—in fact, none of us did
except Miss Allison, I suppose, and you can't seriously
suspect . . ."

Mr Harte drew a shuddering breath and fixed the
sergeant with a glittering and accusing gaze. "I told
you so!" he said. "I *told* you you ought to keep an eye
on him!"

"Keep an eye on who?" demanded the sergeant.

"Pritchard, of course! It's obvious!"

"Pritchard?" said Jim. "My good lad, what on earth
should he have to do with it? He's only been employed
here since old Barker died last year, so he had no expectations of a legacy. Besides——"

Mr Harte danced with impatience. "The Hidden
Killer! He knew when Cousin Silas went out that night,
and of course he followed him! And then he fixed up
this affair to give himself an alibi for doing Cousin
Clement in, and nobody ever bothered to find out where
he was *before* he went to answer the front-door bell

because it looked as though he couldn't possibly have done it!"

"But why?" said Jim.

"Cousin Maud's husband!" hissed Mr Harte.

"Get out!" said Jim scornfully.

"I bet you I'm right! I bet you Mr Roberts will think there's something in it, even if you don't. Because the only thing that put him off Pritchard's scent was his being in the hall when they heard the shot. It's no use you making that face! It's perfectly true! I talked to Mr Roberts about it when you first started wondering about this Leighton bloke, and he said it had occurred to him, quite early on, only it led nowhere, because Pritchard had a cast-iron alibi."

Hannasyde, who had been listening to him with an unmoved countenance, said: "You mustn't mention this to Pritchard, you know, or to any of the servants."

"Rather not! Of course I wouldn't breathe a word to them! I can tell Mr Roberts, can't I?"

"Oh yes, you can tell him if you want to," replied Hannasyde. "Help me to put the tub back, will you, Sergeant?"

Jim said, his brows knit: "Do you think he ought to say anything about this to anyone at all, Superintendent? It's not my affair, I know, but——"

"It doesn't matter what he tells Mr Roberts," replied Hannasyde. "It mustn't come to the butler's ears, though. But he understands that. All right, Hemingway, that's all."

"Are you going back to Portlaw?" inquired Timothy, seeing the two detectives preparing to depart. "Because if you are, I'll come with you as far as Victoria Place."

"All right," said Hannasyde, glancing at his wrist watch. "But we must hurry if we want to catch the ten forty-five bus."

"Look here, just a minute!" said Jim. "What are you going to do about this? I mean, it's all very well for you to waltz off in this airy fashion, but I happen to be rather vitally concerned in the case!"

"I hadn't forgotten that," said Hannasyde. "I am going to the police station to put through a number of urgent inquiries to Scotland Yard. I may be in a position to tell you the result of those inquiries by this evening, or possibly some time tomorrow. Meanwhile, I'm afraid you'll have to possess your soul in patience."

"And what about my precious life?" asked Jim.

"Sergeant Trotter will be answerable for that," replied Hannasyde with the glimmer of a smile. "I don't think it is in immediate danger."

He and Sergeant Hemingway, with Mr Harte between them, walked off at a brisk pace down the avenue and arrived at the lodge gates just in time to catch the omnibus into Portlaw. The omnibus being empty, Mr Harte was able to beguile the tedium of the journey by speculating on the case and trying to coax information out of his two companions. At Victoria Place, in Portlaw, he left them, promising to conduct himself with the utmost circumspection.

No sooner had he alighted from the omnibus than the sergeant drew a deep breath and said: "Well, I never thought I'd live to see this day, that's certain!"

"Pleasant surprise for you," said Hannasyde.

"Super, what's come over you? If anyone had told me you'd go pursuing investigations with a couple of people looking on and, what's more, explain it all to them on top of it, I'd have laughed in their face!"

"Would you?" said Hannasyde, not paying much heed to him.

"I would," said the sergeant emphatically. "You told me not to get rid of Terrible Timothy, and I didn't. But what's your game?"

"Think it out," replied Hannasyde.

The sergeant made a sound suspiciously like a snort. "What do we do now?" he asked.

"Telephone to the Yard first, and get them to put through an inquiry to Colt's, in America. We must know where this gun was bought."

"Well, I'm not surprised young James Kane wonders what you're up to," said the sergeant.

James Kane, however, assuming that Superintendent Hannasyde knew his own business best, did not waste much time in idle speculation. He decided to say nothing either to his fiancée or to his relatives about the discovery of the gun, a resolve that he was soon forced to break, Ogle having informed her mistress of the ravages done to the garden, and Emily, as soon as she came downstairs, dressed for her morning drive, demanded to be told instantly what such conduct meant. As she chose to address Jim in the presence of Miss Allison and Lady Harte, both of whom immediately joined with her in wanting to know the truth, Jim thought it best to disclose the bare fact of Hannasyde's having found the gun in the rain tub.

When Timothy came in an hour later, the first person he encountered was his mother, and he straightway poured the whole story into her ears. By lunchtime everyone but the servants was in possession of all the facts, and Miss Allison, knowing the strength of the bond between Mrs Kane and Ogle, had little doubt that it would not be long before the news spread to the servants' hall.

"I told you Mr Roberts would listen to me!" Timothy said triumphantly.

"Well, I think it's the most crackbrained idea I ever heard," replied Jim. "I can quite easily imagine Roberts lapping it up, because he's been full of crackbrained ideas from the start, but I did not expect the superintendent to run amok over it. What's he up to now? Do you know?"

"No, but I know Mr Roberts has gone to the police station to see him, because as soon as I told him about the silencer and the fuse, he said it put an entirely new complexion on the affair, and he'd have to go and see the superintendent at once. So I came home. Gosh, I do wonder what's happening, don't you? Do you suppose they'll come and arrest Pritchard?"

"No, I don't, and for God's sake be careful what you say! We shall find ourselves had up for libel, or something, if Pritchard hears this sort of chat going on."

As the day wore on without news from Hannasyde Timothy found it increasingly hard to bear the suspense with anything approaching equanimity. He wandered about the house and grounds, propounding theories to anyone whom he encountered, until, in desperation, Jim bore him off to the nearest golf course and gave him an hour's coaching in approach shots. When they returned it was time to change for dinner. During the meal Pritchard's presence precluded any mention being made of the affair, but when the party assembled in the drawing room for coffee afterwards, it was not Timothy only who evinced a strong desire to discuss the subject ad nauseam. So persistent were the comments and surmises made that Sir Adrian, aloof from the discussion behind the evening paper, presently lowered it to say in a bored voice that, since the matter seemed to have become such an obsession with the family, he personally would feel extremely grateful to Hannasyde for solving the mystery.

The words were hardly out of his mouth when Pritchard entered the room to inform Jim that Superintendent Hannasyde had called and would like to see him.

Jim got up but was checked by an indignant outcry from his mother, his stepbrother, and his fiancée. Emily Kane, immovable in the winged armchair by the fireplace, said: "If he wants to see you he can see you here. I've no patience with all this hole-and-corner business." She nodded at Pritchard. "Show him in!"

A couple of minutes later Pritchard ushered Hannasyde into the room. To Mr Harte's chagrin the superintendent made no effort even to detain him. As the door closed softly behind him, Mr Harte, unable to contain himself, blurted out: "I say, aren't you going to arrest him after all?"

For the first time during their dealings with Superintendent Hannasyde the family heard him laugh. "No,

I'm afraid I'm not," he answered. "I'm sorry to have to disappoint you about that."

"Didn't he do it?" asked Timothy, greatly cast down.

Hannasyde shook his head. Jim said: "Won't you sit down? Is the case still in the air, or have you cleared it up?"

"I haven't finished with it yet, but there's so little doubt that it will be cleared up that I came to set your mind at rest, Mr Kane. You're no longer in danger of being murdered."

"Was he ever in danger?" said Lady Harte, laying down her Patience cards and removing the horn-rimmed spectacles from her nose.

"Yes, I think almost certainly."

"You didn't think so at the time."

"You will have to forgive me, Lady Harte, if I—reserved judgment. I did give him a bodyguard, you know," said Hannasyde, recognizing the signs of tigress-in-defence-of-her-young.

Emily thumped her ebony stick on the floor. "That's enough beating about the bush!" she said sharply. "Do you know who murdered my son?"

"I have no proof that your son was murdered, Mrs Kane. I know who murdered your great-nephew, Clement Kane."

"Who?" demanded Timothy. "Did Mr. Roberts put you onto him?"

Hannasyde looked at him rather gravely. "Not quite in the way you mean."

Sir Adrian, rising from his chair, wandered across the room to take a cigarette from a box on one of the tables. "Ah, so it was Roberts himself, was it?" he said, mildly interested.

Hannasyde nodded. A stunned silence reigned for perhaps half a minute. Timothy had gone white and was staring at Hannasyde with his lips very firmly set. Sir Adrian offered the cigarette box to Hannasyde. "Edwin Leighton?" he inquired.

"Yes," replied Hannasyde. "I don't think there's

much room for doubt about that. We can't identify him for certain until we get his fingerprints from Melbourne, of course; but they'll be through almost any day now."

"Roberts?" Jim ejaculated. "But that's fantastic! Are you seriously suggesting that it was he who cut the hole in the Seamew and loosened the nut on my car?"

"Yes, I think so," said Hannasyde.

"But, good Lord, Superintendent, it was he who first warned me my life might be in danger!"

"Clever, wasn't it?" agreed Hannasyde.

Lady Harte got up from the card table and came to sit down in a chair opposite Hannasyde. "I insist upon being told the whole story!" she announced. "I freely admit I never suspected the man. How long have you known it?"

"I've had my suspicions ever since I first considered the Leightons as possible factors in the case, Lady Harte. I wasn't sure till this morning, when we found the gun with the silencer fitted to it and the length of fuse. That seemed to me to be fairly conclusive. I've been busy all the rest of the day collecting proof that the gun did belong to him."

"Tall order, that," said Lady Harte professionally. "A Colt 38, wasn't it? Did you manage to trace it?"

"Yes, we did, after a good deal of trouble. Scotland Yard got an answer from the States at 5 P.M. The American police cabled that the makers had sold that gun to their agents in Melbourne. The Yard then put through a radiogram to Australia. I've just heard the result. The gun was supplied to a retail shop in Melbourne and was bought by a man calling himself Oscar Roberts six months ago."

"Really, I call that marvellous!" said Lady Harte. "Here we are at 10.30 P.M., and since ten-thirty this morning you've been in touch not only with America but with Australia as well. When one considers the difference in time it seems hardly possible!"

"Well, you see, our cable reached the Melbourne police in the small hours, and they probably got the information we wanted as early as they could. As soon as the business houses were open, in fact. There was obviously no difficulty in tracing the gun, for Scotland Yard received the answer by radiogram just on ten o'clock. They rang me up at once, and I caught the ten-fifteen bus out here."

"Yes, very good of you," interrupted Jim; "but never mind about what the Australian police did! You say you've established the fact that the gun belonged to Roberts, and that settles that. He must have shot Clement, and I suppose he must be Edwin Leighton. But I can hardly believe it, all the same. It was he who started every scare we've had. While the rest of us thought my cousin Silas had missed his footing in the fog, he went about hinting that he'd met with foul play. He warned me to be careful———"

"He warned you to be careful," said Hannasyde; "but if you think back, you'll find that he never pretended to know anything until others were beginning to suspect it. The instant he realized that some, at least, of you felt that Mr Silas Kane's death had not been investigated enough, he gave you to understand that he had thought so all along. When your motorboat sank and you, in company with everyone else, were convinced that your stepbrother had run her on the rocks, did he tell you he thought the boat had been tampered with?"

"No, he jolly well did not!" growled Timothy.

"No, not then," said Jim. "But when I told him that Timothy and Miss Allison had got the wind up about it———"

"He said that he had suspected it from the start," interjected Hannasyde.

"Well, yes," admitted Jim. "He did."

"Of course. It was quite safe once the idea of foul play had entered your head. He tried to make you— and incidentally me—think that Mr Paul Mansell was the villain of the piece. He played his part very well indeed, but he slipped up yesterday. Up till that moment I had regarded him in the light of a somewhat tiresome amateur detective—we meet a good many, you know. But that slip of his made me sit up and take a certain amount of notice. You will remember that I came to call on you, Mrs Kane, to find out what you could tell me about the Leightons?"

"Yes," said Emily. "Not that I knew anything about them."

"Roberts was present," continued Hannasyde. "My question must have jolted him badly, for he made a mistake. He hinted, very broadly, that Mr Clement Kane had murdered his cousin and went to some trouble to demonstrate how unlikely it was that two such dissimilar murders should have been committed by the same man. Until that moment he had insinuated that Paul Mansell was responsible for both deaths."

"Quite true," agreed Sir Adrian. "One is led to suppose that he had not anticipated that you would look farther than the Mansells or—er—me, perhaps."

Hannasyde acknowledged this thrust with a twinkle, but Lady Harte said stringently: "I've had enough of that nonsense, Adrian! This whole case astounds me! I'm not squeamish: I've knocked about the world too much to be easily upset; but the idea of a man deliberately setting out to dispose of three people so that his wife would inherit a fortune absolutely appals me!"

Rosemary, who had till then been too much surprised to say a word, now made a contribution to the discussion. "I can believe anything of that man!" she said intensely. "I've had the most extraordinary feeling about him from the moment I set eyes on him. I didn't like to say anything about it, but my instinct is hardly ever at fault."

"So you've said before," replied Emily. "Don't interrupt!" She looked at Hannasyde. "I dare say he thought Maud was Clement's heir, eh?"

"Very probably," agreed Hannasyde. "I, too, find it difficult to believe that at the outset he contemplated the murders of three people. Two he might have got away with; the third, though inevitable once the first two had been committed, made the whole position very dangerous. He was gambling for a big stake; having gone so far, he couldn't think of giving up. So instead of being able to withdraw from the scene and to be next heard of as Edwin Leighton in Sydney, he was forced to remain here until he had succeeded in disposing of Mr James Kane."

"Extremely hazardous," said Sir Adrian. "I suppose, had his wife indeed succeeded Clement Kane, he would have continued to be an errant husband until she was safely in possession of the fortune."

"I imagine so. Of course, we don't know whether she was aware of his plot. I hardly think she can have been; but from what Mrs Kane told me, I gathered that once he elected to return to her she would do exactly as he told her."

"I dare say," said Emily scornfully.

Jim walked over to a side table, whereon Pritchard had set a tray earlier in the evening, and began to pour out drinks. "This has absolutely got me down," he confessed. "Of all the diabolical schemes! . . . He must have calculated to the last second the time it would take him to reach the front door from the study window. He even made an appointment to see Clement at three-thirty that afternoon. I suppose partly as a blind, partly to make it fairly certain that Clement would be in his study. If he hadn't been there, no doubt the murder would have been postponed. He must be a complete devil."

"No, not entirely," said Lady Harte. "He did rescue Timothy. I can't forget that."

"It's beastly!" said Mr Harte violently. "He—he pretended to be trying to guard Jim, when all the time he was waiting to do him in! I think—I think it's the *limit!* I don't care if he did rescue me! I'd rather not have been rescued by him, and I jolly well hope you catch him!"

"Oh, we've done that," said Hannasyde. "You helped a lot, you know."

"Did I?" said Mr Harte. "I say, you're not pulling my leg, are you?"

"No, you really did help. When I found the revolver this morning I was sure Roberts was the man I was after, but I wasn't sure that the department would succeed in tracing the gun. You told him I'd found the gun and the fuse, and that I knew the noise you all heard hadn't been caused by the shot that killed Mr Clement Kane. Once I'd discovered the fuse the game was up, and he knew it. You led him to think that I suspected Pritchard; he saw his one chance of making a getaway and seized it. As soon as he'd got rid of you he shaved off his beard and moustache and caught the eleven-thirty train to town. Sergeant Hemingway was shadowing him, and he was taken into custody at three this afternoon—detained for inquiries."

Mr Harte looked a little dubious. "Well, I don't see that I did much," he said candidly. "I mean, I never knew I was doing anything."

"Never mind," said Hannasyde. "You made him run, and that was what I wanted him to do." He accepted the glass Jim Kane was holding out to him. "Thank you."

Lady Harte got up and shook him vigorously by the hand. "Well, really, I think we owe you a debt of gratitude, Superintendent!" she said. "You've cleared the whole thing up most satisfactorily. I for one am extremely grateful to you."

This sentiment was echoed by Jim and Miss Allison. Sir Adrian, sipping his whisky, said: "I congratulate you, Superintendent. An astonishingly difficult case."

Hannasyde looked a trifle embarrassed and made haste to disclaim any extraordinary astuteness.

"Nonsense!" said Lady Harte briskly. "You've done a very fine piece of work, hasn't he, Aunt Emily?"

Emily, who was feeling tired, said: "I dare say he's been very clever; but I'm not at all surprised. I never did like that Roberts." She gave her shawl a twitch and added with a certain grim satisfaction: "I always said those Australian Kanes were an encroaching lot."